QUEERS DESTROY HORROR!
SPECIAL ISSUE

ISSUE 37 | OCTOBER 2015
GUEST EDITED BY WENDY N. WAGNER

NIGHTMARE MAGAZINE: Queers Destroy Horror! Special Issue   Issue 37, October 2015

Publisher: John Joseph Adams   Guest Editor: Wendy N. Wagner

© 2015 *Nightmare Magazine*

NIGHTMARE
QUEERS DESTROY HORROR!
SPECIAL ISSUE

NONFICTION
edited by Megan Arkenberg

AUTHOR SPOTLIGHTS
edited by Traci Castleberry

MISCELLANY

ON THE
DESTRUCTION
OF HORROR

NOTES FROM YOUR
QUEER EDITORS

WENDY N. WAGNER, GUEST EDITOR-IN-CHIEF AND FICTION EDITOR

WELCOME TO ISSUE thirty-seven of *Nightmare*. It's our second installment of the Destroy All Genres project (see destroysf.com for more information), Queers Destroy Horror!, a double-issue of Nightmare that's entirely written, edited, and illustrated by LGBTQUIA creators. It's been an honor and a privilege to work with this remarkable team.

The first horror story I ever read was Stephen King's "The Raft," a terrifying little gem that appeared in the collection *Skeleton Crew*, a book whose cover instilled in me a sense of disquiet that was only enhanced by the horrible things it contained. I was seven or eight years old, but everything about that book made sense to me. Anything in the world could be dangerous, even toys and dolls and harmless-seeming animals, like the monkey on the cover of that book. I huddled under my blankets and read my books and imagined how I could possibly survive the dangers of the world.

Now as an adult, I turn to horror stories not to train myself to survive the world but to make sense of it. The world is horrible sometimes. Terrible things happen for no explicable reason, and the rules that run society can be unfair and cruel and horrid. But horror stories reframe the terrible things of the world. They hold a mirror up to the revolting so we can put it into some kind of taxonomy. They place wickedness and evil in a context that helps us see their limits and comforts us with the notion that darkness can be labeled, lit, and even survived. The work of the horror story is to define and demarcate the uncanny and the dark.

But to be queer and to love horror stories is not always easy. Those stories are spun out of our culture and our societal norms, and the labels and definitions that come out of horror stories aren't always inclusive or healthy. How many slasher flicks depend on rules about "appropriate" female sexuality? Enough that in *Scream*, the first rule for surviving a horror movie is to never have sex. How many thrillers about psychos rely on the idea of a gender-confused sadist to power their stories to success? Just ask Thomas Harris and Robert Bloch, plus all the writers who've ripped them off over the years.

Be normal!, the tropes tell us. *Be straight! Follow the rules!* The top-level lessons of horror stories can feel stifling with their emphasis on the WASPy, heteronormative society that came to its zenith in 1950s Americana.

But for all those stories that tell us to stop asking questions, stop trying to figure out our own unique relationships to our bodies and our sexualities, there are dozens of other stories that whisper—or even shout—that the way to beat back the darkness and the danger is to be *more* yourself, to break *more* soul-squashing rules, to be as queer as you need to be. The heroes of horror stories are often the oddballs and the weirdos, like the kids in *The Monster Squad* or every character in a Shirley Jackson novel.

This special issue is about celebrating queer work, about breaking rules, and tweaking tropes. It follows in the footsteps of terrific anthologies like *Bending the Landscape: Horror* (edited by Nicola Griffith and Stephen Pagel), *Queer Fear I and II* (edited by Michael Rowe), and *Night Shadows: Queer Horror* (edited by Greg Herren and J.M. Redmann). Do readers really need another all-queer horror collection? My experience editing the personal essays for *Lightspeed*'s Queers Destroy Science Fiction! special edition certainly says they do. In that project, writer after writer spoke on the painful lack of QUILTBAG representation in popular culture, and how much they wanted to see more stories by queer creators and about queer characters. As Jerome Stueart put it: "When we're not there, we're not here."

So here's a collection that puts more of us out there, with terrific essays and nonfiction exploring the role of queers in horror, stunning poems by LGBTQUIA voices, and eight works of short fiction that are dark, timely, and just plain eerie. I hope you will enjoy reading this issue as much as I have enjoyed bringing it together.

I'd like to give special thanks to Ellen Datlow, Ross Lockhart, and Steve Berman for all their assistance with the project. And of course I owe a tremendous debt of gratitude to John Joseph Adams, who is not only the most supportive and encouraging publisher any editor could ever hope to work with, but also the best mentor and friend. Everything I know about this work, I have learned from him.

Now go read the destruction!

MEGAN ARKENBERG, NONFICTION EDITOR

As QUEER WRITERS and readers, we find ourselves feeling both at home and deeply unwelcome in the horror genre. Sexual and gender nonconformity are in the genre's DNA; queer people began writing horror long before it was a recognizable fiction category, and our ranks include some of the biggest names in the contemporary horror scene. There's also something thoroughly queer about the themes that preoccupy the genre, the thrilling or threatening friction between outsiders and communities, attraction and revulsion, sex and violence, power and vulnerability. As people who fall on the ever-expanding spectrum of lesbian, gay, bisexual, asexual, trans, intersex, and nonbinary identities, we think about desire, embodiment, and belonging in ways that are rarely simple and never unexamined. It makes sense that many of us are drawn to fiction that tackles these topics in unexpected and often unsettling ways.

But, as the essays and interviews in this special issue demonstrate, if we often see ourselves reflected in horror stories, it can also feel like the genre wants us gone—or dead. Horror's queer figures include both monsters and victims: the demonically desirable predator and gender nonconforming serial killer, but also the solitary hitchhiker, the disposable gay or lesbian friend, the young woman who has sex in the wrong way or with the wrong people and is punished with death and dismemberment. Queer writers navigate pockets of homophobia or well-meaning ignorance, where our characters' queerness is seen as either a moral failing or an act of exceptional bravery in-and-of itself. Equally frustrating are the readers who dismiss queerness in fiction as an "unnecessary" complication that isn't "integral to the plot." If on the one hand, a certain brand of mainstream horror cannot envision anything but monstrosity or victimhood for queer people, there is also a brand of horror criticism that resents the presence of queerness in the first place, viewing it as an intrusion of faddish political rhetoric into horror's proper sphere.

Of course, there are many possible responses to those who claim that there is no place for queer people, queer relationships, and queer sexuality in horror. We can point to the genre's history. We can insist that representation is a moral issue. Personally, I find myself thinking that the readers who place queerness outside of horror's boundaries are demanding a poorer and duller version of what this genre can be. At its best, queer horror acknowledges the way our vulnerability is shaped by what we desire and how our bodies are recognized. It asks us to dwell in the messy consequences of exclusion and isolation, of family-making and community-building, of finding names for ourselves or coming to recognize that no name fits quite right. It gives us characters with uniquely vexed or uniquely rich connections to their genders, people for whom the body is more than a sack of viscera waiting to be splattered across the walls.

When we say that we belong here, we are insisting above all that this genre can be rich and vibrant—that horror tackles important questions, that it is meaningful to the way we live our lives. Whatever it is that draws you to horror fiction, I hope that these pages remind you why the genre's queerness is something to celebrate.

Robyn Lupo, Poetry Editor

I was asked to do this project by Wendy Wagner. I had done the flash section for Women Destroy Science Fiction! and Wendy brilliantly thought that poetry might serve Horror better as the shorter section here—which makes sense, doesn't it? I feel like nearly everyone I know can quote at least some of "The Raven" by Edgar Allen Poe. As appropriate as the short story is for horror, I feel the short poem has a significant place in the genre, too. Poe, and definitely Lovecraft, sought to capture something particular from language; whether or not their choices are to your tastes is another matter, but I think it's uncontroversial to say that they aimed for the high reaches of feeling through their work; it's no wonder that many horror writers turn to poetry with progenitors like that.

I wish we could have had more room; poets like Mat Joiner, Bogi Takács, and Sonya Taaffe (just to name a few), all have stunning command of language and do exciting things with content—like, if you have a need to read about star-crossed lovers in space with a darker sort of turn, these poets are there for you.

I mentioned the perspective I came in on: pretty conventional, pretty limited. There's a lot more to horror than Poe and Lovecraft, as much as we may owe them. The poets I found still strive for those depths and reaches of feeling. Most of the poems I read this summer had a narrative element, as well, which tickles me as a primarily fiction reader. But they blew the form up; left rhymes behind for jangly line ends and jagged section breaks. And what they talked about was different, too.

These lovely dark pieces capture a sampling of the breadth of dark poetry by queer people and I feel like beyond the lush words and the neat innovations on form, what will hit you is that there's a whole universe of diverse and compelling expressions here. Brit Mandelo takes us into a creepy new house, Shweta Narayan tells us about dark spells, and W.H. Pugmire takes the horror to a near-cosmic level; and each presentation, from the personal horror of us "cerebrated monkeys" to the creeping-horror-behind-the-stars, could be a little awful world of its own.

GOLDEN HAIR, RED LIPS

MATTHEW BRIGHT

I'M NOT IN the photograph. I was off to the side, picture of disinterest, smoking a cigarette, watching passers-by. That was how I passed my days in that part of the century, hovering on the street corner in sight of all those colours. I remember the photographer—button-down shirt, round glasses, mussed hair, the look of someone born away from this city. He was beautiful.

The men were clenched around the window, where the sign had been taped. The photographer's camera clicked, and there they were, stock still in black and white forever.

You might have seen the photograph. There's a good chance, now that we good men of the Castro are the immortalised nameless. Books, documentaries—hell, postcards, probably. This photograph was the vanguard, you see. The seraph's trumpet. Bad times, they were a-coming.

The photographer lowered his camera to roll on the film, and I drew close, unobserved. My eye was on one of the men of the gathering, a hand on his waist as I read, but when I stepped into their circle that feeling—that incessant dressing down, dressing up, undressing behind the eyes—drained away.

There were three photographs, close-ups of body parts, inflicted with vicious looking welts, dark and sick. I'd never seen anything like them before, and I'd lived through them all. TB, scarlet fever, influenza—all the greats. Lesions, they're called. Sarcoma. We didn't know that at the time.

Instead, the poster was labelled, in neat felt-tip capitals, "GAY CANCER." The photographs were of the man who had made the poster, whoever he was. These were the symptoms inflicted on him, all over his narrow body. The poster was a warning.

The camera whirred again, and I turned to face the photographer. He snapped another.

I've seen that photograph, although you won't have. I've tossed back my long hair, and I'm looking straight into the camera. My eyes are quietly confident in the shadows of the sockets. I look fabulous. The other men are still behind me, reading the poster. Concern and fear is in their frame, their worried looks at each other. They're all dead now.

"Good morning," I said to the photographer. "If it's not too bold, sir, I'd like to tell you that you are an uncommonly beautiful specimen of manhood."

"I know," he said, and matched my smile. "But I appreciate hearing it in such an English way." He raised the camera, but I put a hand up to block it, lifting it out of his hands. "You're a long way from home, Lord Fauntleroy."

"I always am," I said, "though that's not my name." I circled him, and lifted the camera up to my eye, pressing the button and capturing him in the frame.

In that one, you can see what's not quite clear in that first—more famous—photograph. The words at the bottom of the page. "Be warned," the felt tip letters read. "There's something out there."

THOMAS MOVES HIS head infinitesimally to rest against my cheek. His skin is cool and clammy, and his face is drawn as if the skin has been pulled inch by inch into every crevice of his skull, the muscle melted away. Every movement feels brittle, as if something will break any second. He looks like a skeleton. He's not the only one in the Castro.

I touch my lips briefly to his forehead. "If it's not too bold, sir," I say, throat tight, "I'd like to tell you that you are an *uncommonly* beautiful specimen of manhood."

The lesions are all over his face, crawling steadily closer to his eyes and nose, as if he's drowning slowly in his own rebellious skin.

"I know," he says, a papery whisper on his shrunken tongue. "But it's nice to hear it in—" He chokes, and there is blood on the pillow. "You're a long way from home, Dorian Gray."

"I always am," I say.

His blood was in my mouth when I stalked the Castro later that night. I had kissed him on the lips until he was gone. He sputtered out, and the beep of the machine solidified. The nurse appeared. She was horrified when she saw the blood on my lips—she pushed my head into the sink, and shrieked words at me that I didn't listen to. They were unnecessary for me, but the poor woman couldn't have guessed.

I wasn't the only one lurking in the corridor outside the ward. Others had been marooned there, dead-eyed and confused. I could hear the electronic fanfare of more lives ending, up and down the ward.

It was no different in the Castro—flatlines everywhere, dressed in their tight shirts and jeans, handkerchiefs in their pockets, sunglasses covering their already dead eyes. I moved between them, brushing against their cadaverous skins, imagining the lesions crawling on their bodies, squirming to escape, to crawl into the pigmentation of my own supple skin.

I found tequila in Twin Peaks, and I found Lewis in the Rooftop Lounge. I was mostly past words by then, but so was he. I kissed him against the bar, and he led me by the hand down the back-stairs, along the alley. In the doorway of Sankeys he slipped his hand down the front of my trousers and gripped me tight, jerking me hard. I breathed hard against his neck.

"Who's he?" Lewis asked.

"Who?"

He bit my neck and jerked a head across the street.

A man was watching us. Golden-blond hair, red lips, flawless skin, half-lost in the shadow.

"Ex-boyfriend?"

"No," I said. I had never seen him before, and yet he seemed curiously familiar.

The blond man moved toward us. "Aren't you afraid?" he asked us.

Lewis laughed, and pulled me deeper into the doorway of Sankeys. "Dizzy queen," he said. "Leave her be." I let him pull me into Sankeys. The gap in the door, at the whim of a slow-close mechanism, narrowed around the blond man, shrinking him from elegant broad shoulders to a glimpse of a piercing face as he followed us.

Sankeys kept up its pretence, mostly; thus, the naked bodies rutting in the damp were lost amongst jets of steam. Lewis pulled me to a corner, pushed me down between his ebony thighs.

"Aren't you afraid?" The blond man had followed us in, taken a place next to Lewis, who hadn't noticed, his eyes closed in ecstasy.

I was. Afraid. Illogically, irrationally. Afraid.

Perhaps the sickness would crawl down my throat, rot my stomach, split my veins into a thousand slender hairs, let me paint the disease in savage brush-strokes over the body of my painting. In my attic by the park, the painting would crawl with lesions like fat, hungry slugs, until there was nothing but the white of my eyes left staring out into the shrouded dark of the sheet that hides it from view.

Whilst I fucked my way from sauna to sauna, my painting would wither and die night after night. And it wouldn't be alone; around it, strung from wall to wall, were hundreds of Thomas' photographs, the ageless black and white faces silently thronged around the decrepitude of my own painted visage—the invert of my own sojourn here on the streets of the Castro.

The blond man watched me defiantly sink to my task, smiled faintly as Lewis filled my mouth. The taste was still slick in my throat when I stumbled home, dragging my aching body up the stairs. I looked in every direction but my covered portrait as I methodically pulled down each of Thomas's photographs, stacked them in a developing tray, and lit the corner with a snick of my lighter.

I left only one untouched—the very first one. The one you've seen, the one that's gone down in history. The men gathered around that sign, back before the real cannibal horror of it all had gripped the street, the words at the bottom of the sheet illegible but stuck fast in my mind.

Especially as, glancing out the window for a moment, I was sure I could see the blond man watching from a doorway.

Be warned. There's something out there.

"I DON'T KNOW how you do it, honey," Lewis said, touching the end of his cigarette to mine. I breathed in deeply to ignite, and I could smell the stale undertone to his aftershave. I wasn't certain, but I could guess. He was perhaps—what?—a few pounds lighter than when I saw him last week. Nothing too noticeable right then. But it wouldn't take long. Six months, and he wouldn't be here either.

"Do what, good sir?" I asked him. They loved the upperclass British schtick here, and it was nice to relax into old patterns of speech. Henry would have been proud. They thought my name was just a part of the act.

"So *handsome*. All the time. Lordy, honey, I wish I knew your secret."

"A deal with the devil," I told him.

Lewis struck a pose, pouting. "'Faustian Pact—for men!'" he quoted. "'Because youth doesn't come cheap.'"

The flower-seller swept up to our table. Lewis scrabbled for a dollar and purchased a rose.

"For the new paramour?" I asked.

"You know it, darling. He's *totally* worth it. I think he might be—" self-consciously dramatic, "—*the one.*"

I pointed at the door. "Is that him?"

It would have been easy to mistake the man who had entered for another Castro clone, but on him the flannel shirt and sandboots had a ring of authenticity, as if he had just stepped right off the farm. Ruddy faced, running a little to fat in a homefed sort of way, blinking in disorientation in the gaudy lights of the bar as I could imagine him blinking as he stepped off the train into the circus of San Francisco. Just my type.

"That's him," said Lewis, and bustled to sweep him into our orbit. "Honey, let me introduce my—" with a schoolgirl giggle "—boyfriend, Luke."

I extended a hand. "A *pleasure*," I said. "And if it's not too bold . . ."

". . . SIR, I'D LIKE to tell you that you are an *uncommonly* beautiful specimen of manhood."

Luke moves his head infinitesimally to rest against my cheek. His skin is cool and clammy, and his face is drawn as if the skin has been pulled inch by inch into every crevice of his skull, the muscle melted away. Every movement feels brittle, as if something will break any second. He looks like a skeleton. He's not the only one in the Castro. He's not the only one in San Francisco.

The lesions are all over his face, crawling steadily closer to his eyes and nose, as if he's drowning slowly in his own rebellious skin.

"Tell Lewis," he says, a papery whisper on his shrunken tongue. "Tell him I'm sorry for what we—" He chokes, and there is blood on the pillow.

"I love you," I tell him. I don't know if I'm lying.

"I'm sure you do, Dorian," he says.

I kiss him, long and hard, and he doesn't fight back.

I CAUGHT SIGHT of Lewis in the hospital waiting room as I passed through. He locked his eyes with me fiercely; his anger was livid and bright, powering the husk of his body. I felt like storming over to him, shaking his bony shoulders, telling him that these days, we should be used to losing things. You can't get too attached to your toys.

He looked rough—bagged eyes, concave chest. Not a sign of the godlike figure between whose legs I had worshipped months ago in Sankeys. But credit to him: he'd lasted more than the six month prognosis I gave him.

Outside, I paused to light a cigarette, and blessed the brush-and-oil lungs of my distant counterpart as I inhaled deeply.

"Aren't you afraid?"

The blond man stepped up to me, though I had counted myself alone on the steps of the hospital.

I exhaled. "Of what?"

He indicated the cigarette. "Dying."

I laughed. "Not really."

The blond man smiled. "That's good," he said.

"Look," I said, "I don't mean to be rude, but you're possessing of a pretty poor sense of timing."

"Oh, my apologies," he said, looking up at the hospital doors. "Another one dead, is it?"

I was too exhausted for anger. "Something like that," I said.

"You'd think you'd be used to it by now, wouldn't you?" the blond man said. He stepped closer, produced his own cigarette from his pocket, motioned to me to light it for him. I extended my lighter. "All those people dying around you. Old hat. The corpses piling up around your *beautiful* face."

He leaned in closer to me, shielding the nascent cherry of the cigarette against the wind. His hand touched mine for a second.

It was as if I had been licked by the slimy, bristly tongue of some foul, preternatural creature; every inch of my skin felt as if it had been turned inside out to puke its stinking contents in the gutter. For a moment his face, leant close to mine, was no longer beautiful; his pale white skin was the hue of maggots in a soldier's wound, his lips the sheets between a miscarried mother's legs.

"Oh, Dorian!" he shouted after me, as I beat a hasty retreat. "Surely you don't believe there's anywhere far enough to run away from all this?"

I meet Freddie in the Rooftop Lounge, and fuck him in Sankeys. Five months later, he moves his head infinitesimally to rest against my cheek. His skin is cool and clammy, and his face is drawn as if the skin has been pulled inch by inch into every crevice of his skull, the muscle melted away. When it's all over, I stalk morosely away from the hospital, and don't dare look to see if the blond man is on the steps.

Leon I meet in the Castro Theatre, his cock in his hand to a grainy video of two bears fucking in a workshop, furtive with the thrill of it. He takes me home to his house on the other side of the city, a respectable, shady tree-lined street, and we pull each other's clothes off as soon as we're in the safety of the cool hallway. We're together for seven months, until his movements become brittle, as if something will break any second. He looks like a skeleton. He's not the only one in the Castro. He's not the only one in San Francisco. He's not the only one in America.

I wonder what my portrait looks like now.

Aimlessly walking the blank corridors of the hospital, I run into Lewis. We hug, anger forgotten, and he introduces me to his new boyfriend, a boisterous drag queen by the name of Tallulah Travesty. I summon the spark of humour to plaster on a charming smile, take her hand, and say, "Why, madam, if I might be so bold as to say . . ." but then Lewis elbows me in the ribs and I laugh it off. She's not my type anyway.

"Aren't you going to introduce me to your friends?" the blond man asks me, when I pass him on the steps, but I ignore him, and sweep Lewis and Tallulah past him, before he can lay a pestilent finger on either one of them.

I meet Nelson in the dark-room of The View, and the low light hides things for a while. He's fresh in the city and I'm the older man—oh, if he only knew. But when he moves into the light, I can see his naked body is already pricked with black patches. As I take him, he reaches behind to hold me, as if marvelling that anyone is touching him. When we're done, I pull my clothes on, kiss him on the forehead, and escape onto the street. I can already see the shape of the hospital bed forming around him.

I search out Lewis and Tallulah in Las Playas, and we go dancing.

The music in the club was hardly what my erstwhile Lord Wooton would have envisioned at even the most debauched of his parties. As we danced in the strobe lights, three drunken men at the centre of a visibly emptying dancefloor, I closed my eyes, and pictured myself eighteen again, clean-cut and freshly enamoured with the indulgences of life. There was Henry, in leather chaps dancing in the corner. Basil, dizzy on poppers, grinding with the leather queens. Sybil a towering drag queen with candy-cane hair piled high. We'd really outdone ourselves, hadn't we?

I could feel the eyes of men on men, but tonight I shrugged it off. I am, and always have been, desirable. I'd already had my fill tonight, and I could still feel the shudder of it, lubricated by fingers and tongues, creasing the lines of my portrait. I'd rather not lay more burden upon it tonight; in fact, it quite appealed, to be dancing there in the centre of the dance floor, an incandescent beauty for all the good men of the Castro to lust after, fruitlessly.

Come on gentlemen, I thought. *Dance to keep the wolf at the door.*

In the gap between lights, I was sure, for a moment, I saw the blond man smiling to himself, waiting for my gaze to alight upon him.

THE LESIONS ARE all over his face, crawling steadily closer to his eyes and nose, as if he's drowning slowly in his own rebellious skin.

"I love you, Lewis," he says, a papery whisper on his shrunken tongue. "I love you—" He chokes, and there is blood on the pillow.

"I love you," Lewis tells him.

"Me too, Tallulah," I say.

Lewis kisses him, long and hard. Neither of them have any fight left in them.

When the nurse draws a sheet over Tallulah's face and ushers us from the room, I escort him to a forgotten corner of the hospital, and let him slump into a heap. We're both getting used to this routine, but I'm still the more experienced.

"It's not fair," he says.

"I know," I said. "He was too young."

"Not that," he said. "You. Untouched. God, you're still so *beautiful*. How have you escaped this . . . this . . . this fucking *thing?*"

I put an arm around his shoulder. It's angular and weak. I wonder how he's still here. He wonders the same thing about me.

"Do you want me to die?" I ask.

"No," he says, and leans into my chest to get the afternoon's sobbing out of the way before we go dancing.

IN MY ATTIC, I stood in front of the covered portrait. My finger twitched at the corner, ready to fling it away, unveil my face.

I could picture it clearly.

My skin would be cool and clammy, and my face drawn as if the skin had been pulled inch by inch into every crevice of my skull, the muscle melted away. Brittle, as if something would break any second. I would look like a skeleton.

The lesions would be all over my face, crawling closer to my eyes and nose, nothing but the whites of my eyes left. As if I was drowning slowly in my own rebellious skin. But then, I'd felt that way for years.

One thought kept me from pulling it away, showing me to myself.

What if it wasn't? What if my face was exactly as it had been the last I saw it? Aged, yes, sick, yes, but not laid low by the plague that had, one by one, snuffed out the lives of all my lovers. What if the portrait had nothing to do with it? What if I had just *survived*?

"HERE HE IS!" Lewis announced giddily. He was practically skipping along the street. It would have been hard to credit that it was only three months since Tallulah's death, but this was a sight common in the Castro these days—nothing lasted long, so you grabbed hold quickly.

"Him?" I asked, and tightened my grip on Lewis' skinny wrist.

"That's the one," Lewis said.

The blond man extended a hand to shake mine.

"I'd rather not," I said.

"Dorian!" Lewis was shocked—properly shocked, not his usual pantomime version. He looked at me pleadingly, shaking himself loose of my hold and wrapping himself around the blond man's arm. I was momentarily torn, but the hurt in Lewis' eyes swayed me. I extended a hand and shook, feeling my skin crawl.

"A pleasure to meet you, Dorian," the blond man said.

"It always is," I said.

"Right, ladies," Lewis said, stringing an arm around each of our shoulders, "it's time to *party!*"

He led us, awkward but compliant, from the street up the spiral steps to the Rooftop Lounge. It was busy that night. In fact, I can tell you exactly how many people were there. Sixty-six. Sixty-seven including me. That's what the newspapers said.

The music was pounding, the drink flowing, but as many shots as Lewis thrust into my hand, nothing could coax me into the party mood. I prowled the floor, placing myself as far away from the blond man as I could at any cost, watching the evening ramp up.

Be warned. There's something out there.

Lewis and the blond man were dancing, increasingly lairy as the night wore on. His fingertips on my friend's bare chest made me shudder, slithering across the corrugated ripple of his ribcage, the crater of his belly. I couldn't begrudge Lewis his happiness, but I didn't have to participate. At eleven, I slipped down the stairs to the bohemian hubbub of the street, seeking solitude amongst the crowds, and lit a cigarette. It was more than the usual partying tonight—the seeds of a protest parade were gathering, marching with placards. Save our lives! Save our lives!

I vowed that when I got home, I would uncover my portrait, look and see what damage should have been done to my body.

"Aren't you afraid?"

I didn't turn.

"I said, aren't you afraid?"

I sighed, and sucked on the cigarette. "Of what?"

"That it's your fault they keep dying?"

"That's not me," I said. "It might be you, though."

"That it might," the blond man said. "But even you couldn't possibly take the blame for all of those bodies in the morgues. But some of them? Maybe." He lit his own cigarette. "Thomas. Luke. Freddie. Leon. Nelson. Tallulah. Lewis—soon."

"It wasn't me," I said. "I'm not sick."

"No," he said. "You certainly don't look as if you are."

We were both quiet for a moment, watching the world go by. A moustached man in tight leather shorts and denim shirt ran his eyes appreciatively up and down the length of me. I returned the gaze, and then his eyes flicked to the blond man; he practically licked his lips with lascivious delight. I sneered inwardly, and mentally rejected him, added him to the stockpile of Men I Would Not Deign To Fuck. He marched on down the road, the placard wavering. *Save our lives! Save our lives!*

"I wonder who *could* take the blame?" the blond man said. "The first rotten seed. Who could possibly be responsible for *all of this.*" The last three words fell from his lips lightly, like a schoolboy proud of his science fair project, beckoning eagerly to his parents to come see.

I didn't answer.

"The devil perhaps?" The blond man smiled. "I don't know, Dorian. You're on better terms with him than I."

I grated the last of my cigarette into the ground.

"If the preachers in the city squares are anything to go by," the blond man said, "then it's God. But I don't really believe in him. I don't think there's anything out there."

I opened my mouth to speak, but I couldn't form a full sentence. Instead, only one word rattled out of my throat, amidst phlegm and spittle. "Monster."

"Probably," he said. "You'd be the one to know." He stepped close to me, and rested a hand against my cheek. Beneath his skin, the maggots squirmed. "It's really not fair, is it?"

he said. "Your face. So pretty, whilst everyone else's wastes away."

He kissed me firmly on the lips, and I vomited sourly in the back of my throat.

I STOOD IN front of my painting, with the lighter burning in my hand. It was not the first time in my century of living I had considered sending my frame up in flames, but I had never been so tempted. You can clean a wound by burning away the dead skin and cauterizing the hole. You can stop an infection spreading.

At the foot of the Rooftop Lounge, I'd laid a thin line of fluid across the doorstep and stepped back. Behind me, people marched, frothing with oblivious indignation.

Lewis nearly made it out alive. He'd squeezed through a window—many of them did. Thirty-two of them, if we're talking numbers. But Lewis went back in, to save his lover, the blond man. His blackened body was found, arms wrapped tight around the blond man to protect him from the engulfing flames.

He wasn't the only one to die. Two brothers, and their mother. A reverend. The man who, trying desperately to squeeze between the bars of the upstairs windows, died screaming, fused to the searing metal.

The cremated bodies of Lewis and the blond man were photographed. You can hang them in a museum with Thomas' last remaining photo.

And here I was, in my attic, squaring up against my painting.

I'm sure I don't need to tell you that the death of the blond man changed nothing. History isn't on my side. You know as well as I that the sickness carried right on spreading. I didn't save anyone. I never do.

I'd branded him a monster, but his skin had crisped and turned to charcoal like any man's would. Except mine. On the streets of the Castro—and the streets of hundreds, thousands of cities across the world—men (and women, and children) were still dying. Their skin would be cool and clammy, and their faces drawn as if the skin had been pulled inch by inch into every crevice of their skulls, the muscle melted away. Their movements would be brittle, as if something would break any second. They would look like skeletons, all the skeletons of the world gathered in adoration around the beautiful monster, Dorian Gray.

Be warned, I thought, as I pulled away the sheet. *There's something out there.*

Matthew Bright is a writer, editor and designer. His short fiction has recently appeared or is forthcoming in *Queen Mob's Teahouse*, *Cairo by Gaslight*, *The Biggest Lover* and *Glitterwolf: Halloween*. He is the editor of the forthcoming anthologies *Threesome* (Lethe Press) and *The Myriad Carnival*, and alongside the poet Christopher Black, he is the co-author of the experimental novella *Between the Lines*. Whilst paying the bills as a book cover designer, he edges slowly closer to completing his first novel. He lives in Manchester, England with his partner John, and a dog with a taste for eating valuable hardback books. Find him on twitter @mbrightwriter or online at www.matthew-bright.com.

ALIEN JANE

KELLEY ESKRIDGE

She came in as a thinskin and we started off badly. Thinskins pissed me off. Everything about them was hopeless: their screams, their red faces, the smell of their blood; and there was always blood because it was night and they came from Emergency. They made me remember where I still was, and that was a terrible thing, a monster thing with nowhere to go but boiling out of me in a cloud of rage that fogged me for hours sometimes. The ward is where they put you when you have the rage.

"Don't you bring her in here."

"Calm down, Rita, go back to your own bed."

"Don't you bring her in here."

"Rita, I won't tell you again to behave yourself." Molasses voice and muscles, and she meant it, Madge the Badge, chief white hat of the night shift. The thinskin lay silent as Madge and a no-name nurse made a sling of the sheet under her and moved her onto the empty bed, the one near the door because I liked the window view: it was just the sidewalk to the parking lot, but I could see people walking away. I thought about *away* for a while until the nurses finished with the sheets and the needles and left me alone with her. Then I got up and took the few steps across the linoleum floor.

"You shouldn't be in my room, I don't want you, and if you give me any hassle I'll hurt you, I swear."

She had her eyes closed until then but she opened them wide, bright blue. And she laughed, laughed. She howled. Two nurses came running into the room, and one held her down while the other shot her up, and the whole time she made noises until her face turned purple. They shot me too, I hate that, but the worst was the thinskin and how she scared me.

She slept almost the whole next day. I got to where I could shake the sleepydrugs off pretty fast, but she was an amateur, down for the long count. The nurses had her under Close Observation; they came in every fifteen minutes to check on her. "She's still gone, what did you people give her, can I have some?" I kept saying, until they finally made me leave the room. I thought maybe she didn't want to come back up, maybe wouldn't, but later I looked in from the hall and there she was cross-legged in the bed, looking fuzzbrained, the blankets and sheets twisted up around her waist.

"You're up. I've been up for ages. You missed breakfast, you missed lunch but it was crap, lunch I mean, so I guess you're better off, and dinner'll be here soon. You wanna come down to the TV room and watch *Remington Steele?*"

She blinked for a while and then she said, "I have to go to the bathroom." She had a low voice, the kind that always makes me want to practice so I can sound like that. You can talk onto a tape to do it. I used to think about being an actress, but that was all crap too, getting up in front of people and letting them see you cry.

I got my first good look at her while she was trying to get out of bed: older than me, maybe twenty-five, yellow dirty hair, and those blue eyes. She was a mess, bandages everywhere, and where she wasn't all wrapped up she was the pastypale color that white people get when they eat meat all the time and don't work it off. She made my fingers itch to stuff an entire head of broccoli down her throat. She moved slow, and she looked at me. She pulled one leg out of the covers, and looked at me, then the other, and looked, until I finally said, "You see something you don't like?"

She shook her head. "Last night . . . you said . . ."

"Oh, hijumadre, forget it, I don't like nights and I don't like thinskins, but I won't hurt you. I was just being mean."

"Thinskins?"

"Yeah. New patients, you know, start by crying and yelling that they don't belong up here with all the rest of us really crazy people, which of course they aren't, crazy I mean, and it's all a mistake. Then they get pitiful for a while and won't talk to anyone and shake all the time. They go off if you say boo to them. Thin skinned."

"Right." She was on her feet by this time, more bandage than body. "Well, I'll just have to remember that I belong here," and then she looked like she might cry, which I hate. I started to drift out and let her get herself back, but I don't know, something about her . . . I don't know. Anyway, I put out one arm and said, "Bathroom's over here," and walked her to the door.

A nurse came in then and took over, she gave me a look and said to the thinskin, "Everything okay here?"

"I didn't do anything," I said.

She was better when I came back, but I didn't want to talk and I guess neither did she, except she said what's your name and I said Rita and she said Jane.

SHE HAD DR. ROUSSEAU who was my doctor and the best, not someone that I wanted to share with creepy Jane; Rousseau, who half of us would have swallowed rocks for, and even the nurses liked. Rousseau spent a lot of time on Jane, but Jane wouldn't talk much more to her than she would to anybody else, which I respected in a way. She wouldn't even talk to Tommy Gee.

"Does she say much to you when you're together on your own, without any doctors around? Does she seem to communicate better with her peers?" Tommy Gee was always doing that, mixing up the stupid patients talk with the doctor talk so you never knew if he meant it for you or some white coat standing behind you. His real name was Gian-something-Italian but we called him Tommy Gee-for-gee-whiz because that's how he was about everything, including being Rousseau's intern.

"If you mean does she relax when she's with the rest of us mentals then no, Dr. Gee, I guess she isn't comm-you-nee-cating well at all. Maybe they don't talk on whatever planet she's from."

"That doesn't sound very supportive, Rita."

"You're the doctor, you support her."

And he tried to. He was always coming around after her sessions with Rousseau to talk to her, see if there was anything he could do to get her to open up. She was his special project.

I got used to having her in my room because she was so quiet I didn't notice her half the time. I talked to Rousseau about that in one morning session, and she just said hmmm and wrote it down.

"I think Tommy Gee likes her, too, but she probably hasn't even noticed how stupid he gets around her."

"Hmmm."

"I guess it'll be okay having her there, I mean, I probably won't even notice when she's gone until two days later."

Rousseau put the cap back on her pen and sat back in her chair. There was a little mended place near the pocket of her doctor coat. The first time I saw Rousseau was twenty hours after I came into Emergency, when they moved me up to the locked ward. She asked me if I wanted to talk and I said no like always, feeling like a rock in the gutter when the rainwater runs over it pushing it little by little toward that big dark hole going down. I said no, and then I saw the mark on her coat, the careful clumsy darn, and I could never explain how it made me feel; but then it was okay to talk to this woman Rousseau.

She turned the pen over in her fingers, gave me a doctor look. "Haven't you thought that you might be the first to leave?" she asked.

I SPENT THE rest of the morning like always, huddled up with Terry Louise on the bench down the hall from the nurses' station: her smoking cigarettes until she could hide behind the cloud they made; me trying to find some way to make my back comfortable against the wood slats, and making kissy noises at the boy orderlies when they went by, because I hated the way they always picked on the little scared ones to rub up against when they thought no one was looking. They walked itchy around me after what happened that one time.

"I hate it when she does that," I said. "Why does she have to talk about me leaving?"

"Just say no, babe," Terry Louise said through a mouthful of smoke.

"Can't keep saying no forever."

JANE'S BANDAGES CAME off, and she was all new pink skin on her arms and legs, like someone had decided she was a big fish that needed scaling. "She did it to herself," Terry Louise said one morning from behind her smoke.

"No way."

"Uh huh. Why do you think she's in here? This isn't a plastic surgery ward."

"No one has the guts to do that to themselves. There's no way she could have got past the first leg."

"Madge the Badge was talking to one of the student nurses last night. So unless the meaning of 'self-inflicted' has changed while I've been away, No Brain Jane is sicker than we are."

"We're not sick."

"Stop squirming around and sit still for half a minute, Rita, you look like something I'd like to bait a hook with," Terry Louise said. The old scars down the inside of her dark arms showed plainly when she raised the cigarette to her mouth. She smiled.

SUSAN CAME TO see me over the weekend. She made me feel like she was holding my soul when she touched me: I wished Jane would disappear, but she was right there, watching.

"Suze, this is my new roommate Jane." I rolled my eyes, but not where Jane could see.

Susan leaned across the gap between our beds and held out her hand. "Hi."

Jane picked lint balls off her blanket.

Susan stood with her hand out. Jane wouldn't look at it.

"You shake her goddamned hand, you pink turd; I'll hurt you worse than whoever did you the last time."

"Rita, shut up." Susan put her hand down. Jane was shaking and squeezing her fingers open and closed around great fistfuls of blanket. Her eyes were shut tight, so she didn't see me reach for her.

"*Back off, Rita.*"

Susan got me out of the room, down the hall. She left bruises on my arm.

"Don't hang onto it. I don't care, I don't even know her. Anyway she must be hurt pretty bad."

"Fuck her. Everybody's hurt."

That was all it took to spoil my day with Susan, just ten seconds of goddamned Jane. When Suze finally left we were both strung tight, dancing around each other like beads on a wire. I glided back into my room like running on electric current.

It came out at Jane then, all my meanness in evil words, and Jane just closed her eyes and bit down on her lip to keep from crying; and when I finally stopped, she opened her mouth and said something that might have been, "I'm sorry, I'm sorry," but it was hard to tell around all the bright red where she had chewed her lip right through.

THE LIP NEEDED stitches. "Frankenjane," Terry Louise chortled up and down the hall, "Frankenjane, feels no pain."

"Shut up, Terry Louise."

"Well, excuse me, honey, I meant to say Princess Jane. Princess Jane, so insane—"

"Shut up!"

"Humph," Terry Louise said, and lit another cigarette.

"She didn't even know she'd done it."

"I know, you told me seven times already—"

"She practically bit her lip *off*, I could see her teeth right through it, and her tongue was all dark red—"

"Rita—"

"Rousseau said it wasn't my fault, but we all have to be careful, we have to be careful, she's always getting hurt and not knowing because she can't feel the pain and you were right, she did that other stuff to herself, to her own self, it's sick, how could anyone do that and not feel it, it's sick, she just chewed herself *up*—" and I couldn't stop talking, faster and faster, couldn't stop even when Terry Louise ran for Madge the Badge.

IT TOOK A long time to wake up from the needlesleep the next day. I was still in bed when Rousseau and Tommy Gee came in with Jane. I wanted to open my eyes, to say I'm sorry, but the drug was like a staircase that I had to climb, and every time I got to the top I would be back at the bottom again: like big wheels in my head turning all night, so I was more tired than if they had just let me cry for a while.

"Thank you for seeing Dr. Novak," Rousseau said to Jane. "Do you have any questions about the kind of testing he wants to do? I know he might not have explained things completely, he's so excited about your condition . . ."

Jane was quiet.

"Please understand how important this is," Rousseau went on. "No one here has had the opportunity to examine congenital insensitivity to pain; it's very rare, and there are so many things we want to know . . ."

"I'm not a lab animal."

"No, you're not. No one will treat you that way. You're a person with an unusual condition, and with your help we can learn the best ways to deal with other people who have it. We may be able to help you find ways to live with it. I promise no one will hurt you . . . I mean . . ."

"I know what you mean, Doctor." Jane sounded a hundred years old, tired and thin-voiced.

"You don't have to do this if you don't want to. No one will make you," Tommy said gently.

"Will you excuse us for a moment, Jane?" Rousseau said. I felt her and Tommy move past me toward the window, their footsteps sending small shudders through the bed and the bones of my skull.

Rousseau kept her voice low. "Tommy, I expect you to back me up on this."

"I just don't think we should push her. She's only just started to connect with us. It's a little soon to ask her to include someone else in that trust."

"Dr. Novak is one of our best research neurologists. I think we should be supporting Jane's opportunity to work with him."

There was a silence that seemed long.

"I don't understand why you're doing this. I know you don't support his research funding, you even wrote a letter about it to the Chief of Neurology last year."

"How did you know about that?"

"Everybody knows."

Rousseau's voice suddenly sounded very close, sharp. "Great. Then maybe everyone should know that I have since retracted that letter and encouraged several of my patients to participate in Dr. Novak's studies. Including Jane, if she's willing."

"I still don't think—"

"Thank you, Doctor," and that didn't sound like any voice I'd ever heard come out of Rousseau; what's wrong I wanted to say but I couldn't open my eyes. I heard Tommy Gee thump out of the room.

Then Rousseau took a deep breath and walked past me to Jane's bed.

"Well, I just need you to sign this release."

I knew I should open my eyes, but I couldn't stop climbing stairs inside my head. No, I tried to say, no no, but I could only make a little noise. "Go to sleep, Rita," Rousseau said, and pulled the curtain across between me and Jane.

SHE BECAME SILENT Jane again, and I saw less and less of her because she had started the testing, and once the lab rats got hold of her they didn't want to give her up. The nurses talked about it up and down the halls, even Madge who was such a porcupine for rules; so we all heard about Jane in the lab being electroshocked and pinpricked and nerve pressed and never feeling a thing, and how it was something you were born with, and that nothing that happened to you ever hurt, no matter how bad it was. Terry Louise said it was kind of neat, and Jane was like the star of one of those old flying saucer movies where the alien takes over your body, so you look like a human but you're not.

ONE DAY IN the room, I wanted to say I was sorry.

"Forget it."

"I didn't mean to hurt you."

"Stupid. Stupid, stupid. No one can hurt me. They've been trying for a week now. Go ahead, do your best."

That wasn't what I meant, I thought, and I couldn't think of anything to say, so I just went on sitting on the edge of my bed rubbing my fingers down the little nubby rows of the bedspread. Jane lay on her back, arms straight by her sides, toes pointed at the ceiling. Her pajamas were dirty around the seams. She looked very thin, greasy with fatigue. She kept absolutely still. She moved only to breathe, and she wouldn't look at me.

I thought I would lie down too like that and look at the ceiling, and be very, very still. The ceiling was gray and restful. I wondered, if Jane and I lay in the same room long enough, would we start breathing together? When I closed my eyes I could hear everything. I heard orderlies wheeling medicine carts past our open door, the pills hissing in the tiny paper cups, little insects full of honey and poison; nurses in rubber soles; Terry Louise in paper slippers; Tommy Gee in his pointy leather shoes; Dr. Rousseau in heels: all stopping at our door, heads bent around the jamb looking in at Jane and me laid out like bodies on the back tables of funeral parlors, waiting to be made pretty enough to be seen by the living. Go away, I thought, go away, and they all did, while Jane and I breathed together and the morning light turned gray under the weight of wet clouds and the light in the room dimmed into something soft and private.

After a long time the old pictures came back into my head, and this time it was okay, okay to let the pictures move through me while the light was cool and the room was quiet with the sound of our breath like slow waves on a beach. The pictures turned into words, and I told myself to Jane.

"When I was little I wanted to wear jeans and climb up the big oak tree onto the garage roof and play pirates for the rest of my life. I could see everything from there. I thought I was queen of the world.

"Down the road from us was a big field where the grass grew as high as my waist, all green and reedy, so it whispered when the wind went over it. I would run through it with my arms flung out wide, as fast as I could, so the wind would pick me up and fly me away. But I would always lose my breath too soon and fall down into the green and the smell of warm wet dirt with just a strip of sky showing overhead, and I would have this whole world that was just for me, just mine."

I breathed gently and thought about my green place, and Jane was there; I could feel her in the grass wanting to run.

"When I was twelve, they took it away. They decided it was time for me to start being a girl like my sisters and my mother, and they took away my overalls and made me put on shoes that hurt my feet. I tried to climb anyway, and my dress got caught around my waist and under my arms so I couldn't move, and I knew I could never run in those shoes. I looked around and saw all the women I knew never running, never moving, weak and tired and bound up, and I couldn't believe my parents would do that to me, that they would tie me up like a box of groceries ready to be delivered. I said I wouldn't do it; I was standing in the dining room in these clothes that felt like ropes around me, and I said I won't, I won't . . . My father took me by the arm and locked me in the hall closet with the winter coats. It was dark, and I couldn't move in those clothes, and the shoes were too narrow for my feet, they hurt . . . I think it was those shoes did something funny to my mind. I think they were why I hung my Christmas doll up by one foot over my father's favorite chair in the living room and set fire to it . . . to the doll, I mean. I lit the match and put it right up against the hair and the whole thing melted and dripped onto the place in the chair that was rubbed shiny from my father. The house smelled for weeks.

"Then I was always in trouble. Always fighting. I burned more things, I tried to run away. I hurt my little sister bad one time with a rake. Everything just got worse. It's better now I'm not with them anymore."

Jane said nothing.

"Maybe it's better you're here now."

Jane breathed.

"I stole things, I got caught. My parents gave me up to the court. My mother cried, said she couldn't do anything with me. She's Catholic, she'll carry it forever. I spit at the judge. That's what got me away from my folks, spitting at the judge. He didn't care about the broken windows and the badmouthing and the knife that time . . . he just didn't like me spitting at him. Spoiled his day."

Maybe Jane smiled, maybe not.

"But it all just hurt too much after a while. When you fall down out there in the world it isn't green and soft, it hurts . . . I met Suze in that place for girls where they sent me . . . but it was too late and I felt so bad and I tried—"

I thought of Jane's legs and arms.

"They have to put you in here for that, and at first I hated it, it was like the closet again. But now there's Rousseau and Terry Louise.

"I don't do those things anymore, not really. I still . . . you know, I still say things sometimes, but even then it's like I only do it to make myself feel bad. I guess the meanness is going out of me. Rousseau says I'm better. She wanted me to leave a few months ago . . . but I screwed up, I did it again . . . one of the orderlies, that stupid Jackson pissed me off. But I could have been out, only I . . . I couldn't remember anymore how it felt, running in the grass."

Wax Jane, silent Jane. Ceiling-staring Jane.

"Suze is what I have left, if I mess that up I don't know what would happen. So I get funny sometimes. I guess you don't have to shake her hand if you don't want to."

I closed my eyes. It surprised me when she answered. Her voice sounded like she hadn't used it in a long time.

"I saw how she held you, how she touched you, you know? And I thought . . . how lucky you were that someone would touch you like that. And then she held out her hand to me . . . I couldn't take it. It would kill me right now to have anyone be that nice to me. I'd rather spend all day with those doctors poking wires in me than one second with your girlfriend's hand in mine."

There was something in the way she said it; I saw again my father's face when he found the doll in a stinking puddle, and my mother saying *how could you, how could you,* but never answering her own question. Jane reminded me of how the world can be so different sometimes from what we expected. I got up and poured her a cup of water and put it on the table by her bed. I knew she wouldn't want me to touch her, even though I would have liked maybe just to hold her hand, not like with Suze, but only because she was scared and in a lonely place. I crawled back onto my bed and turned on my side away from her, blinking against the light. I thought that in my life I had been little Rita, and Rita full of rage, and crazy Rita, and now maybe I would be some other Rita: but I couldn't see her, I didn't know if she would be someone who could run through the world and not fall down.

ROUSSEAU CAME INTO my room the next morning. She looked funny, and she said a strange thing: "Rita, please come with me down to the lab."

"Why?"

"Jane is asking for you. I'd like you to go be with her, if you don't mind."

We walked down the hall. Rousseau started for the elevator and I said, "I want the stairs, okay?"

She turned back so fast she almost caught Weird Bob's visiting sister with her elbow. "Sorry, I forgot about the claustrophobia." She didn't apologize to the sister. That and the forgetting and the asking in the first place made three strange things.

We walked down the stairs. I went first. "Three floors down," she said. She was close, only a step or two behind me. Her smell came down over me like green apples.

"Rita . . . you know that Jane agreed to work on these experiments with Doctor Novak. She's a volunteer. I just want you to remember when you see her . . . I don't want you to think . . . she isn't being hurt . . ." she said in a queer, rushed voice that didn't even sound like Rousseau. I stopped. Her hands were jammed into the pockets of her white coat, and her face was turned to the wall, and she wouldn't look at me.

That was the strangest thing of all, and it scared me. It wasn't Rousseau standing over me, her red hair sparking under the stairwell light. My doctor wasn't scared; my doctor was an amazon, a mother confessor, a carrier of fearlessness that she would breed into me like a new branch grafted onto a young tree. My doctor wasn't this person who was saying, "Just be calm and don't worry, everything will be fine."

"What's the matter with her?"

"Let's go."

My slippers rustled on the stair tread and on the linoleum of the hall when we went through the landing door. I followed the stripes painted on the wall, around and around the hallways like a maze. We came to a locked ward door and a nurses' station beyond it.

The two men behind the desk wouldn't let me in until they checked with Novak on the telephone. The brown-haired one had a badge with a metal clip that he tried to put on me, and I wondered if I would have to hurt him, but Rousseau said, "Don't touch her."

"Doctor?"

"Let her put it on herself."

Brown Hair rolled his eyes and handed me the badge dangling between two fingertips, arm outstretched. Rousseau said nothing, but she was shaking just a little as we went down the hall. We could hear Brown Hair say something to the other one, and they both laughed, and I didn't like being there at all, in a place I didn't know, with strangers.

The hall was long and mostly bare, with only a few metal-backed chairs next to closed doors. The air smelled like ammonia and sweat and burned electrical wires. It was quiet except for our breathing, the *rsshhh rsshhh* sounds of our clothes and Rousseau's hard-heeled, strong step. Then I began to hear another sound, a rise and fall of muffled noise like music, but something about it made me want to walk faster, and then it was Jane screaming and I began to run.

The place where they had her was at the end of the hall, a high-ceilinged room that made an echo out of Jane. The lab was full of white: white-coated doctors, orderlies in white pants and shirts, Jane in her cotton pajamas with her rolling eyes that showed white and blue, white and blue. She sat in a wooden chair with a high back and arms. Thin rainbows of color twisted out of her head, wires running out of her scalp into the machines around her. More wires with small discs on the end lay taped like lollipop strings against her neck; her left wrist; her pink-scarred calf; her ankle; under her nightgown at her heart. She sat very straight in the chair because her shins and forearms and ribs and head were belted against the wood with padded ties the color that white people call flesh, and I wondered if they thought that no one would see the ties because they were the flesh of Jane. Jane was screaming around a rubber mouthpiece that showed tan and wet from her saliva every time her lips pulled back—not terror screams but more like some giant grief, some last precious thing taken away. The room was full of her smell.

I couldn't go in. I stood at the door and I couldn't step into what I saw in that room. Everyone except Jane had stopped in mid-motion; they stared at us with the glazed otherplace look of people caught in the middle of some terrible thing like rape or butchery, the kind of act so horrible that while it is happening the doing of it removes you from all human space. I tried to turn around, but Rousseau was right behind me with her hands braced against the door frame, leaning into it like she would push the whole thing down. Then there was nowhere to go but ahead.

"Goddammit, goddammit," Rousseau was muttering as she moved in behind me.

"What are they doing, what are they doing to Jane?" I said but she didn't hear me. Novak came over and stood in front of us like he was trying to keep us from coming any further in.

"Jesus Christ, what is happening here? I told you to stop the goddamned test until I could get back." Rousseau's voice was low. I felt squeezed between her and Novak.

"Calm down, nothing happened, she's just upset."

"She's still my patient. You had no right."

"Nobody has done anything to hurt her. Christ, Elaine, I'm a doctor, I don't—" Jane stopped screaming, suddenly, like a light turning off. Spit ran down her chin. The machines buzzed and the paper strips whispered onto the floor. A woman with a needle stepped over the coiled electrical cords toward Jane, and I could feel myself tense.

"It's okay, Rita," Rousseau said. "I'll get someone to take you back to the ward."

"No." I pulled out from between them, went toward Jane. Behind me I heard Rousseau start in on Novak. I felt proud of her again, fighting for Jane; then I was standing in front of the woman with the needle and she turned toward me. "Leave her alone," Rousseau said, and the needle went away. Jane saw me and tried to move. I didn't know if she was trying to get away or get closer, and for a moment I remembered the Jane who didn't want to be touched in love, the Jane who would rather stay different in her wires and straps, apart from people, alien Jane; and the Rita who always reached out with hurting hands. Then I unbuckled all the straps and put my arms around her, and she didn't pull away.

The other people in the lab began to move then, but they didn't seem to know what to do or where to go. I didn't want them to touch Jane but they did; they took the wires off her head and peeled them off her legs. They had to reach under me to get to her arms and chest. There was a piece of metal under one white bandage on her arm. They took the metal and left the bandage. They took the mouthpiece, but no one wiped her wet chin so I dried her with the corner of my robe. There was a funny smell about her, something burning; fear-sweat, I thought.

Rousseau came over, with Novak following. They squeezed around me. Jane closed her eyes.

"Let me see her, Rita." And so I had to let go. My hands still felt full of her even when they were empty.

Rousseau said something to Jane I couldn't hear. Jane shook her head, eyes still shut, face pale and moist under the hot lights.

"What's this?" Rousseau said.

She had found the bandage on Jane's arm. When she peeled it back, the arm was white around a stripe of red, and in the center of the stripe was a blister, raw and runny. The smell was worse with the bandage off.

Rousseau looked up at Novak. Being next to her made me feel cold.

"It was an accident," he said. "We were testing her for heat response, one of the techs pushed the dial up a little too high." He shifted, jammed his hands into his coat pockets, rolled his eyes like he thought Rousseau was being ridiculous. She still hadn't spoken. She was so tense I thought she might break apart if she made a sound.

"Oh, come on, Elaine. Nobody got hurt."

"What do you call this?" Her voice was very soft.

"I call it an accident, for chrissakes. It's no big deal. She didn't feel a thing."

Jane began to cry.

Rousseau put the bandage back over the wound and smoothed down the tape. She stood up. "I'm reporting this," she said to him, still speaking softly. "I won't let you harm one of my patients, not that." It was like she was talking to herself.

"She's not really your patient anymore."

"You can't do that."

"I already have. She signed the consent form; she's a volunteer. I can do her a lot of good."

"You don't have enough clout for this. I don't care what kind of strings the Chief of Neuro pulls for you this time."

"Try me," Novak said. "But you'd better be ready, Elaine, because you'll have to go across country to find a job after I'm finished with you."

"Jesus," Rousseau said thickly.

"Jane is the professional opportunity of a lifetime," Novak went on, "and you don't have the slightest idea of what to do with her. But I do."

It felt like a punch in the stomach, the sick-making breathless kind. *It isn't true*, I wanted to say, and then I saw Rousseau's face like still water, and I turned away so I wouldn't have to watch while Novak put one arm around her and led her away, saying softly, persuasively, "Don't be upset. I didn't mean to upset you. Jane will be fine with me, I promise, she'll be fine, and you can still manage her therapy, keep an eye on her, why don't we just go have a cup of coffee and talk it over." I moved closer to Jane and she grabbed me, pulled me in, and I realized she was whispering, her voice becoming more clear as Novak and Rousseau moved away.

". . . it keeps you safe, keeps you safe, the pain keeps you safe, because it hurts and you know something's wrong. People like me die if we're not careful. We pierce our lungs with a broken rib we didn't know we had; we smile and eat dinner while our appendix bursts inside us; we hold our hands out over the fire when we're children and laugh while the skin turns black. Pain keeps you safe. It's how you keep alive, how you stay whole, it's such a human thing, and I don't have it. I don't have it. And you people . . . you think . . . no one ever asked if I could—but I can, I can, I can feel a touch or a kiss, I can feel your arms around me, I can feel my life, and I can feel hopeful, and scared, and I can see my days stretching out before me in this place while they forget and leave the heat on too long again and again and again, just to see, just to see me not knowing until I smell my own skin burning and realize. And when I look at them they aren't human anymore, they aren't the people that bring me ginger ale and smile at me. They're the people that turn up the dial . . . and they hate me because I didn't make them stop, and now they have to know this thing about themselves. They'll never let me go."

I held her tight. "Tell them," I said. "Tell them like you told me. You can make them stop, Jane, you don't have to—"

"I do have to, Rita, I do, I have to be . . . I keep thinking that they'll find a way to hurt me the way they want to, something that will work, and then I'll be okay, I'll be safe, I'll be like everybody else, and I won't have to be alone anymore."

And then I understood that the smell in the room and the rawness under the bandage was her pain, her alien pain; and I suddenly knew how she might have taken a knife and stripped her own skin away, earnestly, fiercely, trying to see what made her different, find it and cut it out and take away the alien and just be Jane.

I held her. There was nothing I could say.

THE NEXT DAY Jane was transferred to the locked ward upstairs. Tommy Gee didn't want to let them take her. "There's a mistake," he said. "Wait for Dr. Rousseau. She'll be here in just a minute." But I knew she wasn't coming. "I'll find her," he said, and went running down the hall.

Jane stood just inside the room, one step from the hallway that would take her further inside her fear and her need, and she smiled. "I'll come see you when I'm better," she said. "You and Susan."

"Yes," I said.

"We'll go to the beach," she said. "We'll spend all day. We'll swim and lie on a blanket and eat sandwiches from a cooler. We'll get ice cream. We'll go for a walk and find crabs and sand dollars. We'll get sunburned and you'll press your finger against my shoulder, it will stand out white and oh, I'll say, oh, it hurts."

"Yes," I said, "it will hurt."

She looked at me like she was flying, and then she went out the door.

I found my jeans and a sweatshirt and sneakers and put them on, and packed my things into my duffel bag that had been stuffed into the back of the closet for so long. I went down to the nurses station, passing Terry Louise on the way. "Where are you going?" she said.

"To the beach."

"What?"

"Bye," I said, and I could feel her watching me all the way down the hall, so surprised she forgot how much she liked to have the last word.

"You can't leave," the day nurse said uncertainly.

"This is the open ward, amiga, I can walk out of here anytime I want."

"You aren't a voluntary patient, you have to have your doctor's signature."

I don't have a doctor anymore, I wanted to say, and then Tommy Gee was there looking pale and tense. He saw my bag.

"I'll sign for this patient."

"Did you find Rousseau?" I said.

"I talked to her." He looked past me down the hall. "She's gone."

I wasn't sure who he meant, Rousseau or Jane, but I nodded.

I WALKED DOWN five flights of stairs to the lobby entrance doors, and stopped. I looked back across the open space, full of people with flowers, new babies, people sleeping on couches, people crying, people going home. Two women went past me, one with a new white cast on her arm, the other one saying, "Are you okay? Does it hurt?"

The hurt one bit her lip and shrugged. "It doesn't matter."

"Oh yes it does," I said. I walked to the door and thought, *I will be Rita running in the grass*, and took the first step out.

———

Kelley Eskridge is a writer, screenwriter, and editor. Her novel *Solitaire* is a New York Times Notable Book, and was a finalist for the Nebula, Spectrum, and Endeavour awards. Her short fiction collection *Dangerous Space* includes two Nebula finalists and three Tiptree Honor stories. "Alien Jane" won the Astraea Prize, was a finalist for the Nebula award, and was adapted by SyFy for television. She is an independent editor with an international client list of established and emerging writers. She attended the Clarion Writers Workshop, has taught the Clarion West Writers Workshop, and served on the board of Clarion West for five years (including three as board chair). The film of her screenplay *OtherLife* is in production, which makes her enormously happy. She lives in Seattle with her wife, novelist Nicola Griffith.

THE LORD OF CORROSION

LEE THOMAS

JOSH HAGEE TOOK a chair as the school counselor composed herself on the other side of the desk. He noted the dandelion yellow file folder, too thick for the average five-year old, and blanched internally when the woman reached out plump fingers to open the cover. Her lip twitched and her mouth set in a slight smile that was meant to project tolerance and patience. She gazed at him over the frames of her glasses, and then returned her attention to the file.

"This is your third visit with us, isn't it?" the woman asked. Her name was Cynthia Pederson, and she wore her brown hair in straight-cut bangs that ran through the pale horizon of her forehead. Her white blouse and powder blue cardigan were either sardonic or anachronistic, and Josh figured the latter was the more likely. Ms. Pederson showed little to no sense of humor, let alone irony.

"Yes," Josh replied. The third time in less than a month.

"I'm afraid this time is particularly serious, Mr. Hagee," she said. "You know our rules regarding hate speech and microaggressions?"

"Yes," he said. The school was very proud of its zero-tolerance-for-intolerance policy. It had been one of the deciding factors in choosing the school for his daughter, Sofia. What he didn't know was how this applied to her.

"This morning, Mister LeBlanc was guiding a free expression period, allowing the students to explore their imaginations through art." Ms. Pederson paused, a calculated act that grated on Josh's nerves. She pushed her glasses high on the bridge of her nose, and then said, "How is everything at home, Josh? Have there been any changes in the household, any new people introduced into Sofia's environment?"

The question landed thick with judgment, though he immediately attributed this perception to his sensitivity to the situation. It was a natural reaction, he felt, to having been summoned from work for the third time in a month to be called a bad father.

"No," he said. "Nothing."

"I see," Ms. Pederson replied.

She withdrew a sheet of paper. Josh could see the bold colors of a child's art project on the face of it. Ms. Pederson eyed the painting and offered Josh a practiced expression of concern, blended with just enough disappointment to be infuriating. She handed the sheet to Josh and then peered over her tented fingers for his reaction.

Sofia had painted a wooded scene. Narrow tree trunks, slashes of brown, rose from the bottom of the sheet to the top. In the center were a series of rectangles, a house or a cabin with a single window and a smudge of pale yellow inside it, perhaps denoting a face. Directly above this figure and laid out along the roof were a series of crosshatched lines drawn with yellow paint. A squiggly line shot toward the thing from the blue sky like lightning striking a television aerial. Light blue, not very different from the counselor's cardigan, filled the gaps between the trees. The image was blunt but rendered well enough for a child of five.

Across the top, in bright red letters, scrawled as if written in blood, were the words:

No Spic Talk

Josh Hagee and Ozzie Dial hadn't known much about Sofia's parents when they'd adopted her. Her mother was Mexican, and the father was "not in the picture." According to the agency, the mother was healthy with no history of serious genetic issues. Josh remembered little of the details regarding the mother's medical history. He'd already switched into father mode, wanting nothing more than to hold his baby after years of wondering if it would ever happen. Naturally, Ozzie had paid attention, which was good. Ozzie always paid attention. Details thrilled him. He'd read every adoption form three times and then had broken the information down for Josh, whose eyes had grown heavy every time he'd been faced with another page of bland, tightly stacked, Times New Roman. "Just show me where to initial or sign," he'd often told his husband.

When Sofia turned three, he and Ozzie decided it would be best if they maintained Sofia's connection to her heritage, so as a family, they'd started Spanish language classes. Though he'd never become fluent, Josh could speak complete phrases and discern meaning from context. His daughter, however, was fluent and often switched to speaking Spanish, sometimes in the middle of a sentence. These days, Sofia continued to practice the language with the online program Josh had bought for her.

All of which made the horrible note on her art project more confounding and terrible. Was it possible she simply didn't know what she had written? *Spic?* Where would she have even heard that word? Though thriving in the heart of Texas, Austin was *not* Texas. It was a liberal blue puddle in the middle of an immense red field, and Josh couldn't remember the last time he'd witnessed an act of blatant racism. Certainly none of the kids in Sofia's school would utter such a terrible thing? Would they?

Ms. Pederson had suggested a bit overzealously that Josh treat Sofia's digression as a teachable moment (a phrase he hated nearly as much as microaggressions). The school practiced what it called a voluntary suspension policy, allowing parents to remove their children from classes to reinforce the severity of certain actions. Josh had taken the option.

As they neared the house, with Sofia rocking back and forth against her seatbelt, Josh returned to the subject that he'd put aside after the counselor's office.

"Who taught you that word?"

"What word?"

"This is serious, Sofia. The word you wrote was a very bad word. It's insulting to a large group of people. People like you and your mommy."

"I don't have a mommy," she said. "I have daddies."

"Sofia, I'm upset with your behavior. Now stop bouncing in your seat. *Spic* is a terrible word. It's used by hateful people to make Hispanic people feel bad about themselves. Now I want you to tell me who taught you that word. Was it one of your friends at school?"

"No," she said, no less animated in the passenger seat.

"Did you see someone say that in a movie or on the television?"

"No."

"Then who was it? Where did you learn that word?"

"From my daddy."

"Sweetheart, I'm your daddy, and I would never use a word like that."

"Not you," Sofia said, rolling her eyes and giggling. She bounced in her seat. "My *other* daddy."

OZZIE DIAL DIED three weeks after Sofia's fourth birthday. He'd been driving home from a late night at the office and suffered a heart attack while changing lanes. His Prius broke through a guardrail and hit a steep incline. The car rolled half a dozen times, ultimately settling on its roof, crushing Ozzie in the process.

After the morgue and the funeral, after the endless paperwork for insurance companies and credit card companies and a hundred other details, Josh had thought it best if he and Sofia spent some time with a grief counselor. He wasn't sure how to manage his own feelings let alone those of a child. He'd found the sessions tedious, the counselor saying nothing he hadn't already told himself hundreds of times.

You seem angry, Josh.

And why the hell wouldn't he be angry? His life had gone from on-track and wholly satisfying to completely fucked in the course of a couple of hours. Instead of building a family with the man he loved, he had become a single parent, and though he loved his daughter beyond words, he felt incapable of raising her alone.

Yes, he was angry. Genius diagnosis, buddy.

Even so, Sofia had loved "Mr. Bob," and she'd continued seeing the man for the better part of six months. The therapist had found a way to speak to her about an issue far too jagged for Josh to handle. For that Josh was grateful.

In light of Sofia's insistence that she'd learned a bad word from her dead father, Josh scheduled an appointment for her with Mr. Bob that afternoon. He took two days off work to spend time with Sofia during her suspension from school. At the therapist's office, they sat on the sofa and waited, Josh checking his email, while Sofia bounced on the sofa cushion, excited to see her friend again.

The therapist opened the door to his inner office and leaned through, beaming a warm smile. "There she is," he said merrily. He was portly, with a thick brown beard and sparkling eyes. Josh often mused that in his retirement, Mr. Bob could build a distinguished career as a department store Santa, if such a thing interested him. "It seems like forever since I last saw you."

Though it had only been a month since her last visit, Sofia leapt from the sofa, shouting, "I know! Forever."

"Hey Josh," Bob said. "Sofia, why don't you wait inside for me?"

"Thanks for seeing us," said Josh.

Bob asked what was happening, and Josh laid it out. He didn't know if scrawling the word was an act of self-loathing or simple innocence. But he wanted to know where Sofia had heard it. More and more, he felt certain the phrase had to have come from one of her friends in her kindergarten class, perhaps another child who'd tossed the phrase out naively, having heard it at home. More disturbing though was the attribution of the slur to Josh's dead husband.

After the therapist returned to his inner office to begin the session, Josh checked his work email and scanned the notes for emergencies. Finding none, he tapped on the euphemistically branded "dating" app and opened a note he'd received that morning:

I'm free tomorrow. If that works for you?

Josh tapped his reply, *Sorry. Busy the next couple of mornings. How does Friday work for you?*

Waiting for the response, he gazed through the window at a mesh of leaves and branches. He cast quick glances at the two doors leading into the room, a reflex of guilt, and then returned his attention to the phone.

Ten minutes later, *Friday works*, appeared on the message screen.

When the door to the inner office opened again, Bob walked through. Sofia remained in the room, engrossed in coloring. Bob closed the door behind him and sat on the sofa next to Josh.

"I'd like to see her again next week," Mr. Bob said. His sparkling eyes held concern.

"What's going on? What did she say?"

"It's nothing serious, so don't get yourself worked up. Essentially, she's manifested an invisible friend. Nothing new or troublesome in that. What makes this interesting is she doesn't suggest the friend is present, like someone she might have a tea party with or play games with. This friend is remote. She talks to him, but he's never actually near her."

"My daughter is hearing voices?"

Mr. Bob held up a hand. "Right now, it seems to be her imagination at work. That's all. I don't get the impression this is indicative of a larger, medical concern. So don't google 'schizophrenia' and think you're going to solve a mystery. I have no reason to believe this is anything but a little girl trying to make sense of her father's death. She's acting out and attributing the behavior to a father figure."

"So she really believes Ozzie is communicating with her?"

"I need more time with her," the therapist said. "It seems she's imagined an abstract notion of 'father.' She wouldn't come out and say it was Ozzie, but that could simply be her unwillingness to accept that he's gone. Clearly, she doesn't mean you, so yes, I would assume her friend is a construct of Ozzie, though one which exhibits negative characteristics."

"Negative characteristics?"

"The racial slur. Some instances of profanity. Nothing she probably hasn't heard a dozen times just walking down a street or through a store. How much access does she have to the internet?"

"Next to none," Josh said. "Why?"

"Just establishing her points of influence so we can get a better idea where some of this messaging is coming from. What do you mean, 'next to none'?"

"Her tablet only has learning apps, a handful of games, and an app to stream kids' movies. I formatted the parental controls on the device before I gave it to her."

"Good. Okay. And she has no access to your home system or any of your devices?"

"No." He considered some of his online chats, and he knew better than to let his daughter anywhere near the content of those. His home computer and all of his devices were password protected, and he kept track of them.

"Good. Then let's get an appointment set up for next week."

"What do I do until then?"

"What you have been doing. If you can get her to say more about this friend, good. But go easy. We don't want her feeling threatened."

THE NEXT EVENING Josh and Sofia had a couch picnic with pizza and juice. On the television, an animated ocean swirled and pulsed with color. For as much as Sofia enjoyed more recent films, her favorite movie, the one she always requested when she was feeling down, was *Finding Nemo*. So Josh watched the movie for the hundredth time as he considered the questions he wanted to ask his daughter.

Sofia had been sullen all day. Her eyes appeared heavy and clouded, and when Josh asked how she was feeling, she just said, "sleepy." Throughout the day, she'd excused herself from activities, telling Josh she needed a nap but in every instance, he'd heard her up and moving around in her room not more than ten minutes after she'd closed the door.

As the screen filled with turtles gliding toward an ominous tide, Josh paused the movie.

"Dude!" Sofia said, doing an uninspired imitation of one of the film's characters.

"I think we should talk about your friend," he said.

Sofia lowered her head and kicked her legs against the sofa. "I don't want to."

"Why not?"

"I don't like him anymore. His voice sounds funny now, like he's mad."

"What's he mad about?"

Sofia yawned and rubbed her eyes and nestled back against the arm of the sofa. "I think he was always mad, but he pretended to be nice, and I don't want to talk about him, because he might hear me, and then he'll start talking again."

"Does he say mean things to you?"

She remained silent, wedged back in the crook of the sofa arm. She twitched as if startled, and then she put her index finger to her lips. "Shh," she whispered.

The man he'd met online, the man who actually looked better than his photos, the man whose real name was Roy though he identified himself online as "Jim," kissed him and petted Josh's chest through the thin cotton shirt.

"I had a good time," Roy said.

"Yeah," Josh said, leaning in for another quick kiss. "So did I."

And while he meant it, and while a part of him wanted to see the man again, he didn't believe it would happen. For five months after Ozzie's death, Josh's sole focus had been on Sofia. He hadn't thought much about his own loneliness. Then, Sofia had spent a weekend in Houston with Ozzie's parents, and Josh had felt an emptiness in the house bordering on the maddening. He'd gone out for a drink with friends, and had met an attractive guy who had looked nothing like Ozzie. Josh had gone home with him. After that tryst, he'd downloaded the dating app and had, on occasion, pursued transient companionship through the service. He never saw the men he met a second time. Part of this was a function of guilt. He had no idea what was considered a respectable mourning period. The other part, the louder more insistent part, was the sad and practical reality that it was far too soon to introduce a new man into the family, into Sofia's life.

He felt relaxed on the drive back to his office. As the familiar scenery of the city fell in around him, his thoughts clicked back into everyday considerations.

His attempts to get more information from Sofia had failed. Though he'd asked several times about her friend, the one Mr. Bob believed to be an abstract of Ozzie, Sofia had said nothing new on the subject. During their time together in those days after the painting incident, Sofia had grown quieter. Removed. Her need to be near him, constantly engaged with him in conversation or action, as she'd been since infancy, had vanished.

Sofia no longer demanded his attention. In fact, she made less than subtle demands to be left alone. When they weren't together, she studied her Spanish lessons and spent long stretches in her room, drawing or claiming to nap, though she never appeared rested. As for her drawings, the pictures were odd for a girl her age, just fields and roads with the occasional car on them, and wooded areas, but gratefully none of them carried hateful captions.

At the office, Josh fell immediately into his routine, immersing himself in scores of emails and documents. Coworkers dropped by his office asking after Sofia's welfare (he'd told them that she was down with the flu), and he assured them all that she was doing much better, a statement he wanted to believe, until Sofia's babysitter called in a panic at ten minutes to five.

THE SHRIEKING, MUFFLED by the walls of the house, reached him the moment he opened the car door. The sound lodged in Josh's throat like a stone. He raced up the walk and threw open the front door.

Chloe, the college student Ozzie had hired two years ago to sit for their daughter, stood in the living room. Broken picture frames and shattered glass littered the floor at her feet. One hand clutched her head, and her thumb was wedged sideways between her teeth. She appeared stricken and confused. Seeing Josh, her hands dropped to her sides, and she hurried to him.

"What happened?" he asked, setting off for the back of the house where the screams still pealed.

"She was fine when I picked her up from the school," Chloe said, following him down the hall. "I got her home, and she ate some crackers and had her juice, and I swear everything was fine. Totally. Then she went to practice her language assignments. It was totally normal. Totally. Then I heard her crying, and when I went to ask what was wrong . . ." Her voice trailed off.

At the end of the hall, Josh pushed open the door to Sofia's room. Toys and books lay scattered about the floor. A porcelain doll, dressed like a Flamenco dancer, lay in ruin. Sofia had torn the doll's ruby red dress with its black lace hems, shredding the skirt and the sleeves. The face was gone, as if shattered to free something from its head, leaving a jagged ridge along the jawline and a partial dome of ceramic to which hair still clung.

Sofia faced the corner, arms locked at her sides with her head tilted up. She screamed at the ceiling, one piercing note after another.

Josh went to his daughter and pulled her into his arms. He turned her trembling body around and hugged her, stroking her hair and whispering, "Shh. What's wrong, sweetheart? What's wrong?"

Her screams subsided but she continued to cry. Small arms locked around Josh's neck, and Sofia sobbed into his collar. He cried softly with her. Josh's chaotic thoughts tumbled and collided. He needed to know what was happening to her, needed to make it stop. She was in misery, and it was his responsibility to soothe her, but this was all beyond his understanding. He knew she was hurting, and he knew with agonizing certainty that he was failing her.

No words of adequate comfort occurred to him, so he just repeated the sound Shh in his daughter's ear. After some time, Sofia's sobs ended, leaving the residue of her misery damp on his collar. He placed her on the bed and then sat beside her.

"Can you tell me what's wrong?" Josh asked. He took her hand in his and held it gently.

"You're going to leave me," Sofia replied, her voice as soft as a whisper.

The dreadful proclamation startled him, and Josh shook his head.

"I'll never leave you, sweetheart. Never. Why would you think that?"

"Because. He said."

Josh knew the *he* she meant—her invisible friend. But if this friend was an extension of Sofia's imagination, then surely the belief he would leave had originated with her, and he needed to know why.

"He's wrong," Josh told her. "He is very, very wrong. We're a family, and I'll always be here for you."

"No. No. No," Sofia said. Anger drew hard lines around the words. "You met a new husband and you're going to leave me and I'm going to be all alone and he said . . . he said . . . and he told me . . ." But she couldn't finish the thought.

"That's not true, sweetheart. It's just not."

"He said," Sofia whispered. "He told me you were going to have a new family and there wouldn't be room for me, and you didn't want me because I was a stain. A dirty little stain, and you and Roy didn't want me."

Roy? The name jumped at him from the mire of Sofia's fearful speculation. How could she know that name? It wasn't possible. And even if she did know the name, why would she believe that his presence in their life presaged her abandonment?

He told her repeatedly that he would never leave her, and he wrapped his arm around her small shoulders and pulled her tight to him. When exhaustion overcame his daughter, he tucked her under the sheets and kissed her forehead and waited for the soft breaths of slumber before standing and turning for the door.

On the wall, written in red crayon, were the words:

Fuckin Faggots
Cant be Saved

JOSH SENT CHLOE home and left a message for Mr. Bob, and then he walked the house, unable to outpace his fear and concern. He poured himself a shot of vodka, threw it back, and then closed his eyes until the sting in his throat subsided. The alcohol didn't help.

He returned to Sofia's room with a garbage bag and quietly, so as not to disturb her nap, gathered up the shattered pieces of the Flamenco doll. Once she was awake, he'd need to run the vacuum to make sure no slivers of porcelain remained in the carpet fibers. As he completed the task, he noted the stack of drawings and paintings on Sofia's desk. Though fearful of what ugly language he might find scrawled among the pages, Josh believed there might be some clues to Sofia's behavior in the artwork. Clearly, at school she'd felt more than comfortable expressing herself through painting. Maybe there were other clues in the buildings and landscapes she'd taken to drawing. Josh gathered up the stack of pages and carried them out of the room.

At the dining table, he spread the papers out and immediately noticed that some of the drawings Sofia had shown him during her school suspension had been altered. They still showed streets and what Josh imagined were fields, but now captions had been added to several of the pieces. The first he examined had numbers and words written along the neatly lined roadways. US 79 was written on a stretch of road running from the bottom of the page to the top. The road that intersected it was labeled Henry B. Oltorf Blvd. Other pictures showed similar intersections, some of which Josh recognized.

What became clear was that Sofia was writing down directions. She was plotting a course.

How had she known about Roy? He wondered. How was it possible? Even if she, or someone else, had managed to hack his phone and read the messages he'd exchanged with the man, they would have seen the pseudonym he used. They would have seen the name "Jim." Josh had only found out the man's real name that morning through a verbal exchange, and he hadn't spoken to anyone about the encounter. Not a single person.

Was someone following him? Was the man who called himself Roy somehow behind all of this? Similarly unlikely threads of paranoia began to knot in his head. He attempted to untangle them with logic, but there wasn't a fucking thing logical about any of this.

What if Ozzie's spirit really was in contact with their daughter? What if he was always just behind Josh, at his shoulder, watching?

No, Josh thought. Ozzie's parents both carried hard, red streaks of prejudice in them, but not their son. Ozzie wouldn't chastise their daughter for learning Spanish. The lessons had been his idea. And he certainly wouldn't coerce their daughter to write a phrase as hateful as the one Josh had read on her bedroom wall.

He was not beyond considering the possibility that his daughter might be haunted, but he refused to believe it was by the ghost of Ozzie Dial. No, if otherworldly forces were acting on the child, they were using Ozzie's identity.

And was he really believing any of this?

He shuffled through more of the drawings until he had extricated all of the images that included road designations. As he did so, another picture caught his eye. It was identical to the one she had painted in school: a house or cabin with a single figure at the window; and trees rising high around the building. Again he noticed a crosshatch of yellow lines, covering the center of the roof above the window. Only this time the squiggled lines that he'd first thought of as lightning seemed to jut away from the design, more like the cartoon interpretation of a radio signal. This drawing also had words on it, but instead of the ugly racial slur she'd noted in red paint, it was a less overtly offensive phrase, yet one that made Josh uneasy.

It read:

Daddy Gundy lives here!

MR. BOB CALLED as Josh worked on the riddle of the street names. Using his tablet's map application, he was able to trace a path from Austin to a small town on the edge of the Davy Crockett National Forest, about three hours away. The town was called Lynnville, and all of the other intersections Sofia had carefully noted lay between their home and this destination.

Before Josh proceeded with the next step of his investigation, the phone rang and he picked up to hear the level, cheerful voice of his daughter's therapist.

Josh explained what had happened—the tantrum, Sofia's unsettling certainty that Josh would leave her, the grotesque slogan scrawled on her wall. He said nothing about Roy or the time he'd spent with the man. Then, he began to describe the pictures he had found.

"And this is a real city?" Mr. Bob asked.

"Yes," Josh said. "It's real."

"She's never been there?"

"*I've* never been there. I don't even know how she would have heard of it."

A pronounced silence filled the line between them, and Josh became impatient.

"What?" he asked.

"Nothing," Mr. Bob replied. "At first, I was thinking about internet predators. You know, trying to lure her away? But if someone were attempting such a thing, they'd know Sofia couldn't get there on her own. She'd have to convince an adult to take her, and then . . . what? Leave her with a stranger? It doesn't connect."

Josh had thought the same thing, but someone had given this information to his daughter. The town of Lynnville existed, and she had mapped a course to get there. Further, he had to believe that her invisible friend—who likely was neither—lived there, or at least she believed he lived there.

"Look Josh," Mr. Bob said, "I'm out of town until Monday. I'm going to email the contact information for a colleague who works weekends. I'll expect to see you Monday afternoon, but if Sofia has another episode, you should call him. Okay?"

"Sure."

"We'll figure this out," the therapist said. "Until we do, just try to hang in there."

Though reasonable, the advice was insufficient. Josh had no intention of waiting for his daughter to endure another episode. He needed to bring her peace, to ease her mind. He wasn't going to wait around hoping the problem fixed itself.

He said goodbye to Mr. Bob, and then he opened a search engine. He plugged in the two words he thought were the most relevant, the name of the town and the name of Sofia's invisible friend. As he hit the return key, he prepared himself for a long slog through dozens of irrelevant websites.

His assumption was wrong. The information he needed came up instantly, and there was plenty of it.

Gundy Morgan had been the mayor of Lynnville, Texas. Six years ago, a woman named Yolanda Ramirez had killed him, shot him in a field on the outskirts of the town. Ramirez was convicted of the murder and currently resided in Mountain View, a correctional facility for women, awaiting the state to carry out her death sentence.

The first article he read was Gundy Morgan's obituary, and it was as generous and fawning as one might expect, honoring a civic leader who had met an ugly end. Then he read several articles, regarding the trial and Ms. Ramirez's sentencing. The bulk of them had the woman convicted before the trial even began, but one article stood out, if only because a less reactionary mind seemed to control the keyboard from which the article had sprung.

Josh wrote down the reporter's name, and then continued reading.

OVER THE YEARS, Josh and Ozzie had wondered about Sofia's birth parents. They'd woven stories about these people at the kitchen table after late night feedings, or while picking up toys in the nursery, or while enjoying the quiet moments during which Sofia slept. The story they decided on, the one that lacked the high drama and ridiculous conjecture of the more entertaining tales, was bland but wholly feasible: two very young people were in love, and Sofia had been the product of that love. They were too young to raise a child on their own, but they were smart enough to know it. Both Josh and Ozzie had imagined a happy life for the couple, now free to grow into adulthood, rather than having it forced upon them too young.

A sixty-three-year-old mayor, murdered by a young woman, had never played into their speculations.

THAT NIGHT, HE sat with Sofia at the kitchen table, pondering the numerous pieces of a jigsaw puzzle that would, upon completion, depict a Disney village and the heroes, the princess, and the villain that resided there.

Sofia looked exhausted. She could barely keep her eyes open as she tested one piece after another, making slow progress on the game.

"Sweetheart, can we talk about your friend?"

She shook her head without looking up from the table.

"Is his name Gundy?"

Her head lifted, revealing wide, frightened eyes. She raised her hands to the sides of her head as if ready to clap them over her ears. Her mouth pinched tightly, and she looked about the dining room as if searching for witnesses before nodding her head.

"Is he the one who told you to draw the roads?"

Again, his daughter nodded, slowly, cautiously. Her palms remained only inches from her ears.

"Does he want you to come visit him?"

"I'm not supposed to say."

"Sweetheart, I'm your father. It's my job to take care of you, and I can't do that if you don't tell me the truth. Does Gundy want you to visit him?"

"He doesn't want me to visit," Sofia said. "He wants me to stay."

"Stay with him?" Josh asked. "For how long?"

"Forever," Sofia whispered. "He said that somebody saved him, and he's pure now, but I'm a stain, and I need to go to him to be clean. And I'm scared, because I don't know what he means, but he keeps saying it." She was working herself up. Her voice trembled horribly. "What's wrong with me?"

Josh leaned forward and wrapped his arms around her. "Shh," he said. "It's okay. There's nothing wrong with you. Nothing at all."

Sofia stiffened in his arms and then began to wriggle free of his grasp. Josh let her go, and she sprang away from him, clapping her hands over her ears.

"Oh. Oh," she cried. "He's back. He's back. Make him stop, Daddy. Make him stop!"

HE PLANNED THE trip to Lynnville without really knowing what he expected to do once he got there. He placed a call to Joan Carter, the reporter who had written the most even-handed, least flattering articles about Gundy Morgan, suspecting she might have background he could use. His cover story was ridiculous, a writer researching a novel about the incident, but it worked well enough to get him a meeting with the woman. After that, he didn't know. He wanted to find the shack Sofia had drawn, because he felt certain that it was important to this mystery, but that was a needle in a haystack, and he didn't even know how to find the haystack.

What was he looking for? Really looking for? A ghost? An evangelical shock jock with a cruel sense of humor and an audience of one?

Sofia's insistence that this specter had been saved added a new layer of dread for Josh. He hadn't expected it, though perhaps he should have. Gundy had no problem transmitting his vile prejudices, and though Josh knew intolerance and religion didn't rely on one another, they'd been woven together enough times to make the connection unsurprising.

Saved? Such a bizarre idea. If Gundy Morgan had been saved why wasn't his spirit comfortably nestled in Redneck Heaven? Why was he tormenting a child?

And what difference did the ghost's motivation make, unless it would help him stop the thing and bring his daughter peace?

If he took Sofia with him, maybe he could show her an empty shack and convince her to ignore the voice, or perhaps use her as a conduit to the spirit, finding some weakness or weapon against it. But he wouldn't bring his daughter anywhere near Lynnville. That was what Gundy Morgan wanted.

He called Chloe and told her he needed to work to make up for the days he'd taken off during the week. Normally Chloe didn't work weekends, and after the horrible tantrum she'd witnessed that afternoon, she was understandably hesitant to say yes. But she needed the money, and she did love Sofia, so she agreed.

Sofia pouted when he told her the lie. In the morning, she asked him to stay, and then she begged.

"I'm just going to work," Josh said, attempting to make light of his daughter's concern. "You and Chloe will have a lot of fun, and I'll be home at the normal time."

JOAN CARTER WAS easy to spot in the diner. An attractive woman in her mid-fifties, she wore her blonde hair in a short, utilitarian cut that framed her face. She looked up from her coffee when Josh entered and eyed him, visually deconstructed him, and put the pieces back together as he approached the table.

They greeted one another, and there were pleasantries, and Josh noted the woman's direct nature, something that had been implied during their phone conversation, but which now came through clearly as he found no hesitation in her manner or words.

"You want to know about Gundy Morgan?" Joan asked.

"Yes."

"And you've read my articles?"

"The ones I could find online, yes."

"There were others," she said, "but my editor, a buddy of Gundy's, refused to publish them. They got to the truth of the matter, but that made his buddy look bad, so he killed them. I spent two years writing about the lumber industry and school bake sales after that."

"So, what isn't in the articles?"

Joan paused, and Josh found the silence discomforting. He gazed at Joan, and only when their eyes had locked did she continue. She wanted his full attention, wanted him to see her face when she spoke.

"Gundy Morgan was a sick, racist prick who terrorized the women in this town. That's the simplest way to put it." She again went silent, allowing the information to sink in. "He took pride in his hate. Didn't mask it. Didn't dissemble. Even by East Texas standards he was an anachronism, but the town loved him. At least the men with power did."

"But the women?"

Joan made a dull, um-hmm sound in her throat and nodded. "A lot of women wished they'd pulled that trigger."

"But only one did."

"Yes. Yolanda Ramirez. She was a young girl who worked at the diner here. Nice enough. She lived with her aunt out on Telegraph Road. She was smart and ambitious, used to say she was saving up for school. She was also strong, not physically mind you, just had that kind of character."

"Gundy raped her?"

"She was one of his victims." At this point, Joan broke eye contact. She drank some coffee and peered out the window, then focused her attention on the table. Josh began to wonder if the reporter also had been a casualty of Gundy Morgan. "But Yolanda was different. She got pregnant, and Gundy wasn't having that."

"Did she want money?"

Joan fought a smile and lost. "No. Yolanda wasn't like that. She intended to have the child and raise it. She was a Catholic girl, so other options weren't even considered. Honestly, she managed as well as anyone could after the attack. She continued working, even served Gundy his bacon and eggs, often at this table right here, but following the attack her aunt met her every night after work and drove her home."

"Then I don't understand," Josh said. "Was the trauma deeper? I mean, did she just let her anger build until she couldn't take it anymore?"

"No," Joan said. "No, Yolanda wasn't avenging herself, she was protecting her baby.

Yolanda told me that Gundy came to her house and demanded she abort the child. He said that if she didn't do it, he'd take care of it himself. When he came at her one night, she was ready for him."

"It was self-defense?"

"No question," Joan said. "And I put that and all of the other pertinent details into several letters I wrote to the defense attorney and to the courts and to the governor. Didn't amount to so much as a fuck you note."

"Did you testify to all of this?"

"I wanted to, but I wasn't even called as a witness," Joan said. "The fact is, Yolanda never stood a chance. Even her defense attorney, that sawed-off peckerwood, was a buddy of Gundy's. He only took it to trial to get the death penalty. Wouldn't even consider arguing the charges down."

"I still don't understand," Josh said. "If Yolanda had kept quiet, if she didn't want anything from Gundy, why was he so intent on her aborting the child?"

"That was a mystery," Joan admitted. "But I heard a conversation between a couple of his buddies after the trial was over, and I think it explained his motivation. These guys were celebrating Yolanda's conviction over beers down to Bowie's. One of them toasted the verdict and said he was glad Gundy got him some justice. The other agreed, but he said something about what a shame it was that Gundy's blood was going to be polluted."

"Polluted?" Josh asked.

"I honestly think Gundy was worried about keeping his bloodline pure. The idea that his whiter-than-white DNA might be carried through generations of mixed-race children genuinely disgusted him."

"That's insane."

"Gundy was a monster," Joan said. "His disease was hate, and it was contagious. It got him elected as mayor and it kept him in office for far too long. Only near the end did he start to lose some of his hold over folks."

"What happened?"

"He *stopped* going to church," Joan said. "Around here, that raises eyebrows."

"Wait a minute," Josh said. "He stopped going to church?"

That didn't exactly line up with talk of salvation.

"Well, he stopped going to Lynnville Baptist. I heard some strange talk near the end there, and I came across something, working on the story. In short, a scary man got scarier. An old boozy lawyer who'd known Gundy for about fifty years said Gundy had found himself a new savior. Wouldn't say anything else about it. In fact, he looked like he was about to shit himself for having said that much."

"A new savior?" Josh mused.

"Can I show you something?" She reached for her cell phone and powered it on before he could answer. After some tapping and swiping along the screen, she handed the phone to Josh. "What does that look like to you?"

The picture on the screen showed an open door and a tight space—a closet of some kind—brightly lit by the camera's flash. On the floor of the closet sat a small, red pillow, likely for kneeling, and a large blue ceramic pot had been shoved against the base of the back wall. Above this, an intricate design of circles and lines had been scrawled in black paint. It looked tribal. No, he thought, it looked mystical.

"What am I looking at?"

"Gundy Morgan's bedroom closet. I managed to get a few pics before the Sheriff's Department ran everybody out. You know what's in that pot?"

Josh shook his head, still examining the insane pattern scrawled across the wall.

"It's animal remains," she told him. "Looked and smelled like he'd coated them in lye. I wanted to get a picture of it, but the sheriff's men ran us out."

"You think he was sacrificing animals?"

"He wasn't making lunch. But again, whenever I tried to talk to anyone about this, I met a brick wall. They weren't interested in the crimes or eccentricities of their hero."

"Can you send me this picture?" He handed the phone back to Joan.

"Sure can," she said.

A moment later, his cell phone pinged and his screen lit up. The notification of Joan's text ran across the picture of Sofia he used as wallpaper.

Joan reached for his phone, taking Josh off guard. "May I?" she asked, already holding the screen to her face.

"Sure," Josh replied, too late to protest. He put her rudeness down to the overstepping curiosity of a journalist, but he still found it impolite.

"She's pretty," Joan said. "Is she yours?"

"Yes. My daughter. Sofia."

"And she's why you're here."

"I told you, I'm—"

"Bullflop," Joan said, setting the phone down. She leaned across the table and whispered, "You may be familiar with yesterday, but I wasn't born there. You haven't taken a single note, and you haven't recorded a word of this, so put away the shovel. Besides, she looks just like her mother."

Josh said nothing.

"You adopted Yolanda's child, and you're looking for background on her parents."

Instructed by her caution, Josh also looked about the diner, checking over his shoulder and ascertaining the whereabouts of their server before saying, "Yes."

This news seemed to please Joan immensely, but the joy on her face crashed a moment later into a stern frown. "Do not tell anyone in this town about that. Gundy's hooks are still in deep with a lot of these people. Some would be more than happy to finish what he started."

BEFORE LEAVING HER at the diner, Josh had asked Joan for directions to Gundy Morgan's property. He'd thought it an easy enough request, but Gundy's children had sold off huge parcels of land in the aftermath of their father's death. Only one small plot, to the northeast of the homestead, was still owned by the Gundy estate. Managed by the eldest son, Gundy's kingdom had been reduced to two acres of wooded area with nothing on it but dirt, trees, and a dying creek as far as Joan knew. She'd given him directions that circled up and around the property.

Her speculation about Gundy's motivation—the effort to keep his bloodline pure—ate at him. It was grotesque, but in a way it explained the messages the monster had been sending to Sofia. He'd called her a stain, something to be cleaned, to be purified. To someone like Gundy those words were likely synonymous with the word *erased*.

Josh parked on the side of the road, next to a sign that had been burned into a scrap of plywood, reading: "We don't call 911 until we're done with you."

Hesitantly, he set off through the trees. He could locate no defined path, but the ground cover was minimal, so he found little in the way of obstruction as he walked deeper into the wood. Under different circumstances, Josh would have found the scent of pine and rich earth relaxing, but the fact he was searching for a ghost, a depraved spirit, erased any pleasure he might have taken from the scene. Branches cracked in the distance. Leaves rustled from low ground cover on his right—a squirrel, a bird, a monster wearing Gundy Morgan's face.

Though two acres wasn't a large area to cover, Josh moved slowly, always conscious of the direction he'd come. He wanted to know he could get back to his car fast if necessary.

It took him ten minutes to find the cabin. In fact, he'd walked past it and had only caught it from the corner of his eye as he'd surveyed the land to his left. The building looked enough like the ones in Sofia's art to tighten the skin at the back of Josh's neck. This was the place Sofia expected to find her "daddy." Hardly large enough to be considered a cabin, really more of a glorified shack, the cracked wooden slats siding the small building were etched with black mold and foul, oatmeal colored fungus. A single black window faced the path. The porch canted dangerously to the side, and the roof above it had caved, partially blocking the door.

His phone sounded, Josh dug it from his pocket.

"Hell—"

"Josh, you have to come home," Chloe shouted. Behind her voice, Josh heard shrill cries. Sofia's miserable wailing.

"What's going on?" he asked.

"Sofia's having another episode."

"Make him stop," Sofia squealed. "Make him stop! He'll die. He'll die!"

"I can't calm her down," Chloe said. "And I really can't handle this. You have to get back here."

"Look, Chloe," he said, still moving toward the dilapidated structure, "I'm not at the office. I went out of town to see if I could find help for her. Please, just try to calm her down."

"She can't even hear me, Josh. It's like I'm not even in the room."

"He's going to die!" The statement was followed by a shrill scream.

The desperate tone of his daughter's voice yanked a cord deep in Josh's chest, pulling painfully on his lungs and heart. Sofia needed him, but he was so far away.

"Oh fuck," Chloe cried. A rattle and crash followed. She'd dropped the phone.

"What's going on?" Josh called. "What's happening there?"

Josh placed his foot on the lowest step. It snapped the plank, sending a tremor up his leg. He stumbled back. Continuing to question the open line between himself and his home three hours away. Shouting now, he walked to the side and lifted his foot high and climbed directly onto the porch, having to duck low to avoid the crumbling roof. A swarm of flies met him. Frantic buzzing accompanied the panicked voice of the babysitter and his daughter's piercing cries.

"Put it down," Chloe said. "Sofia, honey, you have to put the knife down."

"Daddy said I had to or else he'd kill him. I have to or HE'LL DIE!"

"Josh," Chloe called, now a good distance from the phone, "you have to get home. Now. Please, Josh. I don't know what to do."

He swatted at the squadron of insects and edged his way to the door. He had to go in the cabin, but he didn't want to enter the place. It was obvious the building had been abandoned long ago, but he had to open the door and confirm its desolation before returning home to take a more reasonable approach to his child's distress.

At the door, he tried the knob, and though it turned the door was jammed. He put his shoulder to the wood, and with a tremendous shove, the door flew inward.

The odor hit him hard. The interior was dark and his eyes needed time to adjust, but the stench was repugnant—sweet, dusty, fungal, and dense with rot. Josh covered his nose but not before his throat clenched, and he gagged from the reek. He blinked his eyes as he stepped into the shack, trying to speed up the adjustment period.

"Sofia, don't!"

"I have to."

Screams.

Then his eyes adjusted to the contents of the grim little shack. The sight stopped him in his tracks.

An ancient clawed tub ran from the far wall to only a few feet from the door. The tub was filled with a pale doughy substance, the texture of clotted milk. At its center floated a man who seemed made of the same pallid material. Green eyes peered from a doughy face. His arms and legs were as thin as sticks, and his breastbone shown like a grate with shades of the palest lavender tracing each rib. And as the dread of this scene sank in, Josh saw that the man was not floating on the substance, but rather had fused with it, or his flesh had sprouted out like a creeping fungus to fill the basin, which now supported him. A distant thought whispered through Josh's panicked thoughts: *Is this thing a manifestation of Gundy's new savior, or merely the price it demanded to be worshipped?*

A fly dropped to rest on Gundy's sunken cheek and a barely perceptible wisp of smoke rose as if the small, black body had landed in a pool of acid. A moment later, all traces of the insect were gone. Gundy's sharp, bottle green eyes rolled up beneath wrinkled lids until the contents of the man's eye sockets were the same color as the rest of his face.

"He'll die," Sofia cried. Her voice was weak now.

Above the eyes on either side of the man's brow, ugly amber protrusions jutted like slender antlers toward the ceiling. The twisted points joined a foot over Gundy's head, weaving and merging, fanning upward in a sepia mesh that appeared far too heavy to be supported by the frail figure.

Another fly landed on the sickly white chest and was similarly melted and absorbed by the man. A third and fourth followed.

The thing's green eyes lowered to regard Josh in the doorway. They opened wide and a terrible focus entered them, as if Gundy were the one whose senses had come under attack. Then the pit of its mouth opened, revealing a toothless chasm.

Josh leaned against the door for support.

A vaguely metallic rattle sounded from the creature, but this bizarre clamor, like the muffled din of shuffling coins, did not emanate from its gaping mouth; it came from the net of horns above its head. The tone dropped into a hiss of static and then evened out until it faded.

Looking at the trellis of horns, Josh thought of antennas in the way he'd considered them in the scribbles Sofia had included in her drawings. Only now, he realized the things weren't meant to receive signals. They were meant to transmit them. In this context, the crosshatched yellow lines that had seemed incongruous in her pictures made sense. Gundy was sending his messages from this place of hate through the yellowed antlers, and they rode along a hereditary frequency straight to Sofia's mind.

Sofia's screams returned, higher and louder.

Josh put the phone in his pocket, muffling his daughter's pain, and searched the shack for a weapon, but nothing had been left in this space except the tub and its grisly contents. He stepped back onto the porch and spotted a length of two-by-four. Nails jutted from one end of the board. Josh leaned down and grasped it.

Inside he circled the tub and gripped the board like a baseball bat. He cocked his arms to swing, but his determination was immediately canceled. Tendrils of the white substance blossomed into the space above the tub and began thrashing the air. One struck the walls and scarred the wood with a long black slash, no wider than the line of a pencil. A second tendril whipped across Josh's shoulder, cutting through the thin fabric of his shirt.

The burn was instant, the pain intense. He cried out, but maintained his hold on the board. He lunged forward and swung, planting the nails in Gundy Morgan's face as the board concussed tissue with a wet slap. Smoke rose from the board. A tendril lashed Josh's cheek, missing his eye by a fraction of an inch. A stuttering sound, like chuckling, resonated between the mesh of horns. Josh yanked the board free. Splashes of caustic fluid followed the weapon's withdrawal, spattering the ceiling and the wall. Scalding drops landed on Josh's cheek and brow. The holes in Gundy's face filled with doughy, white tissue, quickly healing and shining as unblemished as before the attack.

Josh scurried back. Sofia screamed from his pocket.

"HE'S DYING."

Infuriated by the terror in his daughter's voice, Josh charged forward, meeting half a dozen blistering threads as he came to the side of the tub. Ignoring the pain, he began to swing, not at the remains of Gundy Morgan but on the antlers, the mesh of yellowed twigs.

The board cracked against one edge of the nested horns and a chunk the size of his thumb broke away. From his pocket, both Sofia and Chloe screamed louder and at a higher pitch. He drew the board back and swung at the antlers, cracking and breaking the mesh, as the scalding threads landed across his neck, his face, his ears, his arms and chest.

Josh closed his eyes so the whipping threads didn't blind him, and he bludgeoned the construction rising from Gundy Morgan's head until his board met no resistance except the back wall of the shed. He stumbled away from the lashing tendrils and dropped to the floor.

His entire body burned as if he'd just escaped a shower of acid. The reek of burning fabric and skin filled his nose. Panting against the agony, Josh opened his eyes. Though two small stumps still grew from Gundy's brow, the complex weave of amber sticks had collapsed. A large arcing piece lay against the back of the tub like a headboard. Gundy's green eyes, narrowed in rage, fixed on him.

Josh noticed the silence and dug the phone from his pocket. Chloe had ended the call. He managed to get on his feet, and he leaned against the wall for support as he worked his way back toward the door. Gundy's angry gaze followed him, as Josh punched in Chloe's number.

"You think you're pissed now?" Josh asked, as he waited for the babysitter to answer. "Wait'll I come back and burn this shithole down around your ears."

Outside on the porch, he leaned against the doorframe. When the call went to Chloe's voicemail, he hung up and tried again. On the third try, Chloe answered with a sobbing, "Josh?"

"Is she okay?"

"Josh, where are you?" Chloe asked through wet sobs.

"Is Sofia okay?"

"No, she's not fucking okay. She was cutting herself, Josh. What would make a little girl do that to herself?"

"Cutting herself? How badly?"

"I don't know," Chloe replied. "An ambulance is on the way. I wrapped her arm in a towel. What the fuck is going on, and when are you going to be back here?"

He couldn't possibly explain what the fuck was going on. He wouldn't even try. As for when he was going to be home, he cast a glance back through the doorway of the dilapidated cabin, and said, "I'm heading back soon. I just need to stop for some gas."

⚓

Lee Thomas is the two-time Lambda Literary Award- and Bram Stoker Award-winning author of *Stained*, *The Dust of Wonderland*, *The German*, *Torn*, *Ash Street*, *Like Light for Flies*, and *Butcher's Road*, among others. Lee lives in Austin, Texas with his husband John, and their family of animals. You can find him online at leethomasauthor.com.

RATS LIVE ON NO EVIL STAR

CAITLÍN R. KIERNAN

"I THINK THAT we're fished for," Olan says, menthol cigarette smoked almost down to the filter, and he's sitting at the unsteady little card table by the window, staring out at the high January sky, that disheartening sky like a flawed blue gemstone, and Jessie stops smearing peanut butter on slices of soft white bread and looks at him.

"What?" she asks, and he only nods at the sky so that she has to ask again. "What did you say, Olan?"

"I think we are *fished* for," the words repeated loudly and more slowly, as if she's only deaf and stupid, after all, and he's making perfect sense.

"I don't know what you're talking about," not meaning to sound annoyed, and she puts two pieces of thickly peanut-buttered bread together, another sandwich for this lean and crazy man who lives down the hall, this man to whom she is neither related nor can call her friend. But if no one looks in on him, he doesn't eat. Jessie cuts the sandwich into neat triangles, trims away the crust because he only pulls it off anyhow. She places it on one of the pink saucers that she's rescued from the kitchen's clutter of filthy dishes, wasteland of cracked plates and coffee cups for the cockroaches to roam. She had to bring the soap from her own apartment down the hall, of course, that and a clean dishrag.

"I don't mind listening," she says, setting his sandwich down in front of him. "If you want to try to explain."

Olan exhales, stubbing out his cigarette in a ceramic ashtray shaped like Florida, dozens of butts and cinder-gray ash spilling onto the top of the table. He looks at the sandwich instead of the sky, but his expression doesn't change, the one as much a mystery to him as the other. He takes a hesitant, small sip from the beer that Jessie has brought him. She doesn't often do that, but sometimes, just a bottle of the cheap stuff she drinks while she writes, Old Milwaukee or Sterling or PBR sacrificed to his reliable indifference.

"Never mind," he says and glances at her through his spectacles, wire and some Scotch tape wrapped around one corner, thick glass to frame his distant eyes. He takes a bite of the sandwich and looks at the sky while he chews.

"What are you working on today, Jessie?" he asks around the mouthful of peanut butter as she sits down across the table from him. "Anne Sexton," she says. Same answer as always, but that doesn't matter, because she knows he only asks to be polite, to seem to care. Her eyes are drawn to the window, too, past the dead plant in its clay pot on the radiator, leaves gone to dry and wilt-brown tendrils. Out there, the railroad glints dull silver beneath the white, white sun, parallel lines of steel and creosote-stained cross ties, granite and slag ballast, the abandoned factories and empty warehouses on the other side, a few stunted trees to emphasize the desolation.

She looks away, back down at her own lunch, bread with the crust still on, something mundane to break the spell. "I'm beginning a new chapter this afternoon," she says, not feeling hungry anymore.

"The Death Baby?" he asks, and she shakes her head *no*, "I'm done with the Death Baby for now."

"*There*," Olan says and presses the tip of one finger against the flyblown glass, pointing at something he sees in the sky. "Right there. See it?" And Jessie looks. She always looks, and she's never seen anything yet. But she doesn't lie to him, either.

"I don't see it," she says. "But my eyes are going to shit. I spend too much time staring at fucking computer screens."

"Well, it's gone now," he says very quietly, but only as if to let her off the hook, because his eyes don't leave the window. Olan takes another bite of the sandwich, another sip of beer to wash it down, and his eyes don't leave the window.

THE TINY APARTMENT is on the west side of a Southern city that once knew thriving industry and has seen long decades of decay, foundries and mills closed and the black, smoking skies gone and the jobs gone with them. Not the Birmingham of his childhood, only the shell of the memory of that city, and farther east the hungry seeds of gentrification have been planted. In the newspapers, he has read about the "Historic Loft District," a phrase they use like Hope or Expectancy. But *this* apartment exists on its own terms, or his terms, this space selected twenty years ago for its unobstructed view of the sky, and that hasn't changed.

Three very small rooms and each of them filled with his books and newspapers, his files and clippings and folders. The things he has written directly on the walls with Magic Marker because there wasn't time to find a sheet of paper before he forgot. Mountains of magazines slumped like glossy landslides to bury silverfish and roaches, *Fate* and *Fortean Times*, journals for modern alchemists and cryptozoological societies and ufology cults. Exactly 1,348 index cards thumbtacked or stapled to plaster the fragile, drained color of dirty eggshells and coffee-ground stains. Testaments uncorrelated, data uncollated, and someday the concordance and cross-reference alone will be a hundred thousand pages long.

After the girl has left (The Academic, as he thinks of her), Olan finds the fresh and sticky brown smear of peanut butter on the kitchen window, his shit-colored fingerprint still there to mark the exact spot, and he draws a black circle onto the glass around it. There are other circles there, twenty-three black *and* red circles on this window, and someday he will draw interconnecting lines to reveal another part of the whole, his map of the roof of the sky.

"I don't see it," he whispers, remembering what she said, and something a doctor told him to say years ago, when he was still a boy and might have only have grown to be a man who could say "I don't see it" when he does.

Olan sits at the window, new ink drying as the sun sinks towards twilight. Black ink to indicate a Probable Inorganic, tentative classification of the shimmering orb he saw hanging in the empty sky above the city. A pencil sketch already in one of his notebooks and best-guessed estimates of height and dimension underneath it, something like a bowling ball as perfectly motionless as the train tracks down below.

"Visible for approx. fourteen minutes, 1:56 until 2:10 p.m. CST," he wrote, not sure of exactly how long because the girl kept talking and talking, and then he saw her to the door, and when he got back it wasn't there anymore, had fallen or vanished or simply drifted away.

"I don't see it," he says again, her borrowed words and inflection, and then he takes off his glasses and rubs at his tired and certain eyes.

THIS IS PAGE One. Which is to say—this is where the story begins when he is asked to tell it as a story, when he used to tell it for the doctors who gave him pills and advice and diagnoses. The linear narrative that has as little and as much truth as any necessary fiction ever has, any attempt to relate, to make the subjective objective.

"I was seven, and we lived on my granddaddy's farm in Bibb County, after my father went away, and my mother and I lived there with my grandmother because my granddaddy was already dead by then. It wasn't a real farm anymore, but we did have chickens and grew okra and tomatoes and collards. I had a dog named Biscuit.

"One day—it was July—one July day in 1955, when I was seven, Biscuit chased a rabbit into the woods. And I was standing in the field beside the house calling him, and there were no clouds in the sky. No clouds at all. I'm sure there were no clouds. I was calling Biscuit, and it began to rain, even though there weren't any clouds. But it wasn't raining water, it was raining blood and little bits of meat like you put into a stew, shreds of red, raw meat with white veins of fat. I stopped calling Biscuit and watched the blood and meat hitting the ground, turning it red and black. There was a crunchy sound, like digging in a box of Rice Krispies for the toy at the bottom, a very faint cereal-crunching sound that came from the sky, I think.

"And then my mother was yelling and dragging me back towards the house. She dragged me onto the front porch, and we stood there watching the blood and meat fall from the clear sky, making puddles and streams on the ground.

"No, Biscuit never came home. I couldn't blame him. It smelled very bad, afterwards."

HE HAS A big jar on the table beside the mattress where he sleeps, a quart mayonnaise jar, and inside is the mummified corpse of something like a mouse. It fell out of the sky three years ago, dropped at his feet while he was walking the tracks near the apartment building, this mouse-thing husk from a clear sky, and he has labeled it in violet, for Definitive Organic.

THE GIRL FROM #407 doesn't usually bring him supper, but she did one night a month ago now, and she also brought some typed pages from her dissertation. She cooked him canned ravioli with Parmesan cheese and made a fresh salad of lettuce with radish and cucumber slices. They ate it together, sitting on the paper-cluttered floor while she talked about the work of a poet who had committed suicide in 1974. He had never read the poet, but it would have been impolite not to listen, not to offer a few words when he thought he wouldn't sound too foolish.

"It's a palindrome from a barn somewhere in Ireland," the girl said, answering a question about the title to one of the poems. "Someone had painted it on a barn," and then she produced a tattered paperback that he hadn't noticed among her pages. She read him the poem that began with the title from the barn. He didn't understand it, exactly, Adam and Eve and the Fall, words that sounded good put together that way, he supposed. But, the two words of the title: RATS STAR, those two *particular* words like a hand placed flat against a mirror, like bookends with nothing in between.

"Sometimes she called herself Ms. Dog," the girl said, and he saw the trick at once— Dog, God.

"I would very much like a copy of that poem," he said to her, chewing the last bite of his salad. And three days later she brought him a photocopy of those pages from the paperback, and he keeps them thumbtacked to a wall near the window. He has written RATS and STAR and RAT'S STAR on the wall in several places.

THE SUN IS down, down for hours now, and Olan sits at the card table at the window, studying by the dim fluorescent light from the kitchenette. He has *The Book of the Damned* by Charles Fort opened to page 260, and he copies a line into one of his notebooks: "Vast thing, black and poised, like a crow, over the moon." This is one of the books that makes him nervous—no, one of the books that frightens him. *The Golden Bough* makes him nervous, *Gilgamesh* makes him nervous, and *this* book, this book frightens him. Goosebumps on his arms for a sentence like that: "Vast thing, black and poised . . ." Things that were seen casting shadows on the moon in 1788, things between earth and moon, perhaps, casting shadows.

He flips back two pages and copies another line: "Was it the thing or the shadow of a thing?" Fort's taunting question put down in Olan's obsessively neat cursive, restated in precisely the same ten words. He pauses and lights a Newport and sits smoking, staring out the window, trying to find the sense in the question, the terrible logic past his fear.

There is only a third-quarter sliver of moon tonight, and that's good, he thinks, too poor a screen for anything's shadow.

Down on the railroad tracks there's movement, then, and a flash, twin flashes of emerald, a glinting reflection like cats' eyes caught in a flashlight or headlights. Olan sits very, very still, cigarette hanging limp from his lips, cough-drop smoke coiling about his face, and he does not even blink. Waits for the flashes to come again, and if there were a moon tonight he might see a little better, he thinks, a moment ago happy there was no more light in the sky but now, the not-knowing worse than the knowing, and so he strains his eyes into the night. But he sees nothing else, so in a moment he goes to the buzzing fluorescent bulbs above the sink and switches them off, then sits back down in the dark. There's still a little glow from the next room, but now he can see the tracks better.

"I don't see it," he says aloud, but he does, that thin shape walking between the rails, the jointed, stilt-long legs, and if there are feet he cannot see them. "It *could* be a dog," he whispers, certain of nothing but that it isn't a dog. He thinks it has fur, and it turns its head towards him, then, and smiles, yes, yes, Olan, it's smiling, so don't pretend it isn't, don't fucking pretend. He squeezes his eyes shut, and when he opens them again it's still there. He sits very still, cold sweat and smoke in the dark, as it lingers a moment more on the tracks, and then gallops away towards the row of abandoned factories.

"Did you ever talk about this with your mother or grandmother?" the doctor (not doctor, not real doctor—therapist) asked him, and he shook his head.

"No," he said. "We didn't ever talk about that day."

"I see," the therapist said and slowly nodded her head. She did that a lot, that slow up and down agreement or reassurance nod, and chewed the eraser end of her pencil.

"What else can you remember about that day, Olan?" she asked him.

He thought a moment, what to say, what to hold back, what could never be explained, thoughts sifting, filtering, and finally said, "We went inside, and she locked all the doors and windows. My grandmother came out of the kitchen and watched with us, and she prayed. She held her rosary and prayed. I remember that the house smelled like butter beans."

"You must have had it all over you, then? The blood."

"Yeah," he said. "When it stopped falling, my mother took me to the bathroom and scrubbed my skin with Ivory Soap. She nearly scrubbed me raw."

"Did your mother often give you baths, Olan?" the therapist asked, and he looked at her a while without answering, realizing how angry he had become, the sudden contempt nested in him for this woman who nodded and feigned comprehension and compassion.

"What are you getting at?" he asked her, and she took the pencil eraser from her mouth.

"Was it out of the ordinary, that degree of intimacy between you and your mother?"

"I was covered in blood," he said, hearing the brittle edge in his voice. "Both of us were, and she was scared. We thought maybe it was the end of the world."

"So it was unusual? Is that what you're saying?"

And he remembered his mother dragging him down the hall, a red-black handprint smear he left on the wall, and her crying and stripping off his ruined clothes, the growing suspicion that it was somehow his fault, this horrible thing, and *Where's Biscuit?* he'd kept asking her, *where's Biscuit?*

"I have to go now," he said, and the therapist put down her pencil and apologized for nothing in particular, apologized twice if she'd upset him. He paid her, twenty-five dollars because she was seeing him on a sliding scale, she'd explained at the start. A twenty and three ones and some change, and she gave him a receipt.

"Will you be back next week? I have you down for three o'clock on Thursday, but if that's too late—"

"I don't know," he lied, and she nodded again, and Olan never went back to her office.

"Well?" he asks the girl, The Academic, "Are you going to open it or not?" and she looks up slowly from the brown paper bag in her hands, confused eyes, surprise and a scrap of a smile on her lips. They're standing in the hallway, which seems quieter, stiller, than usual.

"Is this a present?" she asks. "Are you giving me a present, Olan?" And he can hear the caution, the do-I-want-to-encourage-this-sort-of-thing wariness in her voice. But he knows that she will accept what's in the bag, because she's brought him food and beer and talked to him, and rejecting such a small reciprocation would seem unkind. He has noticed that The Academic has a great unwillingness to seem unkind.

"It's not much," he says, and then she opens the bag, and the stillness of the hallway is interrupted by the rustle of the paper. She reaches inside and takes out the padlock and hasp set, the shrink-wrapped Yale he bought at a hardware store seven blocks away. "It's not much," Olan says again, because it isn't, and because he thinks that's the sort of thing you say when you give someone a gift.

She stares at it a moment without saying anything, and he says, "It's a rough neighborhood. It didn't used to be, but it is now."

"Yeah," she replies, and he can see that she's still rummaging for words. "Thanks, Olan. That's very thoughtful of you. I'll put it on the door this afternoon."

"You're welcome," and to change the subject, because it's not hard to see how uncomfortable she is, he asks "How's the new chapter coming along?"

"Ah, um, well, you know. It's coming," she says and smiles more certainly now, shrugs, and, "God, I'm being so rude, letting you just stand out there in the hall. Do you want to come in, Olan? I needed to take a break anyway."

"No," he says, maybe a little too quickly, but he has notes he must get back to, and the walk to the hardware store has already cost him the better part of the afternoon.

"Are you sure? I could make us some coffee."

He nods to show that yes, he is sure, and "It's in the Southern Hemisphere," he says. She looks confused again, and he recognizes the familiar patience in her confusion, the patience that shines coolly from her whenever she doesn't immediately understand something he's said.

"Sextens," he says. "The Sextant constellation. The Rat's Star," and now there's the vaguest glint of comprehension in her, surfacing slow like something coming up from deep water for a breath of air. "I didn't know if you knew that. If you knew much about astronomy," he says.

"No, I didn't know that, Olan. That could be interesting. I mean, I don't think anyone's ever made that connection before," and now she's staring back down at the padlock like maybe she's just noticed it for the first time.

"There are three actually," he says. "Three stars in an isosceles triangle, like this," and Olan tries to show her with his hands, geometry of thumb against thumb, the intersection of index fingers. "Like a ship's sextant," he adds.

"That could be very helpful to know."

"I have books, if you ever need them." He's already turning away from her, can sense that he's made her uneasy, has spent plenty enough years making people uneasy to see the signs. "I have a lot of books on stars, if you ever need any of them. I know you take good care of books."

And she says, "Thanks," as he walks away towards his own apartment door at the other end of the hall. "And thanks for the lock, too, Olan," she says, like an afterthought.

ON ONE WALL he has taken down twenty-seven index cards, accounts of living things found encased in solid stone, toads and worms mostly, and he has written LIVE EVIL where the cards were. Two elements of the palindrome taken out of context and reconnected, like RAT'S STAR. Sometimes the truth is easier to see when things are disassembled and put back together another way. That's what The Academic does, he thinks, takes apart the words of dead women and puts them together differently, trying to find the truth hidden inside lines of poetry. That's what he does with his books and newspapers.

Now Olan lies in the dark on his spring-shot mattress that smells like sweat and tobacco smoke and maybe piss, too, and the only light is coming in through the window above his head, falling in a crooked rectangle on the opposite wall, so he can read LIVE EVIL where he took down the cards.

He lies still, listening to the building and the city outside, and he thinks: There is never any getting closer to the truth, no matter what you write on paper cards or plaster walls, no matter how you rearrange the words. Because the truth is like the horizon, relative to where you're standing, and it moves if you move. And he thinks that he should get up and turn on a lamp and write that in one of his notebooks, because he might forget it before morning. Then he hears the sound: broomsticks thumping on the stairs, that staccato wooden quality to the sound, broomsticks or stilts maybe, and he remembers the long-legged thing from the train tracks the night before. He wonders if its long legs might not make that sound coming up the stairs. His heart is beating faster, listening, as the sound gets closer, not on the stairs any longer, *thump, thump, thump*ing in the hallway, instead. But far down at the other end, near The Academic's door, not his, and he lies very, very still hoping that she has done what she said, that she has put the extra lock on her door.

And then Olan realizes that there is another kind of noise, fainter, but worse to hear, a wet and snuffling sort of noise, like something sniffing along the floor, or at the narrow crack beneath a closed door. A purposeful, searching noise, and he stares across the shadow-filled room towards the door, getting cold from his own sour sweat despite the radiator. In a few minutes, the snuffling noise stops and the thumping begins again, as whatever's in the hall moves on to the next door down.

"I don't hear it," Olan whispers, and he hides his face in his pillow and waits for daylight.

MORNING LIKE CLOTTED milk hanging in the sky, and Jessie, her arms loaded with overdue library books stacked up to her chin, dreading the cold outside and the bus ride to school. Jangle of her key ring in the quiet hallway: key for the doorknob and the dead bolt and the door out to the street, key to the laundry room and mailbox, one more for her shabby little office at the university; all hung together on a shiny loop of brass and a tarnished brass tab with her initials engraved there, a Christmas gift five years old from a now-dead father. It's a sideshow contortionist trick, locking the door, shifting the books, and the one on top slides off, *The World Into Words* falling to the dusty floor. Jessie leaves the key ring dangling in the lock and stoops to retrieve the fallen book, cursing loudly when the rest of the stack almost tumbles over as well, but she catches them by leaning quickly forward against the door.

"Fuck," she says, hard and angry whisper, and her breath fogs in the cold air. It's too fucking early for this shit. She rests her forehead against the wood, swallows, pushing down the camera-flash of rage, knows that she's overreacting, knows that's what her shrink would say.

And then, looking down, she sees the marks in the door, the deep gouges near the floor, and for a second she thinks it's just something that has always been there and she never noticed, that's all. But there are splinters on the floor, too, old wood freshly broken, and a fresh scatter of scaly paint flakes the color of bile. And, the last thing she notices, a faint, unpleasant smell, lingering in the heavy cold, smell like a wet dog and something gone bad at the back of a refrigerator, smell like animal and mildew and mushrooms.

"Jesus," not bothering to whisper anymore. "Jesus H. Christ." She carefully sets the books on the floor and explores one of the gouges with the tip of a finger, the rough and violated wood sharp against her soft skin. Jessie turns and looks down the hall, and there are similar marks on other doors, and a wide diagonal slash across Olan's so big that she can see it all the way from her end. She shivers, not a cold shiver, but a prickling at the back of her neck, short-hair tingle down her arms at the sight of each of the doors with their own individual scars. But all of them are closed, no sign that whoever made the gouges actually managed to break into a single one of the apartments.

Jessie locks her door, thinking of the gift from Olan, unopened and lying useless on her coffee table. *It's a rough neighborhood,* he said, and she picks up her books again, paying more attention to balance this time. She tries not to think about junkies with crowbars, crackheads with tire irons wandering the building while she slept, shit like that. When she gets home she'll dig out a screwdriver and hammer and put Olan's shiny new padlock on the door.

> *"A seeker of Truth. He will never find it. But the dimmest of possibilities—he may himself become Truth."*
> —Charles Fort, The Book of the Damned (1919)

Caitlín R. Kiernan is the author of several novels, including World Fantasy and Shirley Jackson award-nominated *The Red Tree* and the Nebula and Bram Stoker award-nominated *The Drowning Girl: A Memoir*. She is a very prolific short story author, and her stories have been collected in *Tales* *of Pain and Wonder; From Weird and Distant Shores; To Charles Fort, With Love; Alabaster; A is for Alien; The Ammonite Violin & Others; Confessions of a Five-Chambered Heart;* and the forthcoming *The Ape's Wife and Others.* Subterranean Press has released *Two Worlds and In Between: The Best of Caitlín R. Kiernan (Volume One),* with a second volume planned for 2015. Kiernan was recently proclaimed "one of our essential dark fantasy authors" by the New York Times. Her current projects include the next novel, *Red Delicious* and her critically acclaimed Dark Horse comic, *Alabaster.* She lives with her partner in Providence, Rhode Island.

DISPATCHES FROM A
HOLE IN THE WORLD

SUNNY MORAINE

ART BY ELIZABETH LEGGETT

I'M STANDING IN the elevator. The elevator isn't moving. Neither am I. It seems, for the moment, like simply staring at what's in front of me is the simplest and therefore the best immediate project. Far simpler than the dissertation that's supposed to start here.

But I can't avoid it forever.

I'm not sure what I expected, but the place is small. It's tucked into three floors of a generic office building a few blocks from the Library of Congress. From the outside it doesn't look like much of anything; they probably wanted it like that. But what I'm specifically staring at is what looks like the floor of a college library, one of those more

57

industrial ones unconcerned with any popularly conceived aesthetic of Libraryness. White walls, recessed lighting, long desks divided into little cubicles, each equipped with a small, slim computer terminal.

It's empty.

I take a breath, and I step out of the elevator and into an archive of three hundred thousand and seventy-six recorded suicides.

WHEN IT HAPPENED it was like a plague.

No one was sure how it was spreading, or why, or who was going to be next. People feared for their loved ones, their friends and family. People feared for themselves. Pundits proclaimed doom with excited solemnity. Religious leaders got gleeful hard-ons for apocalypse. People blamed technology, peer pressure, the alienation of a generation raised in the midst of crushing debt and recession and increasingly extreme weather and constant war and a general sense of hopelessness.

You know, kids today.

But when that nightmare year was over and things finally began to taper off, all we were left with was questions.

Everyone had at least a tenuous connection with someone who died. That's what happens now—you know people who know people who know people, you follow people without ever actually speaking to them but you communicate in likes and retweets and reblogs. I've had entire friendships that were based around reposting the same series of makeup tutorials. The same collections of gifsets. So suddenly you're watching them die. It scrolls past on your feed, on your dash. It felt like an attack. For a while people thought it *was* an attack. Yet another one, dudebros against the Social Justice Whatevers.

But that wasn't what was going on.

So we watched. Some of us looked away. Some of us said they vomited, said they experienced panic attacks that lasted for hours. It's very hard to explain what it was like for us, because we were *there* in a way our parents weren't, and in a way our kids won't be. You live through a terrorist attack, you live *in* it, you're one of the shell-shocked survivors huddled in blankets, you're brushing ashes and bone-dust out of your hair. Smoke in your eyes.

We survived. We moved on, to the extent you ever can. Those of us academically inclined—who could find places in the decaying zombie corpse of academia—we did what we do. We over-analyze. So we wrote about it. Term papers. Research papers, self-reflective essays. Short stories, poems—for a while there the MFA programs got *really* morbid. We work out our demons however we can. We splash our trauma all over everything.

But as far as I know, I'm the only one to ever take it this far. Because it means going back. Living it. All over again.

My estimated time to completion for this project is two years.

Two years in the Year of Suicide.

IT'S A VINE, from back when Vine was still a thing. Dude put his phone down on a stand or propped it up some other way. He's sitting in a blue beanbag chair. He's white, dark-haired, maybe about fourteen. The room looks like your standard middle-class teenage boy's room. If I looked at the dossier file all the pertinent information would be there, at least what could be collected without special permission from the family—which some gave and some didn't.

I'm not going to look at the file, because that's not how I saw it. I didn't even know it was coming. If I had my way I'd be looking at this in the dark at three in the morning with cold pizza and a bong.

But I'm here. Watching this looping six seconds.

The boy is looking straight at the camera. He has no discernable expression. He lifts one hand; he holds a kitchen knife. He holds it to his throat and slashes his carotid artery. Blood jets to the side and gushes down his shirt. He slumps. Hand twitches and falls.

Repeat.

This boy takes six seconds to die. He dies over and over.

As far as anyone has been able to determine, this is Patient Zero.

WHEN I WAS thirteen I read about Jonestown.

I was a morbid kid to begin with. I hated violence, actually—I was disturbed by gory TV and movies until I was almost in my twenties. Covered my eyes for the chest-burster scene in *Alien*. I was revolted by torture porn horror. I couldn't handle watching animals in pain.

But I was fascinated by history, and the history of murder on massive scales.

So I read about Auschwitz. I read about Hiroshima. I devoured books on the Rwandan genocide. I was fascinated by the gruesomeness of it all, but even more I think I was fascinated by the extremity. What drives people to do things like this? What drives people to slaughter each other?

What drives people to slaughter themselves?

Jonestown was the worst. Because at least according to my understanding at the time, those people *did it to themselves*. I read about it and I imagined myself there in the pavilion with the rest of them, waiting in line for poison, watching people going into convulsions. I imagined watching mothers feeding it to their babies with syringes. I imagined what it would have been like after, sitting there and looking at the empty cup of your death, waiting to feel it and knowing there was nothing you could do. All those people—afraid, not afraid, just . . . in those moments of pre-oblivion.

I imagined those moments as either utterly insane or marked by the most profound sanity a human being can experience. Except that's wrong. *Insanity* isn't so clear-cut. It isn't so simple. Neither is suicide. What suicide means. It's abhorrent to do that to a complex idea. To a lived fact.

We understand that a lot better than we did.

But that pavilion. Nine hundred and thirteen people. Those aerial photographs. I stared at them. For a long time.

I thought, *I am looking at a hole in the world.*

Then the Year. Three hundred thousand and seventy-six holes in the world, opening up one after the other after the other, like bullet holes, like mouths, like eyes.

Except that number isn't reliable. Those are only the ones we know about.

Those are only the ones we saw.

The next one is a girl. Mid-teens, Hispanic, very pretty. Standing on a chair, rope around her neck. It appears to be nighttime; the lights in her bedroom are on. Stuffed animals just visible on the bed. Makeup scattered across the dresser like she was in the middle of messing with some eyeshadow when the idea occurred to her. She lifts her phone, stares expressionlessly into it as she adjusts the angle. The phone jerks. It's clear that she kicked the chair away. The phone swings wildly and falls. You see a shot of her feet swinging. Then it cuts off.

This one went up on YouTube. Within a couple of hours it had over twenty thousand views. You know how they say don't read the comments? Oh my God, do not read the fucking comments.

Those were archived along with the video. They're part of the historical record.

I watch it a couple of dozen times through, and halfway into those couple of dozen times I start going frame by frame, making notes. Of everything I can see. Of what I'm feeling. Part of the point of this project is self-reflexivity. I'll code later. For now I just need to get down everything I can.

About a month into the Year people started asking a very obvious question. Not *why*, and not *how*, and not *how in the hell is this spreading like a virus*—and that was pretty hilarious. Whole new meaning to the term *viral*.

Everyone who documented their own deaths . . . They died. They were dead. Some of them could set things to share automatically and some of them appeared to have done so, but others . . .

Who the fuck was uploading these things?

Like I said. In the end all we had were questions.

Older girl, early twenties, black. Blank-faced. Messy college dorm room. Bottle of pills. She empties them into her mouth gulp by gulp and washes them down with vodka. This one goes on for a while. When she drops to the floor, she manages to prop her phone up where we can see at least part of her. Her face.

This one isn't gory, but it's one of the uglier ones I watch.

Five times, notes, then I need to quit for the night.

I expect to have nightmares. I'm ready for it. I wake up shivering and too hot and I spend a feverish few minutes on my phone, recording my thick, roaring dreams. I manage to fall back asleep. It takes a while. In the morning I save what I wrote for all that coding I intend to do later.

THE ARCHIVE WAS very controversial when it was first proposed, and the controversy hasn't disappeared. A lot of people would just as soon forget that year.

A lot of those people were parents. Adults. People protested, made petitions. But us . . . Even those of us who carried around all our mental scar tissue, stiff and raw, we didn't want to let go. Even if we couldn't look at it, couldn't watch, couldn't even think about it without fight-or-flight chemicals flooding into our blood, we wanted to keep it. The record of our Year.

A lot of it is that this is what we do. We document. We display. It was real. It's ours.

But a lot of it is that, even if we didn't and still don't understand why, those people—our people—wanted to be seen. Wanted those final moments to be out there. Maybe they weren't thinking straight, maybe they were just crazy, maybe something else was going on. Fuck, maybe it was demon possession. But they wanted it.

Pics or it didn't happen. Didn't they used to say that? Maybe it was horrifying. Sure. But it was *ours*.

AGES OF THE victims range from ten to twenty-five, most of them on the lower end. There was something about puberty, went the theory, but of course no one ever verified that in any way aside from what people observed. People noted—repeatedly—the suspicious roundness of those numbers, but no one ever based any concrete conclusions on that either.

For a while people were talking about a particular kind of parasite that infects the brains of insects and drives them to kill themselves. A specific kind of fungus that affects the behavior of ants in bizarre ways and then sprouts from the head, grows and releases spores. They did autopsies, and they found nothing.

They found no drugs. No unusual substances.

Some of the people who died had been exhibiting signs of depression and/or anxiety, sure. A fair number had difficult home lives. Plenty of them were queer, and a lot of those weren't out to anyone but their friends online.

Of course they were going through that shit. They were kids. We were kids, and being a kid is hell, and adults forget that.

We didn't want to forget.

I SPEND MOST of the next day going through more of it. Gifs, Vines, videos uploaded to various places. Still images, selfies; Instagram. Screenshots of Snapchats. Sometimes there's sound and sometimes there isn't, but the common thread running through it all is imagery.

Another couple of clips of people cutting their own throats. I remember hanging being popular. A few people tying plastic bags over their heads. One especially industrious boy douses himself in gasoline in his driveway and lights a match.

I wander outside to eat and get a tasteless hot dog at a lunch truck. I feel dazed. The color seems to be bleeding out of the world.

I have two years of this to go.

I SPEND THE rest of the week on a proposal for a dissertation grant I don't expect to be awarded. This thing is too weird. It's too disturbing. I don't think the NSF is going to want to touch it with a thirty-foot pole. But I need the money, and I badly need something else to focus on.

I WASN'T GOING to read the dossiers carefully until I finished preliminary data collection, but a couple of weeks later I start going through them. I expect it to afford me some distance, but it doesn't. Maybe the information is dry and clinical, but one of the things that makes me good at this is an ability to consume dry, clinical information and translate it into something vital and real and immediate. Something bloody. I sit there in my carrel on the third floor with a pile of printouts—I wanted to work with paper for this, and in here I have to—and I make notes until my eyes hurt, and then I sit back and close them and think about how scared we were and how all we felt like we had was each other, except we didn't know which one of us was going to be next.

I used to wonder if, when my brain started trying to kill me, I would know what was happening.

When I open my eyes it's almost midnight and the woman from the front desk is shaking me. They need to close up. I need to go home.

I DON'T GO home. I wander around downtown until dawn. I look at the Capitol dome and I think about how none of those people in there have anything to do with us. About how, after the Year of Suicide, we all gave up. Voting rates for our generation are the lowest of any generation in history. They bemoan this, our apathy. How disappointing it is. How disappointing we all are.

Look: don't you judge us for opting out of a fucking lie. Don't you ever do that.

We went to war and a lot of us didn't come home, and none of you ever noticed.

I GET THE grant.

IN THE END the thing that allowed the archive to exist was the decision that it would have no connection to any outside network. None. Security is unbelievably tight. We can't bring in phones. We can't bring in any kind of recording device whatsoever. We can bring in paper and pens and pencils and highlighters, and we can make printouts of text. No images. That's it.

It's like the Hot Zone of social media. Because that's what it is, isn't it? It's a giant data quarantine.

They scrubbed the net as clean as they could. They sent in people to confiscate hard drives of all sizes. We're pretty sure they got it all. Once the archive was established, a lot of us voluntarily turned over what we had and deleted everything else. We organized around it. We surprised people, and we baffled people. They didn't understand.

Well, whatever. They don't need to.

The situation is less than ideal, but that was true from the beginning. That was true before the Year. That's always been true.

I GO OUT to dinner with some friends from my program, and as I'm texting them from the restaurant where I've arrived early, I realize that it's my favorite sushi place and I haven't been here in five months, and these are the only remaining friends I ever see face to face and I haven't seen any of them in almost as long.

And I realize I'm only now realizing that, and I think *Huh*.

It's a vague kind of dinner, and that's mostly on my end. They talk about work, about the projects they've hooked up with, about their own dissertations. Kayla has a gig at a marketing firm which is going well. Mike also got that grant I was awarded and we high five.

All these common things that tied us together since the first year in the program are still there, but as the evening proceeds it becomes apparent that there are new things in which I don't and can't share. Mike got that grant; Mike and his husband are also about to adopt a baby. Lissa is getting married in a couple of months and the planning for that is in full swing. With her spot at the firm, Kayla is thinking she might be able to get a down payment on a house in the not-too-distant-future.

And I'm just listening.

So what have you been up to? What you got going on?

Well, after this I'm probably going to go back to my basement apartment and leaf through a binder full of notes I took while I watched fifty-five kids aged thirteen through nineteen erase their faces with shotguns.

So I got that going on.

Sitting there, staring down at my tuna rolls, I feel like darkness is creeping across the table and it's carving me apart from them. Once we used to go out and drink until we were practically falling down, to ease the pain of endless unendurable lectures. We were united by cheerful misery, and there was something wonderful about that union. It felt full and alive.

They moved on. They moved forward. They have lives. But every time I touch this thing I'm getting dragged backward.

And I'm not so sure about *alive* anymore.

KAYLA CALLS ME the next morning. I have an incredible hangover. Not the worst in a while, though, and not from dinner. I came home after, I leafed through the binder, and I drank until I passed out on top of it.

I just want to make sure you're okay.

Sure, I'm okay. Why wouldn't I be okay?

You seemed kind of. She doesn't finish that sentence, and I can't tell if it's because she doesn't want to or she doesn't know how. *I dunno, I just. We hadn't heard from you in a while, and I just wanted to check in.*

Check in. Fuck's sake, I'm fine. She's not my mother, I have a mother. I haven't spoken to her in about three weeks, but I still *have* one.

Kayla's voice drops. *Look, you know . . . You have this thing, and everyone thinks it's kind of . . . Just don't disappear, okay? You remember. You remember what it was like.*

Suddenly she sounds so gentle, and my throat closes up, and I remember the one time she and I got so drunk and so comfortable with each other that a week after meeting for the first time we were sitting in a bar yelling to each other about our worst sexual experiences practically at the top of our lungs.

That was a little over six years after the Year. We were healing but we were all still hurting. We needed each other.

Yes, Kayla, I remember.

Do you?

I HAVE STACKS of binders and I have stacks of highlighters and I have stacks of pens and I have no idea what to do with any of them anymore. I work all the time, but then I stop working and I stare at it and I think, *What exactly is all this? Who left it here? Who would do this?*

Why?

I have a year left.

MY GRANT RUNS out.

IT DIDN'T TAKE us very long to stop looking for answers.

Other people, people outside the trenches—sure, they kept looking. They were desperate. They never stopped looking until things began to taper off and then even after. For a while. Then they did stop. No one officially called off the search. They just . . . stopped.

But we stopped long before that.

Because the *why* didn't matter. We didn't have the luxury of *why*. We didn't have the time or the effort to expend on why. I'm not saying we didn't wonder. Everyone wondered. But after the initial flood of panic, after it became clear that it wasn't stopping, that it was only getting worse, we turned inward and we did what no one else seemed able to do.

We took care of each other.

We stayed in contact. We formed networks of information-sharing and retooled existing ones, and we pooled our resources. We sent people to homes, to sit with and comfort and be with people who were lonely and scared. We helped people in bad situations get out of them. We raised money. We ran seminars and workshops. We got medication to people who needed it. We did highly organized damage control.

We were doing all that before the Year even happened. All the Year did was kick it into high gear.

There did come a point—and it didn't take, thank Christ—where they were talking seriously about going to the sources and shutting everything down. Taking it all away from us.

The death toll was already horrifying. Believe me when I tell you: You don't even want to think about what it might have been.

SITTING WITH MY binders and my highlighters and my pencils and my pens in the dark, looking at my phone on the coffee table. Little screen blinks on. Buzz. Blinks off. Green-purple rectangle, floating in the air in front of me like a ghost.

Blinks on. Buzz. Blinks off.

It's just an alarm. I haven't actually spoken to anyone, in any sense of the term, in over a week.

All these binders full of the dead. All these binders of me in and among and with them. So what does that make me?

HERE'S HOW IT was: We were dying. But we weren't alone.

Suddenly we all knew each other. Suddenly we were all friends. We were all family. Across media and networks and apps and sites and everything you can think of. Sure, some things got seriously ugly, but by the time it became clear what we were dealing with, for the most part people laid down their arms. Truces and ceasefires were declared. We had bigger things to worry about.

We were dying.

I loved those people. I loved every one of them. The people I never met. The people whose names and faces I never knew until I was watching them kill themselves. The people who mourned for them and invited me to mourn with them. We said we loved each other. We all said it. Over and over. Like hands across a chasm, groping in the dark. Knowing that, in the end, we probably couldn't save anyone. All we could do was be there until they were gone, and be with whoever was left.

I remember how it was. I remember it. I remember it so well. I'm drowning in remembering.

Not very shareable.

I love you. I love you.

I love you.

AFTER IT WAS over, I was lonelier than I had ever been in my entire life.

MY NOTES ARE in chaos. My coding is an incoherent mess. None of it makes any sense at all, and I'm not sure it ever did. I have no idea how to organize this into something that could even begin to vaguely resemble something defensible.

I have six months. But that time-to-completion was just an estimate. My advisor is very hands-off. No one is holding me to that deadline but me.

In theory, I suppose, I could just stay here.

SO THERE I am.

I DON'T KNOW how long I stare at it. I know my back starts to hurt and my mouth is dry, and my eyes itch and my head aches, but I'm pretty sure that was all already the case. I sit under those college-library overhead lights and I stare at the screen and it doesn't matter how long I do that because it doesn't change and it isn't going to.

The little clock in the corner of the screen says ten minutes to midnight. I think maybe it's said that for a while.

There I am.

It's a grainy selfie. Poorly lit. It's been put through a filter which has done it no favors. The colors are all fucked and it's hard to make out anything clearly, but I can see enough.

I'm sitting on the floor in front of the coffee table. I can't see the coffee table but I know it's there, just beyond where the phone is. I'm staring into the camera. I have no discernable expression.

I'm not holding the phone.

WE WANT TO wrap things up neatly. We want to come out the other side and look back and be able to make sense of it all. We want to beat fear and pain and loss into narrative submission; this explains the persistence of war stories, and the persistence of their telling.

We record, we write our histories, we analyze and we theorize, we editorialize, we engage in punditry. We publish. We curate and we archive. We do this because we have to, because we can't just leave it all there. We can't just look down at that endless mass of corpses and let that be the last word.

We can't leave the holes in the world.

I wish I could tell you something. I wish I could give you an answer. But in the end no answer could have made any difference. And the questions we were left with never mattered.

All we ever had was each other.

⚓

Sunny Moraine's short fiction has appeared in *Clarkesworld, Strange Horizons, Lightspeed* and *Long Hidden: Speculative Fiction from the Margins of History*, among other places. They are also responsible for the novel trilogies *Root Code* and *Casting the Bones*, as well as *A Brief History of the Future: collected essays*. In addition to authoring, Sunny is a doctoral candidate in sociology and a sometimes college instructor; that last may or may not have been a good move on the part of their department. They unfortunately live just outside Washington DC in a creepy house with two cats and a very long-suffering husband.

BAYOU DE LA MÈRE

POPPY Z. BRITE

THE BAYOU TWISTED through the green sward of Vermilion Parish, brown and slow as a snake basking in the sun. On its left bank sat the town, very small and picturesque, and just now, very very hot. The midday sun bounced off neatly whitewashed buildings and sizzled up from narrow streets like heat rising from a well-seasoned iron skillet. Ancient moss-bearded oaks made shady tunnels over the sidewalk, but if you stood in one of these tunnels too long, a small cloud of midges and mosquitoes would form around you. All in all, it seemed a hell of a place to spend an August vacation, but it had been highly recommended by the bartender.

Said bartender was spending *her* vacation in Colorado, and the two cooks intermittently cursed her name as they trudged around the little town. They had only been successful restaurateurs for about a year. Before that their existence had been pretty much hand-to-mouth, and they'd never taken a real vacation. When they decided to close the restaurant for two weeks during the slowest part of the summer, they felt as if they should go somewhere for at least a week, and friends urged them to get out of New Orleans for once in their lives.

"We can't be more than, like, four hours away," Rickey had said. "Something could come up." Mo convinced them to visit the little town, a three-hour drive from New Orleans.

They were staying on the second floor of a 160-year-old hotel that looked out over the bayou. The place smelled of lemon floor polish and genteelly decaying wood. "I gonna show you up to y'all room," said the proprietress when they checked in. The accent out here was nothing like the exuberant, full-throated New Orleans one; rather, it was low and musical, with a hint of the French spoken here less than a century ago. The woman's jet-dark eyes, curious but not overtly hostile, kept slipping back to them as she showed off the room with its double bed. *We might not like everything y'all do in New Orleans, Rickey imagined her thinking, but we need y'all money.*

When she had gone, G-man set his suitcase on a marble-topped end table and started unpacking. "You think she ever met a couple of fags who were less interested in all these damn antiques?" he said.

"I kinda like the bed," said Rickey. It was a wooden four-poster with knobs carved into tortured flower shapes.

"That's cause you got an interior design queen inside you, just dying to get out."

"Yeah, right." Rickey had decorated the restaurant's dining room almost singlehandedly, choosing everything from the silverware pattern to the shade of green on the walls, but he had never spent more than fifty dollars on anything for their house and couldn't imagine doing so. They weren't home often enough to enjoy nice décor.

Although it was nearing the hottest part of the day, they forced themselves out of the hotel and into the slow-baking streets. That was when they started cursing Mo's name. The bayou, the cannons in the square, the old Catholic church: all were lovely, but all seemed to waver behind a cell-thin, sticky layer of heat. G-man, whose eyes had always been painfully sensitive to light, could hardly see through his dark prescription glasses. Within thirty minutes they were in a rustic but air-conditioned oyster bar gulping cocktails even though happy hour was still far away.

"How can it be hotter here than in New Orleans?" Rickey said.

"It's not," said G-man. "We just got time to notice it here."

"We stand over goddamn stoves all day. I thought I was immune to heat."

"Y'all from New Orleans?" called the manager of the seafood restaurant, who was over in the corner playing video poker. "Y'all don't even know what real heat *is* way up there."

Rickey and G-man looked at each other in half-drunken amazement at having suddenly become Northern aggressors. "I guess that's what we get for calling Tanker a Yankee," said G-man. Their pastry chef had been born in Covington, about forty-five miles north of New Orleans.

They sat at the bar awhile longer, feeling somewhat out of place but not uncomfortably so. There was nothing obviously touristy about them; to all outward appearances they were just a couple of working-class guys in their late twenties. They both wore black chef pants—Rickey's patterned with a thin blue stripe, G-man's with a variety of mushrooms—and they might have been about to work the dinner shift, if this place were slack enough to let workers drink before shifts. However, Rickey felt sure that they were as conspicuous as a couple of dorks in Acapulco shirts with cameras hanging around their necks. He didn't really care, though. He wasn't supposed to feel like a local; he was on vacation.

The thought began to sink in as he sipped his third bourbon and soda. He was on vacation! They didn't have to worry about the restaurant for a whole week. They could drink and eat and wander around aimlessly and do whatever they liked. Thinking about it, he began to feel horny. "Let's go back to the room," he said.

Once there, they cranked up the air conditioner and pulled the curtains shut. The room filled with cool afternoon shadows. Rickey rummaged through his bag. "Did you bring the lotion?" he said.

"I thought you put it in that Ziploc bag of toothpaste and stuff."

"I don't see it." They had used hand lotion as a lubricant since they were teenagers, and had never quite graduated to K-Y, Astroglide, or any of the raunchier products.

"Well, we gotta have it or I'll be walking around here like a guy with fatal hemorrhoids," G-man said sensibly. "I saw a Wal-Mart on the way into town—we could go get some."

"Dude, I don't want to go to Wal-Mart and buy nothing but a bottle of lotion. You know how that's gonna look?"

G-man shrugged.

"Wait a sec," said Rickey, digging deeper into his suitcase. "Here it is. I forgot I put it in its own bag in case it leaked."

They undressed and lay on the bed kissing, but the alcohol, sun, and twelve straight days of work before the vacation had begun to kick in. Their caresses went from languid to exhausted. "Damn, I'm sorry," said Rickey when he realized he had just dozed for a few seconds. "I want to do it, but I can hardly keep my eyes open."

"Me neither. Maybe we could just nap for a few minutes."

They settled against each other and allowed themselves to drift off. By the time they awoke, the room was fully dark, the town outside was still, and every restaurant and bar within a twenty-mile radius had been closed for hours. They went out onto the balcony and sat smoking a joint. At the other end of the street, a traffic signal cycled through its colors several times before a lone car came along, paused briefly at the red light, then went on without waiting for the green. The bayou was invisible in the night, signaling its presence only with a damp organic smell and an occasional flash of moonlight on water.

"Let's go for a walk," said G-man.

"A what?" Rickey wasn't being a smart-ass; the concept of taking a walk late at night simply hadn't occurred to him in many years. It wasn't as dangerous as critics of New Orleans suggested, but it wasn't the sort of thing most people did if they could help it.

"I feel like stretching my legs. Then we can come back here and finish what we started."

The second-floor landing was decorated with an antique mirror, a spray of wildflowers, and a rather large, gory plaster statue of Jesus exhibiting his Sacred Heart. They walked softly down the old wooden staircase and let themselves out of the still hotel onto the silent street. "You know what's different here?" said Rickey after they had gone half a block toward the town square. "Even after a really fucking hot day, it doesn't stink. There's not that shitty garbage vapor rising off the asphalt."

"The bayou stinks a little."

"Well, what do you expect? We're still in Louisiana."

"I don't think these people even believe you and I are from Louisiana. They think New Orleans is a whole 'nother country."

"They might have something there."

"Seriously." As they neared the square, G-man looked up at the spire of the eighteenth-century church. "It's so Catholic out here. I don't think I could live in a place that takes its religion this seriously."

"What you talking about? Your mom takes religion as seriously as anybody I ever knew."

"That's what I'm talking about," said G-man. "That's why I couldn't stand to be around it. Sure, New Orleans is Catholic, but it's different there. More . . . I don't know . . . more adaptable. You're a lapsed Catholic out here, they're gonna make you think about it every damn day of your life. You never really get away from it anyway—they get you by the time you're five, they got a part of you forever."

"Yeah?" As they passed in front of the church, Rickey made a grab for G-man. "Which part?"

"Quit it!"

"How come? There's nobody out at this hour."

But G-man was looking at something on the other side of the square. Following his gaze, Rickey saw a serene-faced white statue of the Blessed Virgin Mary seated in the center of a little bubbling fountain. "Oh, no, dude. You don't want me grabbing your ass in front of *that?*"

"It's just not nice," G-man said uncomfortably.

"Sorry. I didn't know you were still ashamed of me when the goddamn Catholic Church was watching."

"Course I'm not ashamed of you. Don't even say that."

"Don't act like it then."

They walked over to the statue and examined it in silence. Rickey couldn't remember ever seeing the Virgin Mary seated before. People in New Orleans put little statues of her in half-buried bathtubs in their yards, and while her robes might be painted either the traditional blue or a more festive pink, she was always standing. He refused to ask G-man about it, though. Instead he circled the fountain and entered a small floodlit garden behind it. On the whitewashed wall of the nearby church, dozens of flesh-colored lizards lay in wait for nocturnal insects. A little door on the wall was labeled CHAPEL OF PERPETUAL ADORATION, but Rickey didn't know what that meant. G-man followed Rickey into the garden. He saw the sign and the stained glass window beside the door, where the ornate tabernacle holding the consecrated Host cast a weirdly shaped shadow. Remembering the bland dusty taste of the Host on his tongue, he looked away. "This place makes me nervous, that's all," he said. "It's hard to explain. You remember I told you about the last time I ever went to Confession?"

"Yeah. I think that was about a week before the first time I fucked your damn brains out."

Rickey was being crude because his feelings were hurt, and G-man ignored it. "Well, that was what? Thirteen years ago? That was the last time I ever felt like the Church could see what I was doing—"

"The Church?" Rickey said dubiously. He had not been raised in any particular religion. "You mean like God, or what?"

"Sorta. Not exactly. It's more like management." The critical gaze of management was something they both understood all too well. "Like a bunch of 'em all sitting on some kind of advisory board, deciding whether your sins are venial or mortal, how many Our Fathers or Hail Marys you gotta say, counting up every filthy thing you ever done. And even if you leave the Church, your family's still Catholic, so you know you're gonna get a goddamn funeral Mass when you die."

"Dude, you're twenty-nine. What are you thinking about funeral Masses for?"

"I'm not. That's not what I'm trying to say." Frustrated, G-man turned his back on the Chapel of Perpetual Adoration. "It's just that when I walked out of that confessional, I knew it was the last time, and all of a sudden I didn't feel like they were watching any more. Out here, it kinda feels like they are again."

"Yeah, and you're not the first homo tourist they ever saw. Get over it."

They walked the rest of the way around the square in silence and turned onto the deserted Main Street, here called Rue Principale. Rickey stopped to peer through the window of a darkened restaurant. "Cheap-ass flocked wallpaper," he muttered. G-man didn't say anything, and Rickey turned on him. "Well, what? Do you hate it here cause they got a lot of serious Catholics? It's our first ever vacation. I hope you don't hate it."

"No. No, I don't hate it. I'm happy we're here. I just never been to Cajun country before. I didn't know it would be so . . ."

"So what?"

"Catholic."

Rickey threw up his hands in disgust and started walking back toward the hotel. G-man followed, feeling guilty. "It doesn't matter," he said after a few minutes. "It's not gonna ruin anything."

"It better not."

Neither of them said a word until they got back to the room, but it wasn't a particularly uncomfortable silence; they'd been together long enough to get annoyed with each other and get over it in the space of a few minutes. G-man was thinking about a small white rosary his mother had given him for his first Communion. He'd tried to say his penance on it after leaving the confessional for the last time, but had only been able to get through five Hail Marys before realizing he couldn't be a Catholic any more, not if what the priest had just told him was true. He'd put the rosary away and hadn't thought of it for years, until one day Rickey was looking for something in a dresser drawer and found the little velvet-lined jewelry box. Anyone would have thought Rickey had found condoms or maybe a come-stained copy of *Huge & Uncut*. "What do you still have *that* for?" he'd demanded, and G-man finally just said in as sharp a tone as he ever used, "Look, my mom gave it to me. Shut the fuck up about it." But that wasn't the only reason he had kept the rosary. He could no more have thrown it out than Rickey could have gotten rid of his father's old Army dog tags, even though Rickey's parents had been divorced for a quarter-century and he never talked to his father.

Rickey was thinking about a conversation he'd had at the restaurant a few months ago. One of the cooks wondered aloud why G-man (who was elsewhere at the time) wouldn't try to extort a little lump crabmeat or something from a purveyor who'd sent them some wormy fish, and Rickey said, "You gotta understand, G's just a nice Catholic boy at heart." He was surprised to hear himself say that, because he always thought of G-man as his partner in crime, his lieutenant of degeneracy. Not so much in a sexual way—he supposed they were actually pretty vanilla in that respect—but they had gone through a considerable amount of liquor, drugs, scams, and sleaze during their tenure in the kitchens of New Orleans. To suddenly think of G-man in a whole different light was strange and somehow arousing. He went home that night and fucked his nice Catholic boy until they were both sore.

The hotel room felt very cold after the simmering night. The sweat on their skin turned clammy and they burrowed under the covers, shivering. "I don't know about you," said Rickey, "but I'm wide awake now."

"Same here. You want to do something?"

"Yeah."

It was years since they'd had sex in unfamiliar surroundings—usually they were lucky if they could find the time and energy to do so in their own bed. They'd done it once in the restaurant before opening night, but that was mostly just to make the place theirs, and Rickey had been too worried about the carpet to really get into it. Now, though, he found that he liked being in a strange room. There was something vaguely illicit about it, something that hinted at affairs and assignations without any of the pain these things would cause were he to actually seek them out. The mattress was a little too soft, but it was wider than the one they had at home, allowing them to roll around without fear of falling off the edge. Only after several minutes did they notice that one of the bed's wooden legs was banging quite loudly against the floor.

"Goddamn uneven floorboards," said Rickey. "Goddamn broken-down place. We should've stayed in a Holiday Inn."

"Don't worry about it," said G-man. "Here, let's try that daybed by the window."

They moved over to the daybed. "That's better," Rickey said, testing its firmness. "The springs aren't all busted in this one."

"I'm sure we'll bust 'em."

"Probably so . . . oh. There. You like that?"

"Yeah," said G-man. "I like that a lot." He braced himself against the windowsill as Rickey fucked him. He could barely make out the dark slow shape of the bayou through crooked oak limbs, and above it all, a crescent moon hanging high in the predawn sky. For the first time in years he remembered his mother telling him the moon was God's eye, and that whenever he saw it, he should remember God was watching him. He closed his eyes, but the white crescent's afterimage still hung there. "Let me turn over," he said to Rickey.

"Aw, c'mon G, we *never* do it this way—"

"Okay, let me lay down then."

Rickey did. G-man pressed his face into the upholstery and concentrated on Rickey's mouth against his neck, Rickey's hand on his dick, Rickey's dick in his ass. God wasn't watching them, and if He was, it didn't matter. G-man had not stopped believing in God when he left the Church; he'd left because he did not believe that God wanted him to have a loveless life, and he'd never once felt that being with Rickey was wrong. He didn't feel it now. He just felt more self-conscious out here, somehow, than he'd ever felt in New Orleans.

They returned to the old four-poster bed to sleep, but their dreams were not peaceful. Rickey dreamed he was back at the restaurant on reopening day. Dinner service was about to start, but no one else in the kitchen had shown up, not even G-man. Rickey was on the line by himself, wondering how in hell he was going to work all the stations, trying to stifle his fury at his negligent crew because he knew it would incapacitate him if given free rein. He could already see the tickets piling up, could hear the waiters yelling for their orders.

Didn't I go on vacation? he thought, but realized he had no memory of it.

G-man dreamed of Sts. Peter and Paul, the church he had attended as a child. His name was still Gary Stubbs, he had just barely started learning to cook, and his knees were sore from kneeling, waiting to take Communion. Again he tasted the crumbling wafer, the musky sweet wine. He could smell the sweat on the priest's palm, could count every hair on his wrist. It was supposed to be flesh, blood. *Wasn't that as intimate as anything you could do with a person?* he had always wondered.

It was Sts. Peter and Paul, but for some reason the Stations of the Cross were all in French. *Jésus condemné à mort. . . Jésus chargé de la Croix. . . Jésus tombe une le fois. . .* He wasn't sure if he was reading the words or if a voice was whispering them to him. The Stations themselves were set into walls that towered high above his head, the carved wooden faces of the figures precise in their anguish.

Then he was outside the church, out in the night long past even midnight Mass, and it was no longer Sts. Peter and Paul; it was the old church in the bayou town. The weirdly backlit tabernacle rose up behind the window, wavering as if an unseen figure had passed between it and the glass. The statue of the Blessed Virgin sat placidly in the center of the fountain. Her mantle and her shoulders were worn almost smooth, like the soapy-looking lambs that mark children's graves. *Jésus recontre sa Mère*, the voice whispered, or had he just thought the words? Her eyes were wide, blank, white, fixed upon him as she began to rise, her stone knees crumbling, her lap cracking apart. Her shadow appeared on the stained glass window, blotting out the tabernacle. She reached out to him—

"Jesus!" he said, sitting up in bed, his heart hammering, his right hand at his throat. A second later, he realized he was groping for the St. Christopher medal he hadn't worn since he was twelve.

"G? You okay?" He felt Rickey's hand on his back. "What's a'matter?"

"Nothing. I'm fine."

"Sure?"

"Yeah."

"C'mere . . ."

Rickey pulled him down and wrapped a warm arm around his chest. Fitted into the curve of Rickey's body like a spoon, G-man began to relax, his heart slowing, his eyes growing heavy again. By morning he remembered nothing of the dream, and Rickey did not remember waking at all.

Since they'd never had a proper meal the day before, they woke up ravenous and headed immediately to the oyster bar, which was just opening for lunch. "Y'all cooks?" the waitress asked, noticing the baggy shorts they had made from worn-out chef pants. In her musical half-French accent she chatted to them about local restaurants, recommended the boudin, warned them away from the crawfish stew. Throughout the meal she kept their cups filled with strong chicory coffee. By the time they finished eating, the strangeness of yesterday had receded and they felt almost comfortable in the town.

Out on the square, they stood looking up and down Rue Principale. It began to dawn on them anew that they had absolutely no responsibilities, no plans, nothing to guide them except whatever they felt like doing. "You want to check out the church?" said

Rickey, though he had shown no interest in it the day before.

G-man looked up at the wooden spire. He realized he really didn't want to go in there; certainly he'd been in Catholic churches since his last Confession, but he felt a reluctance to enter this one. Almost an aversion, for what reason he couldn't imagine. "What for?" he said.

"Well, I don't know. It's old. It's one of the things you're supposed to see—Mo said so." Rickey pointed at a nearby sign. "Look, it's on the Historic Register."

"I guess," said G-man with no enthusiasm. But Rickey had already set off toward the church, apparently determined to be a dutiful tourist despite his lack of experience. G-man followed as he always had. The heavy front doors sighed shut behind them and they were enveloped in dimness, in the smell of candles and old wood. G-man could not help dipping his fingertips in the font and genuflecting as he entered; it was as automatic as brushing his teeth or wiping the edge of a plate after he had arranged food on it.

"Hey, check it out," said Rickey. "The whaddaya call 'em, the Stations of the Cross are in French."

G-man edged into a row of pews; he didn't feel quite capable of walking around the church. He sat there and watched Rickey roam around the place admiring the architecture, the history, the craftsmanship of the carved and painted wooden statues. It must be nice to enjoy such a beautiful place at face value, without the heaviness of lost faith. His head had begun to ache dully. He could not think why this church felt so much more oppressive than others he had been in.

"May I help you?" someone said. G-man looked up and saw an old priest with eyes nearly as blue as Rickey's. The priest was smiling benignly at him, offering no threat.

"Uh, we were just looking around," he said. "It's a beautiful church . . . Father."

"Yes, it is. You're from New Orleans?" G-man nodded. "I recognize the accent. I was pastor of St. Rosalie's in Harvey for ten years before I came here. What brings you to our town?"

"We're just tourists."

"Well, I'm so glad you stopped in. The church is very old, you know. So many stories about it. Some of them are even a little crazy." The priest chuckled. "Did you see the statue of the Blessed Virgin out front? The one by the fountain?"

"Sure. It's kinda unusual—"

"Because she's seated, right. You don't see that too often in America. The statue was carved in Italy in the style of the Pietà, but alone, without the body of Christ in her arms. It represents her sorrow after He was taken from her. Anyway, there's a legend about it."

"I bet there is," said G-man. He really didn't want to hear it, but he knew he was about to.

"It's said that the Virgin will stand if a sinner comes before her." The priest chuckled again, then broke into a hearty laugh. Up near the altar, Rickey turned to see what was going on. "But she's never stood up yet, so apparently all of us in town and all who visit us must be without sin!"

G-man rose and stumbled out of the pew. "I'm sorry, Father," he said. "The sun . . ." But he welcomed the sun after the shadows of the church and sat with his face turned up to it until he heard the door open behind him. He tensed, afraid it might be the priest, but it was Rickey.

"You okay?"

"Yeah."

"You sick?"

"I'm fine."

"I'm sorry I made you go in there. I guess you didn't really feel like it."

"No," said G-man. "I really didn't."

He rubbed his hands over his face. Rickey patted him on the back, and G-man could feel the worry in his touch. After a few minutes he let his head fall back against Rickey's shoulder.

Out of the corner of his eye he could see the fountain and the soft eroded shape of the statue. Its blank gaze was upon him again, but the Virgin stayed seated. He wondered if she understood that she must either sit forever or stand up for everyone in the world.

⚓

Poppy Z. Brite, who is the author of eight novels, four short story collections, and much miscellanea, lives in New Orleans with a motley krewe of cats and reptiles. Read more at poppyzbrite.com.

HUNGRY DAUGHTERS OF STARVING MOTHERS

ALYSSA WONG

As my date—Harvey? Harvard?—brags about his alma mater and Manhattan penthouse, I take a bite of overpriced kale and watch his ugly thoughts swirl overhead. It's hard to pay attention to him with my stomach growling and my body ajitter, for all he's easy on the eyes. Harvey doesn't look much older than I am, but his thoughts, covered in spines and centipede feet, glisten with ancient grudges and carry an entitled, Ivy League stink.

"My apartment has the most amazing view of the city," he's saying, his thoughts sliding long over each other like dark, bristling snakes. Each one is as thick around as his

Rolex-draped wrist. "I just installed a Jacuzzi along the west wall so that I can watch the sun set while I relax after getting back from the gym."

I nod, half-listening to the words coming out of his mouth. I'm much more interested in the ones hissing through the teeth of the thoughts above him.

She's got perfect tits, lil' handfuls just waiting to be squeezed. I love me some perky tits.

I'm gonna fuck this bitch so hard she'll never walk straight again.

Gross. "That sounds wonderful," I say as I sip champagne and gaze at him through my false eyelashes, hoping the dimmed screen of my iPhone isn't visible through the tablecloth below. This dude is boring as hell, and I'm already back on Tindr, thumbing through next week's prospective dinner dates.

She's so into me, she'll be begging for it by the end of the night.

I can't wait to cut her up.

My eyes flick up sharply. "I'm sorry?" I say.

Harvey blinks. "I said, Argentina is a beautiful country."

Pretty little thing. She'll look so good spread out all over the floor.

"Right," I say. "Of course." Blood's pulsing through my head so hard it probably looks like I've got a wicked blush.

I'm so excited, I'm half hard already.

You and me both, I think, turning my iPhone off and smiling my prettiest smile.

The waiter swings by with another bottle of champagne and a dessert menu burned into a wooden card, but I wave him off. "Dinner's been lovely," I whisper to Harvey, leaning in and kissing his cheek, "but I've got a different kind of dessert in mind."

Ahhh, go the ugly thoughts, settling into a gentle, rippling wave across his shoulders. I'm going to take her home and split her all the way from top to bottom. Like a fucking fruit tart.

That is not the way I normally eat fruit tarts, but who am I to judge? I passed on dessert, after all.

When he pays the bill, he can't stop grinning at me. Neither can the ugly thoughts hissing and cackling behind his ear.

"What's got you so happy?" I ask coyly.

"I'm just excited to spend the rest of the evening with you," he replies.

THE FUCKER HAS his own parking spot! No taxis for us; he's even brought the Tesla. The leather seats smell buttery and sweet, and as I slide in and make myself comfortable, the rankness of his thoughts leaves a stain in the air. It's enough to leave me light-headed, almost purring. As we cruise uptown toward his fancy-ass penthouse, I ask him to pull over near the Queensboro Bridge for a second.

Annoyance flashes across his face, but he parks the Tesla in a side street. I lurch into an alley, tottering over empty cans and discarded cigarettes in my four-inch heels, and puke a trail of champagne and kale over to the dumpster shoved up against the apartment building.

"Are you all right?" Harvey calls.

"I'm fine," I slur. Not a single curious window opens overhead.

His steps echo down the alley. He's gotten out of the car, and he's walking toward me like I'm an animal that he needs to approach carefully.

Maybe I should do it now.

Yes! Now, now, while the bitch is occupied.

But what about the method? I won't get to see her insides all pretty everywhere—

I launch myself at him, fingers digging sharp into his body, and bite down hard on his mouth. He tries to shout, but I swallow the sound and shove my tongue inside. There, just behind his teeth, is what I'm looking for: ugly thoughts, viscous as boiled tendon. I suck them howling and fighting into my throat as Harvey's body shudders, little mewling noises escaping from his nose.

I feel decadent and filthy, swollen with the cruelest dreams I've ever tasted. I can barely feel Harvey's feeble struggles; in this state, with the darkest parts of himself drained from his mouth into mine, he's no match for me.

They're never as strong as they think they are.

By the time he finally goes limp, the last of the thoughts disappearing down my throat, my body's already changing. My limbs elongate, growing thicker, and my dress feels too tight as my ribs expand. I'll have to work quickly. I strip off my clothes with practiced ease, struggling a little to work the bodice free of the gym-toned musculature swelling under my skin.

It doesn't take much time to wrestle Harvey out of his clothes, either. My hands are shaking but strong, and as I button up his shirt around me and shrug on his jacket, my jaw has creaked into an approximation of his and the ridges of my fingerprints have reshaped themselves completely. Harvey is so much bigger than me, and the expansion of space eases the pressure on my boiling belly, stuffed with ugly thoughts as it is. I stuff my discarded outfit into my purse, my high heels clicking against the empty glass jar at its bottom, and sling the strap over my now-broad shoulder.

I kneel to check Harvey's pulse—slow but steady—before rolling his unconscious body up against the dumpster, covering him with trash bags. Maybe he'll wake up, maybe he won't. Not my problem, as long as he doesn't wake in the next ten seconds to see his doppelganger strolling out of the alley, wearing his clothes and fingering his wallet and the keys to his Tesla.

There's a cluster of drunk college kids gawking at Harvey's car. I level an arrogant stare at them—oh, but do I wear this body so much better than he did!—and they scatter.

I might not have a license, but Harvey's body remembers how to drive.

THE TESLA REVS sweetly under me, but I ditch it in a parking garage in Bedford, stripping in the relative privacy of the second-to-highest level, edged behind a pillar. After laying the keys on the driver's seat over Harvey's neatly folded clothes and shutting the car door, I pull the glass jar from my purse and vomit into it as quietly as I can. Black liquid, thick and viscous, hits the bottom of the jar, hissing and snarling Harvey's words. My body shudders, limbs retracting, spine reshaping itself, as I empty myself of him.

It takes a few more minutes to ease back into an approximation of myself, at least enough to slip my dress and heels back on, pocket the jar, and comb my tangled hair out with my fingers. The parking attendant nods at me as I walk out of the garage, his eyes sliding disinterested over me, his thoughts a gray, indistinct murmur.

The L train takes me back home to Bushwick, and when I push open the apartment door, Aiko is in the kitchen, rolling mochi paste out on the counter.

"You're here," I say stupidly. I'm still a little foggy from shaking off Harvey's form, and strains of his thoughts linger in me, setting my blood humming uncomfortably hot.

"I'd hope so. You invited me over." She hasn't changed out of her catering company clothes, and her short, sleek hair frames her face, aglow in the kitchen light. Not a single ugly thought casts its shadow across the stove behind her. "Did you forget again?"

"No," I lie, kicking my shoes off at the door. "I totally would never do something like that. Have you been here long?"

"About an hour, nothing unusual. The doorman let me in, and I kept your spare key." She smiles briefly, soft compared to the brusque movements of her hands. She's got flour on her rolled-up sleeves, and my heart flutters the way it never does when I'm out hunting. "I'm guessing your date was pretty shit. You probably wouldn't have come home at all if it had gone well."

"You could say that." I reach into my purse and stash the snarling jar in the fridge, where it clatters against the others, nearly a dozen bottles of malignant leftovers labeled as health drinks.

Aiko nods to her right. "I brought you some pastries from the event tonight. They're in the paper bag on the counter."

"You're an angel." I edge past her so I don't make bodily contact. Aiko thinks I have touch issues, but the truth is, she smells like everything good in the world, solid and familiar, both light and heavy at the same time, and it's enough to drive a person mad.

"He should have bought you a cab back, at least," says Aiko, reaching for a bowl of red bean paste. I fiddle with the bag of pastries, pretending to select something from its contents. "I swear, it's like you're a magnet for terrible dates."

She's not wrong; I'm very careful about who I court. After all, that's how I stay fed. But no one in the past has been as delicious, as hideously depraved as Harvey. No one else has been a killer.

I'm going to take her home and split her all the way from top to bottom.

"Maybe I'm too weird," I say.

"You're probably too normal. Only socially maladjusted creeps use Tindr."

"Gee, thanks," I complain.

She grins, flicking a bit of red bean paste at me. I lick it off of my arm. "You know what I mean. Come visit my church with me sometime, yeah? There are plenty of nice boys there."

"The dating scene in this city depresses me," I mutter, flicking open my Tindr app with my thumb. "I'll pass."

"Come on, Jen, put that away." Aiko hesitates. "Your mom called while you were out. She wants you to move back to Flushing."

I bark out a short, sharp laugh, my good mood evaporating. "What else is new?"

"She's getting old," Aiko says. "And she's lonely."

"I bet. All her mahjong partners are dead, pretty much." I can imagine her in her little apartment in Flushing, huddled over her laptop, floral curtains pulled tight over the windows to shut out the rest of the world. My ma, whose apartment walls are alive with hissing, covered in the ugly, bottled remains of her paramours.

Aiko sighs, joining me at the counter and leaning back against me. For once, I don't move away. Every muscle in my body is tense, straining. I'm afraid I might catch fire, but I don't want her to leave. "Would it kill you to be kind to her?"

I think about my baba evaporating into thin air when I was five years old, what was left of him coiled in my ma's stomach. "Are you telling me to go back?"

She doesn't say anything for a bit. "No," she says at last. "That place isn't good for you. That house isn't good for anyone."

Just a few inches away, an army of jars full of black, viscous liquid wait in the fridge, their contents muttering to themselves. Aiko can't hear them, but each slosh against the glass is a low, nasty hiss:

who does she think she is, the fucking cunt

should've got her when I had the chance

I can still feel Harvey, his malice and ugly joy, on my tongue. I'm already full of things my ma gave me. "I'm glad we agree."

OVER THE NEXT few weeks, I gorge myself on the pickup artists and grad students populating the St. Marks hipster bars, but nothing tastes good after Harvey. Their watery essences, squeezed from their owners with barely a whimper of protest, barely coat my stomach. Sometimes I take too much. I scrape them dry and leave them empty, shaking their forms off like rainwater when I'm done.

I tell Aiko I've been partying when she says I look haggard. She tells me to quit drinking so much, her face impassive, her thoughts clouded with concern. She starts coming over more often, even cooking dinner for me, and her presence both grounds me and drives me mad.

"I'm worried about you," she says as I lie on the floor, flipping listlessly through pages of online dating profiles, looking for the emptiness, the rot, that made Harvey so appealing. She's cooking my mom's lo mien recipe, the oily smell making my skin itch. "You've lost so much weight and there's nothing in your fridge, just a bunch of empty jam jars."

I don't tell her that Harvey's lies under my bed, that I lick its remnants every night to send my nerves back into euphoria. I don't tell her how often I dream about my ma's place, the shelves of jars she never let me touch. "Is it really okay for you to spend so much time away from your catering business?" I say instead. "Time is money, and Jimmy gets pissy when he has to make all the desserts without you."

Aiko sets a bowl of lo mein in front of me and joins me on the ground. "There's nowhere I'd rather be than here," she says, and a dangerous, luminous sweetness blooms in my chest.

But the hunger grows worse every day, and soon I can't trust myself around her. I deadbolt the door, and when she stops by my apartment to check on me, I refuse to let her in. Texts light up my phone like a fleet of fireworks as I huddle under a blanket on the other side, my face pressed against the wood, my fingers twitching.

"Please, Jen, I don't understand," she says from behind the door. "Did I do something wrong?"

I can't wait to cut her up, I think, and hate myself even more.

By the time Aiko leaves, her footsteps echoing down the hallway, I've dug deep gouges in the door's paint with my nails and teeth, my mouth full of her intoxicating scent.

MY MA'S APARTMENT in Flushing still smells the same. She's never been a clean person, and the sheer amount of junk stacked up everywhere has increased since I left home for good. Piles of newspapers, old food containers, and stuffed toys make it hard to push the door open, and the stench makes me cough. Her hoard is up to my shoulders, even higher in some places, and as I pick my way through it, the sounds that colored my childhood grow louder: the constant whine of a Taiwanese soap opera bleeding past mountains of trash, and the cruel cacophony of many familiar voices:

Touch me again and I swear I'll kill you—

How many times have I told you not to wash the clothes like that, open your mouth—

Hope her ugly chink daughter isn't home tonight—

Under the refuse she's hoarded the walls are honeycombed with shelves, lined with what's left of my ma's lovers. She keeps them like disgusting, mouthwatering trophies, desires pickling in stomach acid and bile. I could probably call them by name if I wanted to; when I was a kid, I used to lie on the couch and watch my baba's ghost flicker across their surfaces.

My ma's huddled in the kitchen, the screen of her laptop casting a sickly blue glow on her face. Her thoughts cover her quietly like a blanket. "I made some niu ro mien," she says. "It's on the stove. Your baba's in there."

My stomach curls, but whether it's from revulsion or hunger I can't tell. "Thanks, ma," I say. I find a bowl that's almost clean and wash it out, ladling a generous portion of thick noodles for myself. The broth smells faintly of hongtashan tobacco, and as I force it down almost faster than I can swallow, someone else's memories of my childhood flash before my eyes: pushing a small girl on a swing set at the park; laughing as she chases pigeons down the street; raising a hand for a second blow as her mother launches herself toward us, between us, teeth bared—

"How is it?" she says.

Foul. "Great," I say. It settles my stomach, at least for a little while. But my baba was no Harvey, and I can already feel the hunger creeping back, waiting for the perfect moment to strike.

"You ate something you shouldn't have, didn't you, Meimei." My ma looks up at me for the first time since I walked in, and she looks almost as tired as I feel. "Why didn't you learn from me? I taught you to stick to petty criminals. I taught you to stay invisible."

She'd tried to teach me to disappear into myself, the way she'd disappeared into this apartment. "I know I messed up," I tell her. "Nothing tastes good any more, and I'm always hungry. But I don't know what to do."

My ma sighs. "Once you've tasted a killer, there's no turning back. You'll crave that intensity until you die. And it can take a long time for someone like us to die, Meimei."

It occurs to me that I don't actually know how old my ma is. Her thoughts are old and covered in knots, stitched together from the remnants of other people's experiences. How long has she been fighting this condition, these overwhelming, gnawing desires?

"Move back in," she's saying. "There's so much tong activity here, the streets leak with food. You barely even have to go outside, just crack open a window and you can smell it brewing. The malice, the knives and bullets . . ."

The picture she paints makes me shudder, my mouth itching. "I can't just leave everything, Ma," I say. "I have my own life now." And I can't live in this apartment, with its lack of sunlight and fresh air, its thick stench of regret and malice.

"So what happens if you go back? You lose control, you take a bite out of Aiko?" She sees me stiffen. "That girl cares about you so much. The best thing you can do for her is keep away. Don't let what happened to your father happen to Aiko." She reaches for my hand, and I pull away. "Stay here, Meimei. We only have each other."

"This isn't what I want." I'm backing up, and my shoulder bumps into the trash, threatening to bury us both in rotting stuffed animals. "This isn't safe, Ma. You shouldn't even stay here."

My ma coughs, her eyes glinting in the dark. The cackling from her jar collection swells in a vicious tide, former lovers rocking back and forth on their shelves. "Someday you'll learn that there's more to life than being selfish, Meimei."

That's when I turn my back on her, pushing past the debris and bullshit her apartment's stuffed with. I don't want to die, but as far as I'm concerned, living like my ma, sequestered away from the rest of the world, her doors barricaded with heaps of useless trinkets and soured memories, is worse than being dead.

The jars leer and cackle as I go, and she doesn't try to follow me.

The scent of Flushing clings to my skin, and I can't wait to shake it off. I get on the train as soon as I can, and I'm back on Tindr as soon as the M passes above ground. Tears blur my eyes, rattling free with the movement of the train. I scrub them away angrily, and when my vision clears, I glance back at the screen. A woman with sleek, dark hair, slim tortoiseshell glasses, and a smile that seems a little shy, but strangely handsome, glows up at me. In the picture, she's framed by the downtown cityscape. She has rounded cheeks, but there's a strange flat quality to her face. And then, of course, there are the dreams shadowing her, so strong they leak from the screen in a thick, heady miasma. Every one of those myriad eyes is staring straight at me, and my skin prickles.

I scan the information on her profile page, my blood beating so hard I can feel my fingertips pulsing: relatively young-looking, but old enough to be my mother's cousin. Likes: exploring good food, spending rainy days at the Cloisters, browsing used book stores. Location: Manhattan.

She looks a little like Aiko.

She's quick to message me back. As we flirt, cold sweat and adrenaline send uncomfortable shivers through my body. Everything is sharper, and I can almost hear Harvey's jar laughing. Finally, the words I'm waiting for pop up:

I'd love to meet you. Are you free tonight?

I make a quick stop-off back home, and my heart hammers as I get on the train bound for the Lower East Side, red lipstick immaculate and arms shaking beneath my crisp designer coat, a pair of Mom's glass jars tucked in my purse.

HER NAME IS Seo-yun, and as she watches me eat, her eyes flickering from my mouth to my throat, her smile is so sharp I could cut myself on it. "I love places like this," she says. "Little authentic spots with only twelve seats. Have you been to Haru before?"

"I haven't," I murmur. My fingers are clumsy with my chopsticks, tremors clicking them together, making it hard to pick up my food. God, she smells delectable. I've never met someone whose mind is so twisted, so rich; a malignancy as well developed and finely crafted as the most elegant dessert.

I'm going to take her home and split her open like a—

I can already taste her on my tongue, the best meal I've never had.

"You're in for a treat," Seo-yun says as the waiter—the only other staff beside the chef behind the counter—brings us another pot of tea. "This restaurant started as a stall in a subway station back in Japan."

"Oh wow," I say. "That's . . . amazing."

"I think so, too. I'm glad they expanded into Manhattan."

Behind her kind eyes, a gnarled mess of ancient, ugly thoughts writhes like the tails of a rat king. I've never seen so many in one place. They crawl from her mouth and ears, creeping through the air on deep-scaled legs, their voices like the drone of descending locusts.

I'm not her first. I can tell that already. But then, she isn't mine, either.

I spend the evening sweating through my dress, nearly dropping my chopsticks. I can't stop staring at the ugly thoughts, dropping from her lips like swollen beetles. They skitter over the tablecloth toward me, whispering obscenities at odds with Seo-yun's gentle voice, hissing what they'd like to do to me. It takes everything in me not to pluck them from the table and crunch them deep between my teeth right then and there, to pour into her lap and rip her mind clean.

Seo-yun is too much for me, but I'm in too far, too hard; I need to have her.

She smiles at me. "Not hungry?"

I glance down at my plate. I've barely managed a couple of nigiri. "I'm on a diet," I mutter.

"I understand," she says earnestly. The ugly thoughts crawl over the tops of her hands, iridescent drops spilling into her soy sauce dish.

When the waiter finally disappears into the kitchen, I move in to kiss her across the table. She makes a startled noise, gentle pink spreading across her face, but she doesn't pull away. My elbow sinks into the exoskeleton of one of the thought-beetles, crushing it into black, moist paste against my skin.

I open my mouth to take the first bite.

"So, I'm curious," murmurs Seo-yun, her breath brushing my lips. "Who's Aiko?"

My eyes snap open. Seo-yun smiles, her voice warm and tender, all her edges dark. "She seems sweet, that's all. I'm surprised you haven't had a taste of her yet."

I back up so fast that I knock over my teacup, spilling scalding tea over everything. But Seo-yun doesn't move, just keeps smiling that kind, gentle smile as her monstrous thoughts lap delicately at the tablecloth.

"She smells so ripe," she whispers. "But you're afraid you'll ruin her, aren't you? Eat her up, and for what? Just like your mum did your dad."

No, no, no. I've miscalculated so badly. But I'm so hungry, and I'm too young, and she smells like ancient power. There's no way I'll be able to outrun her. "Get out of my head," I manage to say.

"I'm not in your head, love. Your thoughts are spilling out everywhere around you, for everyone to see." She leans in, propping her chin on her hand. The thoughts twisted around her head like a living crown let out a dry, rattling laugh. "I like you, Jenny. You're ambitious. A little careless, but we can fix that." Seo-yun taps on the table, and the waiter reappears, folding up the tablecloth deftly and sliding a single dish onto the now-bare table. An array of thin, translucent slices fan out across the plate, pale and glistening with malice. Bisected eyes glint, mouths caught mid-snarl, from every piece. "All it takes is a little practice and discipline, and no one will know what you're really thinking."

"On the house, of course, Ma'am," the waiter murmurs. Before he disappears again, I catch a glimpse of dark, many-legged thoughts braided like a bracelet around his wrist.

Seo-yun takes the first bite, glancing up at me from behind her glasses. "Your mum was wrong," she says. "She thought you were alone, just the two of you. So she taught you to only eat when you needed to, so you didn't get caught, biding your time between meals like a snake."

"You don't know anything about me," I say. The heady, rotten perfume from the dish in front of me makes my head spin with hunger.

"My mum was much the same. Eat for survival, not for pleasure." She gestures at the plate with her chopsticks. "Please, have some."

As the food disappears, I can only hold out for a few more slices before my chopsticks dart out, catching a piece for myself. It's so acidic it makes my tongue burn and eyes itch, the aftertaste strangely sweet.

"Do you like it?"

I respond by wolfing down another two slices, and Seo-yun chuckles. Harvey is bland compared to this, this strangely distilled pairing of emotions—

I gasp as my body starts to warp, hands withering, burn scars twisting their way around my arms. Gasoline, malice, childish joy rush through me, a heady mix of memory and sensory overstimulation. And then Seo-yun's lips are on mine, teeth tugging gently, swallowing, drawing it out of me. The burns fade, but the tingle of cruel euphoria lingers.

She wipes her mouth delicately. "Ate a little too fast, I think, dear," she says. "My point, Jenny, is that I believe in eating for pleasure, not just survival. And communally, of course. There are a number of us who get together for dinner or drinks at my place, every so often, and I would love it if you would join us tonight. An eating club, of sorts."

My gaze flickers up at her thoughts, but they're sitting still as stones, just watching me with unblinking eyes. My mouth stings with the imprint of hers.

"Let me introduce you soon. You don't have to be alone anymore." As the waiter clears the plate and nods at her—no check, no receipt, nothing—Seo-yun adds, "And tonight doesn't have to be over until we want it to be." She offers me her hand. After a moment's hesitation, I take it. It's smaller than mine, and warm.

"Yes, please," I say, watching her thoughts instead of her face.

As we leave the restaurant, she presses her lips to my forehead. Her lips sear into my skin, nerves singing white-hot with ecstasy. "They're going to love you," she says.

We'll have so much fun, say the thoughts curling through her dark hair.

She hails a cab from the fleet circling the street like wolves, and we get inside.

I RUN INTO Aiko two months later in front of my apartment, as I'm carrying the last box of my stuff out. She's got a startled look on her face, and she's carrying a bag stuffed with ramps, kaffir lime, heart of palm—all ingredients I wouldn't have known two months ago, before meeting Seo-yun. "You're moving?"

I shrug, staring over her head, avoiding her eyes. "Yeah, uh. I'm seeing someone now, and she's got a really nice place."

"Oh." She swallows, shifts the bag of groceries higher on her hip. "That's great. I didn't know you were dating anybody." I can hear her shaky smile. "She must be feeding you well. You look healthier."

"Thanks," I say, though I wonder. It's true, I'm sleeker, more confident now. I'm barely home any more, spending most of my time in Seo-yun's Chelsea apartment, learning to cook with the array of salts and spices infused with ugly dreams, drinking wine distilled from deathbed confessions. My time stalking the streets for small-time criminals is done. But why has my confidence evaporated the moment I see Aiko? And if that ravenous hunger from Harvey is gone, why am I holding my breath to keep from breathing in her scent?

"So what's she like?"

"Older, kind of—" kind of looks like you "—short. Likes to cook, right." I start to edge past her. "Listen, this box is heavy and the van's waiting for me downstairs. I should go."

"Wait," Aiko says, grabbing my arm. "Your mom keeps calling me. She still has my number from . . . before. She's worried about you. Plus I haven't seen you in ages, and you're just gonna take off?"

Aiko, small and humble. Her hands smell like home, like rice flour and bad memories. How could I ever have found that appealing?

"We don't need to say goodbye. I'm sure I'll see you later," I lie, shrugging her off.

"Let's get dinner sometime," says Aiko, but I'm already walking away.

CATERERS FLIT LIKE blackbirds through the apartment, dark uniforms neatly pressed, their own ugly thoughts braided and pinned out of the way. It's a two-story affair, and well-dressed people flock together everywhere there's space, Seo-yun's library upstairs to the living room on ground floor. She's even asked the caterers to prepare some of my recipes, which makes my heart glow. "You're the best," I say, kneeling on the bed beside her and pecking her on the cheek.

Seo-yun smiles, fixing my hair. She wears a sleek, deep blue dress, and today, her murderous thoughts are draped over her shoulders like a stole, a living, writhing cape. Their teeth glitter like tiny diamonds. I've never seen her so beautiful. "They're good recipes. My friends will be so excited to taste them."

I've already met many of them, all much older than I am. They make me nervous. "I'll go check on the food," I say.

She brushes her thumb over my cheek. "Whatever you'd like, love."

I escape into the kitchen, murmuring brief greetings to the guests I encounter on the way. Their hideous dreams adorn them like jewels, glimmering and snatching at me as I slip past. As I walk past some of the cooks, I notice a man who looks vaguely familiar. "Hey," I say.

"Yes, ma'am?" The caterer turns around, and I realize where I've seen him; there's a picture of him and Aiko on her cellphone, the pair of them posing in front of a display at a big event they'd cooked for. My heartbeat slows.

"Aren't you Aiko's coworker?"

He grins and nods. "Yes, I'm Jimmy. Aiko's my business partner. Are you looking for her?"

"Wait, she's here?"

He frowns. "She should be. She never misses one of Ms. Sun's parties." He smiles. "Ms. Sun lets us take home whatever's left when the party winds down. She's so generous."

I turn abruptly and head for the staircase to the bedroom, shouldering my way through the crowd. Thoughts pelt me as I go: Has Aiko known about me, my ma, what we can do? How long has she known? And worse—Seo-yun's known all along about Aiko, and played me for a fool.

I bang the bedroom door open to find Aiko sprawled out across the carpet, her jacket torn open. Seo-yun crouches on the floor above her in her glorious dress, her mouth dark and glittering. She doesn't look at all surprised to see me.

"Jenny, love. I hope you don't mind we started without you." Seo-yun smiles. Her lipstick is smeared over her chin, over Aiko's blank face. I can't tell if Aiko's still breathing.

"Get away from her," I say in a low voice.

"As you wish." She rises gracefully, crossing the room in fluid strides. "I was done with that particular morsel, anyway." The sounds of the party leak into the room behind me, and I know I can't run and grab Aiko at the same time.

So I shut the door, locking it, and mellow my voice to a sweet purr. "Why didn't you tell me about Aiko? We could have shared her together."

But Seo-yun just laughs at me. "You can't fool me, Jenny. I can smell your rage from across the room." She reaches out, catches my face, and I recoil into the door. "It makes you so beautiful. The last seasoning in a dish almost ready."

"You're insane, and I'm going to kill you," I say. She kisses my neck, her teeth scraping my throat, and the scent of her is so heady my knees almost bend.

"I saw you in her head, delicious as anything," she whispers. Her ugly thoughts hiss up my arms, twining around my waist. There's a sharp sting at my wrist, and I look down to discover that one of them is already gnawing at my skin. "And I knew I just had to have you."

There's a crash, and Seo-yun screams as a porcelain lamp shatters against the back of her head. Aiko's on her feet, swaying unsteadily, face grim. "Back the fuck away from her," she growls, her voice barely above a whisper.

"You little bitch—" snarls Seo-yun.

But I seize my chance and pounce, fastening my teeth into the hollow of Seo-yun's throat, right where her mantle of thoughts gathers and folds inward. I chew and swallow, chew and swallow, gorging myself on this woman. Her thoughts are mine now, thrashing as I seize them from her, and I catch glimpses of myself, of Aiko, and of many others just like us, in various states of disarray, of preparation.

Ma once told me that this was how Baba went; she'd accidentally drained him until he'd faded completely out of existence. For the first time in my life, I understand her completely.

Seo-yun's bracelets clatter to the floor, her empty gown fluttering soundlessly after. Aiko collapses too, folding like paper.

It hurts to take in that much. My stomach hurts so bad, my entire body swollen with hideous thoughts. At the same time, I've never felt so alive, abuzz with possibility and untamable rage.

I lurch over to Aiko on the floor, malice leaking from her mouth, staining the carpet. "Aiko, wake up!" But she feels hollow, lighter, empty. She doesn't even smell like herself any more.

A knock at the door jolts me. "Ma'am," says a voice I recognize as the head caterer. "The first of the main courses is ready. Mr. Goldberg wants to know if you'll come down and give a toast."

Fuck. "I—" I start to say, but the voice isn't mine. I glance over at the mirror; sure enough, it's Seo-yun staring back at me, her dark, terrible dreams tangled around her body in a knotted mess. "I'll be right there," I say, and lay Aiko gently on the bed. Then I dress and leave, my heart pounding in my mouth.

I walk Seo-yun's shape down the stairs to the dining room, where guests are milling about, plates in hand, and smile Seo-yun's smile. And if I look a little too much like myself, well—according to what I'd seen while swallowing Seo-yun's thoughts, I wouldn't be the first would-be inductee to disappear at a party like this. Someone hands me a glass of wine, and when I take it, my hand doesn't tremble, even though I'm screaming inside.

Fifty pairs of eyes on me, the caterers' glittering cold in the shadows. Do any of them know? Can any of them tell?

"To your continued health, and to a fabulous dinner," I say, raising my glass. As one, they drink.

SEO-YUN'S APARTMENT IS dark, cleared of guests and wait staff alike. Every door is locked, every curtain yanked closed.

I've pulled every jar, every container, every pot and pan out of the kitchen, and now they cover the floor of the bedroom, trailing into the hallway, down the stairs. Many are full, their malignant contents hissing and whispering hideous promises at me as I stuff my hand in my mouth, retching into the pot in my lap.

Aiko lies on the bed, pale and still. There's flour and bile on the front of her jacket. "Hang in there," I whisper, but she doesn't respond. I swirl the pot, searching its contents for any hint of Aiko, but Seo-yun's face grins out at me from the patterns of light glimmering across the liquid's surface. I shove it away from me, spilling some on the carpet.

I grab another one of the myriad crawling thoughts tangled about me, sinking my teeth into its body, tearing it into pieces as it screams and howls terrible promises, promises it won't be able to keep. I eat it raw, its scales scraping the roof of my mouth, chewing it thoroughly. The more broken down it is, the easier it will be to sort through the pieces that are left when it comes back up.

How long did you know? Did you always know?

I'll find her, I think as viscous black liquid pours from my mouth, over my hands, burning my throat. The field of containers pools around me like a storm of malicious stars, all whispering my name. She's in here somewhere, I can see her reflection darting across their surfaces. If I have to rip through every piece of Seo-yun I have, from her dreams to the soft, freckled skin wrapped around my body, I will. I'll wring every vile drop of Seo-yun out of me until I find Aiko, and then I'll fill her back up, pour her mouth full of herself.

How could I ever forget her? How could I forget her taste, her scent, something as awful and beautiful as home?

Alyssa Wong is a Nebula-, World Fantasy-, and Shirley Jackson Award-nominated author, shark aficionado, and 2013 graduate of the Clarion Writers' Workshop. Her work has appeared in *The Magazine of Fantasy & Science Fiction, Strange Horizons, Tor.com, Uncanny Magazine,* and *Black Static.* She is a first year MFA student at North Carolina State University, and can be found on twitter as @crashwong and at crashwong.net.

LET'S SEE WHAT HAPPENS

CHUCK PALAHNIUK

ART BY ELIZABETH LEGGETT

IN HINDSIGHT, THEIR mistake seemed obvious. Heather's parents had weighed the pros and cons before choosing Missoula, Montana over Eugene, Oregon and Moscow, Idaho. They'd managed the question of immunizations. They'd even reached a resolution on the issue of standardized testing. It wasn't until Heather had come home from the second grade at her new school, hugging a paper, a pamphlet printed with rainbows, that they'd recognized their slip up. She showed it to them, after naptime, as they ate oatmeal cookies in the kitchen.

The front of the pamphlet showed a group of smiling kids more or less Heather's age. Seven years old. The kids were the standard mix of skin colors. A balanced number of small boys and girls. Photoshopped among them were a tiger, a lamb, a male lion, some kind of brown bear, a panda bear, a large colorful parrot and a sleeping fawn with a white-spotted rump. Even a stegosaurus, which loomed over the group. A rainbow arched above everything, and superimposed on the rainbow were the words "Join Us!" The two facing pages inside the pamphlet promised love. A family. Life after death. On the back, in a blank square clearly set aside for the purpose, someone with a rubber stamp had added the name and address of a local church in bleary, blue ink.

Montana was their new beginning. It didn't offer the same perks as Seattle, but all the Waldorf schooling in the world wouldn't compensate Heather for living in a broken home. But by the time Heather's parents read the pamphlet, their daughter already believed in life everlasting. She knew all about demons, and guardian angels, and how she, Heather, was the beloved of a vast unseen holy host. How could her parents compete, now that Heather knew that the path to her real, celestial family lay in attending church services? Helping himself to another cookie, her father snuck her mother a look. She was drinking a cup of coffee at the last moment in the day when it wouldn't wreck her night's sleep. Clearly they'd fallen down on the job of child rearing.

"The best part of church," said Heather, "is when the Holy Spirit comes all over you."

Her mother wasn't certain she'd heard right.

Her dad didn't miss a beat, asking, "Does the Holy Spirit come all over the little children?"

Heather's mom gave him a sour glance. What she meant was, *Mister . . .* To their daughter she said, "You shouldn't say the word 'all.'"

Heather asked, "How come?" Meaning, *Since when was "all" a dirty word?*

Her dad pushed on, now giving his wife a smirk, next saying, "At least the Holy Spirit knows to pull out in time." By this he meant Brian. By *Brian*, he meant the reason they'd left Seattle.

"Be serious," Heather said, sighing as if they were idiots. She shut her eyes and smiled sweetly, as if she, only Heather, knew the secret behind the mystery of everything visible. Patting a little hand against her heart, she said, "The spirit, he comes *inside* me!"

Her dad started to choke on the cookie he'd been chewing, now crossing the kitchen and the living room in three long-distance strides, next shutting himself in the bathroom, where even with the fan running and the shower spraying full blast and him flushing the toilet, all at the same time, now they could still hear his laughter.

Not that Heather's parents were idiots. In their experience it was crucial to expose a child to religion, in particular to religious services so boring, in a setting so stifling, in clothing so uncomfortable in the presence of self-righteous, bullying, bad-smelling old people, that the child in question would be scarred for life. If a kid hated church it made the whole God issue all the easier. People wanted to believe, kids in particular. A bad church memory, scarred deep in their psyche did the trick better than a lifetime of rational arguments explaining why mommy and daddy and all the really smart humanists were atheists.

Heather's parents had started with a basic idea: A child raised with enough self-esteem wouldn't need the crutch of any god's love. To keep things simple, they'd just never introduced their daughter to the idea of a deity. Neither had they pushed atheism, because the denial of something automatically cemented that idea in place. To mention that they didn't believe in any god would ensure that someday Heather would latch onto religion, if only as an act of teenage rebellion.

Animals, they reasoned, didn't automatically worship anything. A human had to be socialized. A church offered the promise of inclusion and acceptance, and God's love was the trophy everyone got simply for showing up. They'd only just moved to Missoula, and here was a ready-made circle of friends.

Their next step was crucial. They couldn't gamble that the rainbow stegosaurus church would be miserable enough. God forbid their daughter have a great time and want to go back. God only knew what that would lead to next: Running with a pack of fresh-faced young Bible thumpers and doing missionary work, now fishing for more converts in soup kitchens and charity car washes, next bringing Heather into contact with some apple-cheeked God-fearing boy, and the two getting married, in a church no doubt, with no birth control and no college for Heather, not even a two-year undergraduate degree, always this was how a pair of rational sensible progressive thinkers could fuck up and raise a kid who'd just become another part of the on-going problem.

To ensure their daughter's first taste of religion was truly bitter, her father made inquiries which brought the three of them to the doorway of The Temple of the Prophet's Blood, a church audible from miles away due to the size of its loudspeakers and the shouting of its prophet, a man who stood behind the wooden table that acted as an altar, and he held a snake, a real snake, maybe not a poisonous one, God knows what species, but a live snake in one hand and a Mason jar of some clear liquid, most likely moonshine, but God knows it was just as likely strychnine or gasoline they'd all be called to come forward and test their faith by tasting, and wouldn't that be a perfect memory for Heather, her dad whispered to her mom: Getting jawed on by a biting snake. A kid going to her first worship service and watching while one of her folks drinks Christ's blood and falls over dead, now that, that kind of image was the take-away they needed seared into Heather's fresh, impressionable little brain.

They'd taken seats in the back row of pews, Heather clutching her Stegosaurus pamphlet. Now she wasn't smiling, not that she seemed scared either, no, her eyes were riveted on the snake. She whispered, "Where are the pandas?" as she studied the people who'd already walked up the center aisle and knelt down and now flopped face-down on the bare pine boards of the floor, people spread out like Jim Jones, like the People's Temple, around the feet of the snake man, people shaking in their clothes, and now pitching full-out fits, flopping like fish, now turning full-fledged convulsive, to which Heather's dad whispered, "Jesus wept," now happy in the certainty they'd picked the perfect church for his kid's first and last taste of religion.

The Jesus freaks really knew how to bust out their crazy. Bedlam old ladies rolled, their skirts bunched up around their waists, exposing cotton panties and blue-veined thighs and men barked and howled like werewolves, thank God, until Heather's mom whispered to her husband, "Wish me luck," now getting to her shaking feet, now advancing up the central aisle, now knee-deep in lunatics, sweaty smells, lunatic hands clutching at her hands, lolling mouths babbling gibberish while maniac eyes tried to hold her gaze, now almost to the altar table she turned to look back at her little family, now her husband nodding, eyes wide, expecting her to upstage zealots who had a lifetime of practice going bat-shit, now a glimpse of her daughter smiling, next waving, and mommy waving back, now that little wave morphing into a single jazz hand, fingers spread, a move she recalled from high school dance team, now that long-ago muscle memory triggering both jazz hands, next a shoulder roll, next a cheerleading jump, arms flung wide, next landing in a crouch, something leftover from some Drama Club audition for "Cats" where she'd strutted, always bellowing a medley of snippets from the score of "Annie," now by accident kicking some fallen Christian in the ribs. Now even the most-feverish congregants edged their antics away from her, now giving her some Saturday-Night-Fever space to cut up, now that she was revving up some fitness class pole dancing routine, now Heather's mom broke out the little bit she still knew of the Electric Slide, next segueing into the Macarena, now a couple moves leftover from the Hokey Pokey between a couple fan kicks, now the disco dance, the Y.M.C.A., now belting out the chorus of "Don't Cry for Me, Argentina," now Heather's mom was doing that thing Madonna did, squaring her hands around her face, now moon walking backward, now the whole congregation going quiet, gradually falling still and silent as she, Heather's mom, Ms. One World Fair Trade Rational Atheist, always cutting up pure break dancing, pure krumping, now full-on mosh-pit pitching herself around the sanctuary, singing twinkle-twinkle, singing happy birthday.

Another stolen glance revealed Heather cowering, drawing her feet up on the pew, going fetal with her knees tucked to her little chest at the sight and sound of mommy now channeling every two-all-beef-patties television jingle, now somehow up atop the altar table swinging the snake around her head like a venomous lasso, executing a high-energy buck-and-wing, now a flash of her daughter's weeping face, now her own blouse ripped open, her bra cast aside to cheers, now shaking her breasts, now launching a series of high kicks, now one Prada stiletto sent flying, now her mouth making its own words, now the sound of breaking glass, now her shoe punching a hole in the stained glass window, caught there by the heel, now hanging there hooked by the heel where an angel's face used to be, now Heather's mom stuck for a big finish, her escape, now drenched, now dripping in sweat, her hair flogging her bare shoulders, now out of breath, the church and congregants getting dark around the edges, everything pin-holed, by now mostly gone, now nobody, next nothing.

The snake man shook hands with them at the door. He said faith among parishioners had been waning. Since their previous shepherd had been taken, lured away by the Devil to a false church, their numbers had dwindled. His eyes darted toward a group standing near the front of the church. These dregs of the former church membership, they were stooped with age. Among them were younger people confined to wheelchairs, some with slack faces or twitches that suggested dementia. The minister brought his focus back to Heather's mother. He asked if she'd consider witnessing in the coming weeks. He said they'd be honored if she'd testify to them. Someone from the group came forward, limping and drooling and walleyed, and this afflicted stranger knelt to kiss her bare foot.

In the car, strapped in the backseat, Heather cried the entire trip home. Her mother was driving, saying, "It's a perfect laboratory." She was irked her husband couldn't see that. Here they had a mob of believers, desperate to kowtow to something. Honest, everyday people. She could twist their faith in a socially positive, earth-friendly direction. What she meant was *Let's see what happens*. Her eyes never leaving the road, she said it would make a great sociology study. Possibly a memoir. A blog at least. "I'm tired of playing house," she said, "and looking after everyone's needs." This would be dipping a toe back in the labor market. It felt weird to work the clutch pedal with a bare foot. "Every week," she resolved, "I just need to call down my inner crazy."

Her husband disagreed. "Not a book," he said. He nodded as he spoke, his eyes focused on some distant goal. Neither of them mentioned the crippled, the aged and the dying people who'd be involved. Instead, Heather's father said, "It would make a great documentary film."

After lunch, after they'd spent the afternoon getting ready for school the next morning, after they'd put Heather to bed, her father asked her mother, "Did you mean what you said up there?"

She waited. They were in bed. She was reading a textbook about Margaret Meade she'd saved since college.

He said, "During your show." He had his laptop open, surfing something. Search word: Choreography. Search word: Gigging.

"I said a lot of stuff," she countered.

He said, slowly, implying a quote, *"Yes, I fucked Brian."*

She turned away, now her lips sucked between her teeth, now her insides hollowed out, becoming a vacuum, now poised between fight or flight, always playing opossum. Composed, she asked, "Why would I say that?"

Now he waited. His eyes didn't leave the screen, but he'd stopped keyboarding.

She marked the place in her book and set it aside. She advised, "You should get your ears checked," and shut off the bedside lamp.

The next Sunday found them back at the temple place. Heather's mother didn't say as much, but it was clear she hoped to stage an encore. Recapture the magic. In preparation, she'd done thirty minutes of stretching to warm up. Her clothes, she'd dressed nicely, but this blouse and skirt weren't anything she couldn't rip off her body and cast to the wind, and underneath she wore a new matching bra-and-panty set. This time, she'd upped the ante by having her legs waxed. People looked to her as the music blared, now thundering louder, masking everything but the loudest screaming wail. The hole in the stained glass window had been patched with brown cardboard. Before she could make her move, Heather's father stepped into the aisle and staggered toward the altar.

It was clear that he was reenacting the zombie chorus line sequence from the Thriller video. His hands hovered as if leading him. His feet dragged. Heads turned to follow his progress. The gauntlet had been cast down. The Holy Ghost had found a new vessel. Heather's mother plucked a digital recorder from her purse and held it forward, activated, as her husband channeled Sid Vicious, now aping Mick Jagger. He strutted and flapped his arms. Once, his eyes found her still seated beside their daughter in the back of the church. His look was full of gloating and triumph, now tearing open his shirt and plucking at his own nipples, next reliving a few steps of the Lindy Hop they'd practiced for months to perform as the couple's dance at their wedding reception, now falling, blam, into a full James Brown splits against the pine floor, a stunt that proved he had to be wearing an athletic supporter, not boxers, probably a cup, too, proof he'd premeditated this up-staging. Now doing that maniac dance from *Flashdance* that's more-or-less running in place, now seizing the Mason jar of clear moonshine or deadly gasoline and, splash, dashing himself in the face, now shaking back his wet hair, like Jennifer Beale, just another exotic dancer-slash-welder who dreams of Pittsburgh ballet school and oh-what-a-feeling. Next Heather's mother recognized the chicken dance they'd learned at Oktoberfest in Seattle the year prior. He sang a medley of Nine Inch Nails and Christmas carols. Playing a scene from Magic Mike, he shucked his pants and threw them into the cheering crowd, always doing, almost step-for-step, the sexy black guy dance from *A Chorus Line*, a movie he'd always before now claimed to hate but had clearly been studying like a textbook, until, red-faced, panting, now he was sweating like a pig stripped of everything except ankle socks and his jock strap.

Seated beside her mother, Heather curled her body into a ball, holding both hands in little fists to cover each ear. Rocking herself gently. Both her eyes were closed, her pursed lips humming a series of loud, long bursts as if to further block out the scene.

Her mother looked down but didn't come to Heather's aid. In a way this was a punishment. If Heather's parents were honest, they were punishing their child for bringing God into the happy, happy enough, home they'd made. They were getting their revenge on her for implying that two bright, loving parents wasn't enough. No, Heather wanted someone bigger. A love bigger than their love. They'd given her life, but now their greedy kid wanted immortality.

When Heather's father collapsed in a heap, the worshippers rushed to his aid. Heather's mother was fuming. The opportunity to match his performance had passed. An uncountable number of hands, liver-spotted, palsied, were reaching forward with scraps of fabric. They'd divided his shirt and pants among themselves. They were using the shreds to blot sweat from her husband's forehead. People clutched the damp rags against their lips.

The snake man of the temple place, he approached them afterward. He shadowed them across the gravel parking lot back to their car, cradling something in his hands. Something glossy black. Other parishioners watched as the snake man handed the object to Heather's mother without a word. It was the shoe she'd lost the previous week. She couldn't help but feel a little insulted. While other churchgoers fanned themselves and spit tobacco as they pressed sweat-soaked scraps of shirt between the pages of their Bibles, here the snake man was giving her back her shoe.

Bare-chested, Heather's dad drove them home in a borrowed pair of denim pants. Hillbilly bib overalls dug out of the charity barrel in the church entryway. One back pocket showed the faded circle from years of carrying a can of chewing tobacco. It was hard for him to imagine anyone in more poverty than the donor. He didn't slouch the way he usually drove. Instead, he sat as if riding a horse, his spine so straight it hardly touched the seatback. "Those people aren't worshipping a god," he said. "If anything, they need the gestalt acting out."

His wife nodded. Wagging a finger in the air, she said, "Their lives are nothing but suppress, suppress, suppress."

Heather's sobbing had triggered an attack of hiccups, and between them she asked,

"Why only one snake?" What she meant was: *Where was the stegosaurus?* Her pudgy hands had clutched the rainbow folder until the grubby paper was edged with mush. The address on the back, smeared to blue fingerprints.

"Hold your breath, sweetheart," her mother suggested. Already, Heather's mom worded together a book pitch in her head. She knew all about holding her tongue, at least in front of you-know-who. She was plotting her holy roller comeback the next week, a razzmatazz Bob Fosse routine, part Martha Graham, part Jackie Chan. She'd wow the faithful and lure them away from adoring her husband. Without turning to address him, she watched the houses scroll past, little cracker box places with cars parked on parched, yellow lawns the size of a postage stamp. To her, houses seemed to occur in inverse proportion to churches: neighborhoods with dinky houses had huge churches. Conversely, their own distant suburb with its half-acre lawns, its three-car garages and great rooms, it didn't have a single church. As they neared the street on which they lived, she asked, "Did you mean what you said back there?"

Wearing a stranger's pants, Heather's dad kept his eyes on the road. As if he were only a careful driver, he squinted at the rearview mirror, the side mirror, and the speedometer before he ventured, "What?" Heather's hiccups broke her sobs at regular intervals. Like a broken record, he thought but didn't say. It was too much to tackle, explaining a record album to his kid.

"Never mind," said his wife. What she meant was *You can lie to me, later.*

At dinner, Heather announced that she never wanted to go back to church, but the matter was out of her little ink-stained hands. At bedtime she refused to kneel down and say any prayers. Her father stood over her with his video camera, his shoulders hunched, elbows jutting out like stubby wings. He caught a glimpse of himself in her bedroom mirror. With the camera pointed down like a droopy beak he could pass for a vulture menacing a tyke. "Come in here," he yelled to her mom, "and tell your daughter to pray for daddy's goddamn documentary!" Heather hated God, but she still believed in Him.

In their own bed, her mother told her father he smelled like a brewery. She meant his hair, the corn liquor or whatever he'd doused himself with on the altar. He combed his fingers through the strands and smelled his hand. "The Holy Spirit came in my hair," he said and offered her the open hand to lick, but Heather's mom had her laptop open, propped on her knees, watching clips of Kung Fu movies, the flying kicks and karate chops, trying to memorize them and not make yelling Kung Fu faces that might give away her strategy. She pictured herself throwing her fists around the sanctuary and cleaving the altar table with a single downward punch. Ignoring his open palm, she asked, "What you said, this morning, is it true?"

Heather's dad sighed and looked at the ceiling as if stymied, telling her, "I was talking gibberish." He bunched his eyes shut until he hit on the correct word. "I was speaking in tongues."

His wife said, "You said it twenty times." She had it on digital recorder. And he said, "It didn't mean anything." She said, "You kept repeating it." He told her, "I was babbling." She said, "*I'm fucking Gloria?*" He paused, one, two, too many beats too long before insisting, "I didn't." His wife wouldn't give up, "You *didn't* fuck your teaching assistant?" To which he parried, "Is that what I actually said, or what you heard?" She watched a martial arts actor kick over villains like ten pins, trying to control her voice before she said, "It's what you said." Each time she spoke his fingers tapped a few keys as if collecting her words for his screenplay. And if so, she wondered, were they actually her words or was he keyboarding words into her mouth? She cut her eyes sideways without turning her head, trying to read what he'd written. He craned his neck, trying to see her computer screen and said, "You heard what you wanted." He waited, adding, "Isn't that what religion is all about?" She knew what he meant was *projection*, and that she was the problem. She took the digital recorder from her bedside table, touching a button on the controls, triggering his voice, unmistakable, shouting, ". . . so much booty she got them buns, them bum-bum-bums so full and stuck-out I get a dick's worth of hot, tight squeeze even before I officially touch hole . . ." In the distant background, they could hear Heather's steady, raspy church breathing.

When Heather's dad heard the words his eyes and mouth exploded wide. His cheeks ripening, red as a tomato. At last he spoke, asking, "Can I use that in my film?"

On her laptop a karate master drove a dagger through the heart of an adversary. Heather's mom, her hand wanted to bridge the space between them and touch the hair on her husband's arm. Her tongue wanted to lick the hand he'd offered. The problem was how one thing would lead to the next and this struck her as the wrong moment for a sex scene. It wasn't enough to let events run their natural course. Heather's mom knew an audience expected a certain shape in a page turner. Rising tension. Obstacles. Triumph, transformation and relief. The simple truth wasn't true enough. She could wait. If that's how he was playing this, she'd wait and deliver her retribution the next Sunday. She could spout cruel gibberish as well. "Fine," she said, and toggled to another screen where she typed the night's argument into the first chapter of her book.

Heather's father stepped aside the next week. A realist, he'd brought his video camera and needed to shoot footage. He knew his wife was eager to strut her stuff.

Heather's mom brushed past him, leaving the pew, sprinting down the aisle, now leaping, now hand springing, now catching air, her skirts flying, now a flash of her hot-pink thong, next sticking her landing a perfect ten in front of the altar table, the church music blaring from the piled-up speakers, now she was bouncing parkour moves off the sanctuary walls, next covering Paula Abdul straight-up dance steps, next Ruby Keeler tap steps, Shirley Temple tap dancing, revving up to zumba, bringing home The Red Shoes, delivering hot and ready Gypsy Rose Lee, ready to bake, kicking it, serving up, laying down, now busting out her best robot, her husband's camera trained on her, his wife, his competition for authority, his collaborator, for this, the battle over who would be the narrator of their true story.

Every glance toward the back pew found Heather weeping, always shuddering, her face cupped behind her hands, now hyperventilating. Always her mom felt pulled to console her but there were bigger fish to fry. Boiling out of her mother's mouth came words, slug lines, signature catch phrases, now a song refrain, now a Dr. Seuss hop-on-pop nursery rhyme, now that Dr. Pepper I'm-a-pepper ditty, now O Canada. Next shedding her blouse, now shimmying out of her skirt, watching the faithful rend her clothes to rags, playing to the camera, now digging deep, always hitting her mark, she swayed Marilyn Monroe style, Diamonds Are a Girl's Best Friend slithering, all pink-satin rattlesnake, now exhausted, now executing a perfect shuffle-ball-change, next overdosed on adrenaline, her knees rubbery, her vision filling with spots, achieving ecstasy, always seeing Heather in the distance, seeing her husband's camera-masked eyes. Heather's faced masked with tears. Her husband's cheeks puffed up with rage. Now seeing nothing.

That night, Heather's father had only had to press playback and there she was tap dancing, kicking jujitsu, the shuffle-ball-change, shouting, "... I never loved you." Shouting, "Heather's father is Brian ..."

Brian, she wrote in her book that night. By Brian she meant *adultery*. He'd been studying on a baseball scholarship. Heather's mom forgot the field of study, Geology or Geography; however, she could remember how his trainer had ordered him to throw a ping pong ball, fast and straight, some Karate Kid counterintuitive exercise, insisting that if he could throw something weightless, fast and level, across the plate, then his pitching arm would make the big leagues. When Heather's mother had skipped her period, Brian wasn't thrilled. He'd gotten wasted and cracked up on his bike, some kind of motorcycle, before the fetus even had a heartbeat. Him and that motorcycle, both so loud and alive, next so not. She understood some edict that a good story had to include both a birth and a death. Good-bye Brian. Hello Heather and Montana.

Heather's mother typed the words into her draft of the current chapter. Wondering what actor would play her, touch typing, planning what she'd wear to be interviewed by Oprah Winfrey, she almost didn't hear the screams.

In the next room Heather wailed, and her father, now perhaps not her real father, now he collected his camera and tripod and took them to her bedside and set them up, now getting the focus perfect, now tweaking the exposure before kneeling down in the shot, hitting his mark in the perfect composition of little Heather screaming in bed, now as if he'd rushed straight in to comfort her. Leaving a cheat for the camera, he took her in his arms, now rocking her gently, mindful not to look into the lens as Heather coughed out the words, "God's chasing me!" In broken sentences she said how God wanted to make her an angel in Heaven because He loved her so much. She begged her father not to take her back to church, and he shifted her slightly in his arms so the microphone could better catch her words. "God will get me at church," she sobbed, breathless with terror. "God wants to kill me."

Her fingers looked blue from clutching the smeared address on the pamphlet. She must've touched her face, too, because her cheeks were a pale, bloodless grey. Her fingers had been in her mouth so even her little tongue had turned purple. Her lips looked like those of a corpse. He'd fix that in post.

In the week that followed, both parents plotted and trained. Video meant forever so Heather's mom went four times to a tanning salon, unconvinced that an orange spray tan wouldn't streak and run once she broke a heavy sweat. Her husband got his hair cut, next covering the grey, next submitting to a session of ultraviolet teeth whitening.

Now as the church bell called the faithful, Heather's father mounted his camera on a tripod. He told Heather, "Shoot coverage for daddy, please." Her mom propped her digital recorder where it would collect every sound. Ready, raring to compete, now everything hung in the balance as both parents, now everything at stake, now hot-footing it down the central aisle like a wedding march on fast-forward, him breaking beats, now going off the rails, his pelvis off-the-chain bumping. Now his hands gesticulating sign language with no meaning. The pair of them now elbowing aside lame children propped on crutches, now strong-arming old ladies to make more room. Next storming the sanctuary, Heather's mom mad free-styling, now wrecking the air as some sphincter in her head lets loose every graphic detail about her and Brian, dead Brian, now her playing it quiet, standing by while her husband goes pantomiming some mime feeling his way around inside a not-there box. Her butt now seized by an attack of uncontrolled twerking. Now both of them locked in the ultimate Holy Spirit face-off. Now the two competitors showered with shouted hallelujahs, now praise be's. Now Heather's dad crowing all Gloria, Gloria, not half-stepping, now stomping the yard, full-blown crunking, making his confession, the way only cracks make clean glass visible. Now he throws a glance to find Heather. Now his hips humping and bucking air porno. Her mom Grateful Dead twirling, dervish whirling, delirious, delusional, now tranced-out transcendent. Now her mother looking, too, and Heather not there. Both Heather's parents not finding her, now finding their child gone.

Her parents boogie back to find their daughter turned blue on the pine floor, her face beyond just smudged ink, now indigo blue and still all over, now inert. Her hand pricked in two spots no larger than staple holes leaking blood, the church viper now slithering away, off the pew, under another pew, now snaking through a knothole in the boards, now gone. Next Heather's head flops loose on her neck, now her lips turning cold under her father's mouth-to-mouth, her hands cold to her mother's touch, next her father collecting her in his arms, next her mother scrambling for the phone in her purse, now dialing 9-1-1, now scream-asking the snake man for the temple's physical address, where they're located, now her father finding no pulse in Heather's neck, always the whole congregation kneeling around them, now her mom listening for a siren coming here, now no siren, now the hum of low prayers, now still no siren, now the faithful all reaching in to lay hands on Heather's cold body, now her mother listening for the words of everyone's prayer, now her father adding his whisper to those same words, next everyone present not just pretending to pray, now the paramedics kicking open the front doors, asking the species, meaning, now louder *What kind of snake?* Next flashing a penlight and finding her pupils fixed and dilated, next sticking a needle into her little arm and injecting something clear, now no heartbeat, now still no heartbeat, now nothing but people praying, no beeps from the cardiac monitor, now Heather's mother and father both weeping, always the camera and the digital recorder still spying on them, now documenting a story they never wanted to tell.

Now a cry beneath the layer of everyone praying, now even the paramedics praying a little, next a little cough, now Heather whispered, "Amen."

That night in her hospital bed, Heather wore a white gown, angelic, calm and composed, saying, "God sent me back." They were all there in Heaven, she said, the panda, the parrots, the rainbows and stegosaurus. Sitting to one side, her parents held the video camera so she couldn't see the little screen, how the camera no longer trained on them, how the autofocus had slipped to watch the snake biting her, Heather crying out, her distress lost in the roar of the show, her calling for them, her eyes falling closed, her body collapsing to one side, sliding to the floor, her breathing slow, now slower, now stopped. On video, one dying hand giving a twitch, a spasm, now frozen still. On video, rewound and replayed, Heather dying alone, dead, dead for minutes ticking away on the video counter. As if just trying to cure hiccups, holding her breath while her mother's recorded voiced screamed, "Breathe!" Dead too long to ever be anything else.

The attending physician in the ER gave credit to the anti-venom, and he wanted her admitted, at least for overnight, for observation. In regard to her experience, he shrugged, now explaining about how Heather's pineal gland had flooded her brain with a serotonin-like hallucinogenic. How when the brain perceives a serious threat to itself, this chemical triggers a vivid psychedelic reaction in the neocortex. Not coldly, not too coldly, he now dismissed Heather's vision as the reaction of the primitive brainstem to impending death. Now a self-comforting sort-of final bedtime story. Hers was a vestigial behavior leftover from when humans were prey animals and had to evade predators by playing dead. One final euphoric party for Heather's central nervous system.

Unbelieving, the snake man whispered how the doctor was wrong. Eyes closed, he whispered, "It's a miracle."

Smiling sweetly, now that she, only Heather, knew the secret behind the mystery of everything visible, she cupped a little hand to one side of her mouth, now waving for her father to lean close, now whispering, "Don't tell mommy." She paused next, thinking hard, her brow furrowed. Now saying, "In Heaven, Mommy's friend can throw the ping pong."

Whispering to her father, Heather said, "Mommy doesn't know . . ."

All her parents' hand waving and leg shaking, their singing, now recitations, next doing confessions, always taking up space, always filling silence, making a world of themselves, themselves the center of the world, always twitching and prancing to hold the attention, spouting nonsense. It was all about denial. About how one snake bite could stop everything. Something like a snake bite would arrive at any time and deliver them to a still, silent eternity.

Now Heather whispering, "But he told me he couldn't make babies."

Now, hearing this, her dad started to choke, now crossing the hospital room in one long-distance stride, now shutting himself in the bathroom, where even with the fan running and the shower spraying full blast and Heather's father flushing the toilet, all at the same time, everyone could still hear him cry.

<hr>

Chuck Palahniuk is the author of thirteen novels—*Doomed, Damned, Tell-All, Pygmy, Snuff, Rant, Haunted, Diary, Lullaby, Choke, Invisible Monsters, Survivor,* and *Fight Club*—which all have sold more than five million copies in the United States. He is also the author of *Fugitives and Refugees,* published as part of the Crown Journey Series, and the nonfiction collection *Stranger Than Fiction.* He lives in the Pacific Northwest. Visit him on the web at chuckpalahniuk.net.

ON MOVING INTO
YOUR NEW HOME
BRIT MANDELO

If on the first night
her sorrow-sounds wake you
the echo of a cry fading to silence
drawing a chill sweat up your spine
leaving you shaking in your bed—

If on the second night
her sobs tumble you
from your cobwebbed dreams
to the moon-silvered shadows
of a cold room, a lonely hour—

If on the third night
the edge of her keening moan
worms slick into your ear
as you begin to drift off
and pries your eyes wide open—

If on the fourth night
her hitching struggling breaths
seem to brush like cool fingers
down the back of your neck
spreading a fear like ice—

If on the fifth night
her desperate whimpers
cease like they never were
cut off when you turn on the lamp
the sudden light stabbing at your retinas—

If on the sixth night
her begging intrusions
become too awful to bear
and you must stop the noises
before you go ravening mad—

Check the attic up its narrow stair,
the secret spaces and cellar shadows
hunting clues, hunting bones, hunting
for anything at all of her
that could explain the visits.

Or—on the seventh night,
if you came up empty-handed,
light the lamp
and huddle tight,
waiting for her whispers.

❧

Brit Mandelo is a writer, critic, and editor whose primary fields of interest are speculative fiction and queer literature, especially when the two coincide. She is the senior fiction editor for *Strange Horizons* and has two books out, *Beyond Binary: Genderqueer and Sexually Fluid Speculative Fiction* and *We Wuz Pushed: On Joanna Russ and Radical Truth-telling*. Her other work—fiction, nonfiction, poetry; she wears a lot of hats—has been featured in magazines such as *Stone Telling*, *Clarkesworld*, *Apex*, and Ideomancer. She also writes regularly for Tor.com and has several long-running column series there, including Queering SFF, a mix of criticism, editorials, and reviews on QUILTBAG speculative fiction. She is a Louisville native and lives there with her partner in an apartment that doesn't have room for all the books.

THE GREAT UNKNOWN

JOEL LANE

It must have been a kind of folk myth
from colder times, when winter held echoes
of the Ice Age. I'm sure I heard it
some night in my fearful childhood.

A terrible winter gripped the coast
and the sea froze from the land outward
until the boats were shells of ice
tethered in a dead harbor, and mist

breathed over miles of frozen waste
where gulls stiffened in mid-flight
and packs of wolves made the crossing
from the North, silent and lean;

and where, as the winter deepened
and the skies turned greyer, the dead
came back as a blizzard of ashes.
I used to think such things impossible

until I lost you. Until our love became
a fragile echo on the telephone
and an occasional touch of your hand
late at night, after too many drinks.

I miss the loneliness that was ours
to share, when we walked in the city
and explored its waste lands. I miss
your cold hand, your bitter mouth,

the rock salt between your thighs.
I know the myth is yours too. I know
there is only one date left for us.
Let's meet before dawn, and walk

together, hands linked, from the shore
through the mist and the dying gulls,
and kiss once as the wolves approach
over the frozen waves, and belong.

Joel Lane (1963-2013) was the author of four poetry collections, *The Edge of the Screen* (1998), *Trouble in the Heartland* (2004), *The Autumn Myth* (2010), and *Instinct* (2012); several collections of short fiction; and two novels, *The Blue Mask* (2003) and *From Blue to Black* (2000). Lane was also the editor of three anthologies. He received the British Fantasy Award twice and in 2013 won the World Fantasy Award for his short fiction collection, *Where Furnaces Burn*.

WORM AND MEMORY

LUCY A. SNYDER

It'd be nice to flourish
a wand in clever magic,
gracefully draw a caustic
gray thread from the head
and drop it, splashless,
in a cool gazing pool.

We cerebrated monkeys
seldom find any witchy
pennies for our thoughts;
our long-tailed guilts,
shames and rages grow
like *Dracunculus* worms:
burning, blistering, itchy.

Milky little demons are best
twisted out in private, a bit
at a time; in the healthy light
the worms can spin to gold.

Lucy A. Snyder is the Bram Stoker Award-winning author of the novels *Spellbent, Shotgun Sorceress, Switchblade Goddess,* and the collections *Orchid Carousals, Sparks and Shadows, Chimeric Machines,* and *Installing Linux on a Dead Badger.* Her story collection *Soft Apocalypses* was released by Raw Dog Screaming Press in July 2014. Her writing has been translated into French, Russian, and Japanese editions and has appeared in publications such as *Chiral Mad 2, What Fates Impose, Once Upon a Curse, Strange Horizons, Weird Tales, Hellbound Hearts, Dark Faith, Chiaroscuro, GUD,* and *Best Horror of the Year, Vol.* 5. You can learn more about her at lucysnyder.com.

IN MEMORIAM:
ROBERT NELSON

W.H. PUGMIRE

Under the unmoving cloud, I wait. Still, I taste the nectar of that lake of blood, wherein I washed my innocent hands, and then my face, with gore that spilt from hands that knew no crime as yet. I take up one perfumed blossom from the lake of blood, a bloom wherein is curled a fetid serpent that, rising, kisses my eye. White mist of moon sinks down to copulate with crimson mist of lake, and I rise at last, barefoot, a phantom lost in mournful youth. I creep beneath unmoving cloud, into the woodland of neglected souls, and shake from my splintered skull my crumbled dreams. I drift on naked foot through rotting gloom, beyond joy and sorrow, into a realm of ecstasy and pain. I find the vacant tomb beside the vat of gore, that tub before which kneels a clumsy skeleton that has dropped its skull into the silo's mess. I push my hand into the thick liquid debris and pluck the skull, but turn my eyes away from its too-wide grin. I walk, barefoot, upon the soft floor of that mephitic woodland, sucking in its fumes, until my calloused toes touch mausoleum marble. How sad the crimson candles look, unlit. I set the skull onto a ledge and place one candle in its jaw. Striking flint, I summon sparks that kiss my eye, that lick the several candle wicks. The tiny scarlet flames are beads of blood on fire. They shimmer as did the lake of blood, and I clutch with innocent hands into the air of carnage. One candle alone remains unlit, reposing in a death's-head jaw. I strike the flint a second time and wonder why this candle's flame is black. I feel that glacial flame upon my eye, that eye that peers onto the sharp edge of the flint stones, that hard unyielding edge. I strike that edge against my pulsing wrist and watch the mist of mortality rise from me and conjoin with crimson air. I move my naked foot in pool of blood and peer at that one midnight flame that ushers me, at last, into glad deliverance.

Wilum Pugmire has been writing Lovecraftian weird fiction since the early 1970s, determined to show that one can write in the Lovecraft tradition and still remain original and audacious. His many books include *The Tangled Muse, Some Unknown Gulf of Night, The Fungal Stain and Other Dreams*, and *Gathered Dust and Others*. 2013 saw the publication of two new hardcover collections, *Encounters with Enoch Coffin* (Dark Regions Press, written in collaboration with Jeffrey Thomas) and *Bohemians of Sesqua Valley* (Arcane Wisdom Press). Willy also has many tales in numerous forthcoming anthologies.

FLOURLESS DEVIL'S FOOD
SCHWETA NARAYAN

Oranges: you'll have to grow your own, love, feed them
finger-cut, moon-flow, any blood will do. The neighbour's cat
—just say coyotes got her—
and mice who skitter now across her silence.

Migrant workers' daughters when your tree grows
thirsty. Say coyotes got them
—and just don't take a blonde.

When fruit hangs heavy, love, copper-bright as screams
grind leftover bones to meal. Add baking soda
and somebody's sacred food (their children's captive sweat
adds notes of salt and steam; their children's
hollow eyes bring out the bitter).

Follow your normal recipe from there. Invite the neighbours, and match
napkins to their baby's dappled fur. They'll taste

that citrus bite, love. Tell them
it's a welcome home.

I'll be there.

Shweta Narayan was born in India, and has lived in the liminal spaces of Malaysia, Saudi Arabia, the Netherlands, Scotland, and California. Their poetry has appeared in places like *Strange Horizons*, *Goblin Fruit*, and Tor.com, and their short fiction in places like *Strange Horizons*, the *2012 Nebula Showcase* anthology, and *We See a Different Frontier*. Shweta received an Octavia E. Butler Memorial Scholarship, co-edits the speculative poetry zine *Stone Telling*, and feels old on tumblr at shwetanarayan.tumblr.com.

THE SKIN-WALKER'S WIFE

LISA M. BRADLEY

Behind the roadhouse
her lips drag over flannel
mouth skimming a seam, shoulder to collar
until he pushes too hard, drives
her hip into the clapboard siding
and she gasps, sucking down
the cig smoke trapped
in his worn-soft shirt.

She doesn't smoke but it tastes better
than the blood in her mouth
the ulcers she's chewed
inside her lips, waiting for her husband
to come home, wondering what—
who—he'd become,
if she'd recognize him this time
or if he'd be a perfect stranger.

This other one, he bumps his forehead to hers
a quick forced tilt so he can see
her eyes, and he huffs, "You okay?"
still fucking but concern edging
into lust-hazed eyes, eyes that earlier
across the pool table
had flickered with something—
someone—
she'd thought she recognized.

She nods, focuses on the wet oval
on his shirt. "More,"
she whispers, and he kisses her through
his grin and the sweet whiskey still slicking
his tongue. She knows as he rocks her
steady pressure against splintered planks
his breath and hers fogging the dark
she knows he is not
her perfect stranger.

But he numbs the gnawing ache
that grows every time her husband goes
in search of a stronger body
a vessel that won't creak under the demands
of his soul, such weighty cargo,
and, stranger still,
tonight she finds that going numb
is enough.

She notes how this one fits inside her
fits so familiar inside his skin
not like her husband: stretching bone
and gristle beyond their limits
and not like her: clamping down on each
homesick wish, heart furling tight around
new hurts and leaving great, echoing
chambers of herself behind.

When he groans against her shoulder,
filling the rubber, he remains
himself
relieved but not expended
softening yet undiminished.
She wants to learn this trick.
She watches him pull out, step back
shed his latex skin without concern.

After he tucks in his shirt, he offers
her another beer "or maybe a ride home?"
She shakes her head, shifts
her weight, feeling off-balance in her
chest not her legs.
Something is unfurling.
"Busy day tomorrow," she decides. "Leaving town."

His eyes flicker like luck. He grins again.
"Wasn't that bad, was it?"
"Baby," she says, grinning back, "it changed my life."

Lisa M. Bradley's first collection of short fiction and poetry is *The Haunted Girl* (Aqueduct Press). Her poetry has appeared in numerous venues, including *Strange Horizons*, *Stone Telling*, *Cicada*, *Mothering*, and *Weird Tales*. A Latina writer of Tejano heritage, Lisa lives in Iowa with her spouse, child, and two cats. She is currently working on a fantasy novel set on the Texas-Mexico border in the 1930s. Her website is lisambradley.com. You can also find her on Twitter as @cafenowhere.

NO POISONED COMB

AMAL EL-MOHTAR

The tale is wrong. I bear no grudge.
A story in the teeth of time
will shift its outlined shape, be chewed
to more palatable stuff.
Thus death; thus cold demands
for a hot hot heart,
for slivers to simmer in warm plum wine
on winter nights.

Nonsense.

They say I told him to bring me her heart,
but I didn't.

It is a fact well known
that the fashion for wearing hearts on sleeves
has passed. Young girls today,
with their soft looks, their sharp lashes,
wear their hearts as cunning hooks
in their cheeks—that supple flesh
so like to apples, so red, so white,
smelling of fall and summer both,
of sweet between the teeth.

My huntsman hungered.
So did his knife.
Do you eat the red cheeks,
I said to him that day,
and I will eat the core.

I cored her. Oh
her looks might've hooked
the hearts of mirrors, of suitors
in dozened dimes, but my huntsman
hooked her looks, carved sweet slices,
blooded the snow of her face, and I
gave her the gift of a fabled room
whose walls were mirrors.
The tale is wrong. Their way
is kinder, I confess.

But mine is fair.

—For Caitlyn Paxson and Jessica P. Wick

Amal El-Mohtar is the Nebula-nominated author of *The Honey Month*, a collection of poems and very short fiction written to the taste of twenty-eight different kinds of honey. Her poetry has won the Rhysling award three times and the Richard Jefferies Prize once, and her story "The Truth About Owls" is presently a Locus Award finalist. Her fiction has most recently appeared in *Uncanny* and is forthcoming in *The Bestiary*, edited by Ann VanderMeer. She writes reviews for *NPR*, *Lightspeed*, and *Tor.com*, narrates fiction and poetry for *Uncanny's* podcast, edits *Goblin Fruit*, and has occasionally been known to deadlift genre professionals. She is also, with Scott Lynch, Liz M. Myles and Michael Damien Thomas, part of *Down and Safe*, a Blake's 7 podcast. She divides her time and heart between Ottawa and Glasgow. Find her online at amalelmohtar.com or on Twitter @tithenai.

THE ROTTEN LEAF CANTATA
ROSE LEMBERG

(1) I cannot cry.

(2) The leaves fall. Over the long winter they rot under snow, they give birth to new ground.

(3) The winters are gone; the leaves, paperbag brown and rigid, clog my front yard, too heavy for raking.

(4) I have never loved you.

(5) I want to buy a piece of furniture. A leather sofa, a Chesterfield, handsome and dignified and enveloping in all the right places. Upon it I will huddle, covered in a blanket of last December's foliage.

(6) The dying leaves cocoon me. I transform—a mermaid, a unicorn, a slug, a hedgehog.

(7) I do not transform. I stay the same, fat and graying, all my colors bled into the dead leaf wash.

(8) My new piece of furniture warps under the weight of the snow. I take the crowbar to take it apart—isn't that what one is supposed to do in fairytales?

(9) I have never owned a crowbar.

(10) It hurts too much to wrap my fingers over the handle. My hands and arms no longer obey me. I do not remember if they ever did.

(11) Inside the hacked-up Chesterfield there is a heartbox of ormolu and enamel, delicate and filled with the finest perfume of fig and peppery musk. You say I have never seen the heart of you, never cared enough to dab it on my wrists in movements quick and precise, but if I do—if I do—can the smell-thread spell the way home?

(12) There never was a you. You don't know about ormolu, or how enamel is an anthology of sunsets layered upon each other in waves of translucent color.

(13) You don't understand poetry, you say. Have you ever told a lie? The ormolu box, its sides coral and pink like the edges of a sunset, that is yours; it has come from you, shaped itself perfectly and secreted itself away. It left you bereft and confused, like a heap of wet leaves that will never see snow. You are always waiting to hear the softness of it falling, and yet you hate snow, you say.

(14) I will not miss you when you go. The winter will send me crocuses, wrapped in white paper that will melt under my fingers. I will buy a piece of furniture and give my crowbar away, plant crocuses like succulents upon the windowsill and wait for them to wilt. Under the oaks outside the last-year leaves will warp themselves into birds, and lift off, heavy and limping, into the inscrutable air.

Rose Lemberg is a queer bigender immigrant from Eastern Europe. Her work has appeared in *Strange Horizons*, *Beneath Ceaseless Skies*, *Interfictions*, *Uncanny*, *Sisters of the Revolution: A Feminist Speculative Fiction Anthology*, and other venues. Rose co-edits *Stone Telling*, a magazine of boundary-crossing poetry, with Shweta Narayan. She has edited *Here, We Cross*, an anthology of queer and genderfluid speculative poetry from *Stone Telling* (Stone Bird Press), and *The Moment of Change*, an anthology of feminist speculative poetry (Aqueduct Press). She is currently editing a new fiction anthology, *An Alphabet of Embers*. You can find Rose at roselemberg.net and @roselemberg, and support her work on Patreon at patreon.com/roselemberg.

THE H WORD:
A GOOD STORY

LUCY A. SNYDER

EARLIER THIS YEAR, I asked Facebook friends to leave comments if they (or those they love to read) are queer horror authors. It was a popular post. While remarks like "Me! I'm gay!" or "Heck yes! Clive Barker is my favorite!" dominated the thread, there were also several comments like this: "*I don't care about the author's sexuality; I just want a good story.*"

A good story. Doesn't every reader of popular fiction want that? And that plea for a good story seems pretty broad-minded at first glance, doesn't it? These readers are all about the narrative! It doesn't matter if we writers are black or white, male or female, liberal or conservative, gay or straight! Story is queen.

Story is royally critical, no question. But it doesn't exist in a vacuum separate from the writer. Writing good fiction isn't like baking cookies or assembling a model car kit. It's *personal*. We write what we know. Our hopes, our dreams, our fears, our obsessions, our experiences . . . it's all material for our tales. We horror writers are cutting ourselves open and spreading ourselves out there on the page.

Any given story of mine is a mix of the completely imaginary and the deeply intimate. And that's true for any other horror or dark fantasy author in service to his or her craft. A reasonably attentive reader of my fiction could guess that I'm either queer or am thinking a whole lot of queer thoughts.

Horror is the literature of fear. And if you're queer, and if you write fiction about your darkest fears while also doing your very best to tell a good story, a funny thing happens. Many of those readers who claimed to just care about story are now all squirmy. Sure, the plot's exciting . . . but you made it all weird! Why couldn't you just write a good old-fashioned entertaining story where the monsters are uncomplicatedly monstrous and the heroic guy gets the trophy girl at the end? Why couldn't your story be *straight*, darn it?

All of us who write horror have to find that middle road between art and commerce. Satisfying art means striving to meet a high craft standard for our work while being true to ourselves, but satisfying commerce means producing a piece of writing that will sell. Those two goals are not mutually exclusive, but the further your writing strays from what readers and publishers are comfortable with, the more difficult it is to reconcile the two.

LGBTQ authors have made tremendous strides into the mainstream in the past few decades. But our cultural image of the average person is still someone who's straight, white, and male, with the emphasis on straight. And that cultural default can affect publishers' perceptions of the kinds of characters readers want to see in their books.

The only time I've ever argued with an editor's request for revisions was when one asked me to straighten the female protagonist of one of my stories. This was just a few years ago, and the tale was for a horror anthology aimed at adults and teens. Here are the relevant parts of the email he sent me:

> [Publisher Redacted] will have a hard time with a few issues that I think are easily fixed and really don't have that much bearing on the story.
>
> The second thing, and I know it is very subtle with no action, is the lesbian aspect. I don't have a problem with it myself, but at the same time, I think you would have a stronger character if she was straight . . .
>
> The reason [Publisher Redacted] will have a problem is (honestly) their personal beliefs, and the contracts they have with local school systems, which purchase large quantities of books.

While I appreciated his candor—it's likely I'd had stories rejected for queer themes before but the editors wouldn't be straight about it—my jaw was on the floor.

My story's viewpoint character was a violent survivor; her love for her partner was the only remnant of her humanity, and that love was at the core of all her motivations. The only way my zombie-slaying, bandit-murdering, weapons-stealing protagonist would be a "stronger" heroine as a heterosexual . . . would be if queerness is a defect.

So, I wrote him back:

> I'm glad you enjoyed the story. I can change the magic details, no problem there. But I have personal objections to straightening my character to make her more acceptable. I'm sad that you would ask that of me (I'm queer). Lesbian, gay, and bisexual children and teens exist (and make up a nontrivial portion of the kids who read SF and fantasy) just as black and Hispanic and Asian teens exist, and asking me to make a lesbian character straight to make her acceptable is not any different than asking me to make a black character white for the sake of a publisher who thinks black people bear the mark of Cain.
>
> And as for the books being purchased by schools—gay and lesbian characters regularly appear in YA and middle grade books that appear in libraries and schools around the country; I just don't see that having a lesbian character is really that unusual these days: "There are so many queer characters in YA lit now, including manga and graphic novels, that the topic doesn't seem nearly as controversial as it once did. At

conferences and conventions where educators and librarians gather, there are always sessions with LGBTQ topics. Inclusiveness is all the rage." (see bit.ly/lo_afterellen for the whole article).

> *I do want to be a part of the book. I am willing to make some changes to make her orientation more subtle, but I won't straighten her. I hope you will reconsider your request in that regard.*

He wrote me back with a heartfelt apology, but made it clear that business concerns trumped everything else:

> *The school system orders these books for every student (in specific grades) in the county. I assure you it is a large purchase and projects are cultivated to fit into this program. The County Commission actually purchases the books . . . they have a board that approves the books before they are purchased. They are very strict. . . . [Publisher Redacted] can't afford the projects without the County Commission purchases. Therefore, if they turn down a project, the project will not make it to the light of day.*

The subtext I read was, "Don't be difficult, Lucy. This is just how the world works. Obviously brain-fiending zombies and plagues and murder and decapitations are good clean fun as far as the school system is concerned. But a woman feeling romantic love for another woman? Heavens no! They have to think of the children!"

After my initial flush of frustration at his response, I started thinking of my own childhood. I went through my first suicidal depression at the age of twelve. If I'd been just a little more resourceful, a little less fearful, I would not be here right now. I would not have written this column or anything else.

Why was I suicidal? I felt completely isolated and unwanted and defective. I was fat. I was a nerd. I was weird in so many ways. And deep down, I knew I was queer.

Being queer was the worst. I couldn't admit it to anyone, not even myself. Back then in that little dust-blown town in Texas, queers were at best morally weak crazy people who needed years of shameful psychiatry to straighten out. At worst, they were perverts and predators, innately evil and not really human. If someone killed a queer, well, that wasn't what proper law-abiding folks did, but it was still doing the world a favor, wasn't it?

I escaped into books. I could pretend to be someone else for a while, someone who mattered in their world and had amazing adventures in fabulous places. All those characters I wanted to be were arrow-straight, and mostly male. While I got temporary comfort from these novels, they ultimately reinforced the image I had of myself as being defective because I wasn't a boy (and therefore wouldn't ever do anything really cool) and I wasn't like the other girls, either. Not at all. I was something else, something nobody wanted around. Something that probably didn't deserve to be alive.

So when I hear someone tell me that characters have to be heterosexual to keep them fit for younger readers? I'm hearing that person tell me that the world was a right and proper place when it made me want to commit suicide before I'd even turned teen.

If I'd had queer female protagonists in my books? They would have been signs that there might be a future where I belonged and could be happy. I'd have still had plenty of problems as a fat nerdy kid who consistently failed to perform her gender correctly. But I'd have felt I deserved to breathe air.

Despite my self-loathing, I didn't kill myself. A decade later I escaped to a college town that tolerated gays and lesbians. Life got better. Eventually I came to grips with my own queerness. I wrote hard, and earned myself a career as a professional horror writer.

Being a pro writer is as integral to my public identity as my sexuality is to my private identity. And when you're a pro, you make the sale. When an editor who's offering you hard cash tells you to change something, you change it.

Even if it means you wouldn't be able to look your twelve-year-old self in the eye.

Even if it means you can't really look your grown-up self in the eye, either, because you just erased your own existence from your story. For six cents a word.

But this is America, and while story is queen . . . business is king. So I did the best I could: I made the queer aspects of the character as subtle as anything you'd find in a 1950s film hiding in the celluloid closet. The editor accepted my rewrite, and life went on.

The good news is that since then, I haven't had another editor reject a story for containing queer characters or themes. For instance, Jason Sizemore operates Apex Publications from Kentucky and frequently calls himself a hillbilly. Despite the socially conservative climate in his state, he's supported LGBTQ authors and he originally published my Stoker-winning queer tale "Magdala Amygdala."

So, publishers who want to be allies and see the value in publishing diverse voices are managing to do that just fine. Hopefully before too long we'll be living in a world where other publishers' beliefs (whether about religion or reader expectations) and County Commissions across the land aren't keeping queer characters out of books and limiting the scope of human stories that readers get to choose from.

And then, we can all be sure that it's really the story that matters.

Lucy A. Snyder is the Bram Stoker Award-winning author of the novels *Spellbent, Shotgun Sorceress, Switchblade Goddess,* and the collections *Orchid Carousals, Sparks and Shadows, Chimeric Machines,* and *Installing Linux on a Dead Badger.* Her story collection *Soft Apocalypses* was released by Raw Dog Screaming Press in July 2014. Her writing has been translated into French, Russian, and Japanese editions, and has appeared in publications such as *Chiral Mad 2, What Fates Impose, Once Upon a Curse, Strange Horizons, Weird Tales, Hellbound Hearts, Dark Faith, Chiaroscuro, GUD,* and *Best Horror of the Year, Vol. 5.* You can learn more about her at lucysnyder.com.

THE LANGUAGE OF HATE

SIGRID ELLIS

STEPHEN KING TAUGHT me how to hate.

I was, oh, twelve or thirteen years old when I found the novels of Stephen King. *Firestarter* was the first. I was a fan of the *X-Men* comics, you see, and the cover blurb for *Firestarter* promised a young girl with superpowers. I was game. I checked the book out of the library, read it overnight. Stephen King changed my world.

Those changes were, and remain, complicated. I recently told a friend of mine that Stephen King introduced me to theory of mind. This isn't entirely true—Chris Claremont, writer of the *X-Men* comics, also contributed. But it's more true than a person might want to publicly confess. Wikipedia defines theory of mind as "the ability to attribute mental states—beliefs, intents, desires, pretending, knowledge, etc.—to oneself and others and to understand that others have beliefs, desires, intentions, and perspectives that are different from one's own." In short, theory of mind is the idea that other people are as fully and independently human as oneself. It's the ability to imagine what another person might be thinking—including what they might be thinking about me.

I was a bit hazy on this as a kid. Most kids are at some point. It's a developmental stage, narcissism. But even past that developmentally appropriate stage I was unsure on how this worked. I knew other people were independent humans, different from me, because they did utterly inexplicable things. They made jokes that were not funny, they presumed I knew things I did not know, they expected actions from me that they had never explained they wanted. Humans were weird and confusing black boxes of unpredictability. Stephen King changed that for me.

I expect many people hear the name "Stephen King" and think "bestselling author of horror fiction." They might imagine an intricately-crafted tale of suspense. But what avid readers of his work know—the dirty little secret—is that King's strength is not his plots. He occasionally pulls out a tense, tightly-run story, but mostly his plots meander. From time to time he publishes books that just fail to have an ending, entirely. What King is best at is writing characters. His characters, whether protagonist, antagonist, villain, or minor cameo, are richly developed with complex inner lives. Their thoughts, feelings, and motivations are clearly stated no matter how small the part played.

I recently spent some time catching up on King's more recent novels. I read *Mr. Mercedes*, and *Finders Keepers*, and *The Colorado Kid* (one of those aforementioned novels that simply skips any sort of plot resolution). I loved returning to the world of King's imagination. I love the way he creates living, breathing people on the page. But this time around I noticed how often his characters think in hateful terms about weight, fatness, and infirmity. In *Mr. Mercedes*, the point-of-view antagonist uses specifically hate-filled terms for his alcoholic, overweight mother and for his disabled younger brother. This being a horror novel, he then kills both. In *Finders Keepers*, fatness and softness are used as terms of contempt equivalent with homophobic hate speech.

In both of those books, and in many (if not most) of King's novels, the most hate-filled language exists in the minds and voices of villains and antagonists. Tom Rogan, one of many antagonists in *It*, taught me most of the insulting language for lesbians. It was also the source of all my anti-black racist terms—many of them obsolete by the 1980s, but many unfortunately still perfectly current.

But it's not merely the villains whose minds are filled with contempt and hatred. Most of King's protagonists feel that weight gain is indicative of moral laxity. Fatness means weakness, addiction, and giving up. Fatness is a form of dependence on food for emotional satiety, and thus a form of addiction and thus a moral failure. His protagonists and narrators put on weight when they are weak or depressed or helpless. Losing weight is a sign that they are fit to combat evil once more.

Addiction in general is treated with complicated feeling in King's work. No surprise there, since his own experience of addiction is an indelible part of his work. But King's characters, overall, seem ambivalent about the notion that addiction is a disease. Most of his characters think of it as a failure of will. This is perhaps most evident in *Doctor Sleep*, in which our protagonist is an addict who tries a number of different strategies to stay clean and sober. The language King uses to describe white-knuckling is . . . ambivalent. Dan Torrance seems very committed to simply being stronger than his addiction. He's proud of it. When he ultimately goes to meetings and tries to work AA, there is an element of shame for him. I am pretty sure that this reflects the feelings King himself has.

And, yet, still, other characters describe addiction with absolute contempt. All of the stereotypes and tropes of addiction are in King's work. Brady's mother in *Mr. Mercedes* is a neglectful incestuous drunk. The alcoholic hobo in *It* is a puke-covered child molester. When Andy McGee in *Firestarter* is addicted to pills, he is a fat, emotional slob.

Women are also objects of hate in King's work. One of the clearest markers the reader has as to whether a character is a bad guy is how they think about women. Antagonists think of women as bitches and whores, and that's merely a starting point. The descriptions get incredibly detailed and biological, the view of women as objects omnipresent in the villains' minds.

But the good guys, the protagonists, they also constantly objectify women. The men who narrate King's stories are always eyeing the women around them, contemplating their attractiveness, their sexual orientation, their sexual availability, the relative merits of their various individual body parts. These are the heroes, you understand. The men we are to admire and cheer for.

And let's not even ponder how Stephen King characters think of and describe homosexuality. Fags or lesbos are sort of the best descriptors a queer character can hope for from another character. From there the invective gets wildly and specifically creative. (It reminds me of the weirdly specific concerns anti-gay politicians seem to come up with, the sort that make me question exactly how much time these extremely heterosexual folks have spent daydreaming about queer sex.)

When I assert, therefore, that Stephen King taught me how to hate, I mean that in a very specific and instructional sense. The language of hatred is a thing I learned from King.

Being taught how to hate is an odd thing. I learned not only what the words for hatred were, I learned why these things were to be hated in the first place. Fat is to be hated because it is weak, selfish, and uncaring for the needs of others. Addiction is to be hated because it puts the self above others at all costs. People with disabilities are to be hated for the burden they are on others. People of color are to be hated for having possession of any single thing a white person might hypothetically desire. Queers are to be hated because they are intrinsically aberrant. Lesbians are specifically hated for not wanting men. Gay men are specifically hated because they reject being proper men and therefore threaten the masculinity of all other men. Women are to be hated because they are desirable, or not desirable enough. Because they are available for sex or because they are not. Women are to be hated for loving men or for loving women. They are to be hated for being strong and for being weak. For speaking their minds and for remaining silent. For raising children and for abandoning them. For living and for dying.

There is no thing a woman in a Stephen King novel cannot be hated for. There is no way of being a women in his novels that avoids hate.

How odd, how very odd, to learn the rich tapestry of things a person could be hated for.

I should note, here, that I do not think Stephen King himself personally hates all of these people. In fact, I sense a great deal of benevolent humanist comprehension from his writing. In King's nonfiction I find him to view the world with a constant sense of wonder, of appreciation. He seems to be trying to understand all of human nature, all of the time. It's not his fault that human nature includes vileness. And yet, when every protagonist views women as objects, when every bit character takes a moment to ponder the queer or addict with disgust . . .

Well, a theory of mind develops.

This, then, is how other people view the world. When other people think, this is what their thoughts must look like. If everyone in all of these novels, good guys and bad guys and bit players who are instantly dead, share these views, this must therefore be the nature of reality.

As a younger person I would read Stephen King as a guide to other people's motivations. His characters are so richly written, their motivations so cleanly explained! I read his novels and tried to figure out how the people I knew in my life could possibly work. What were the real people I knew thinking? Why did they make these jokes? What did they expect from me? What did that smile mean, or that frown? What on earth was I supposed to say or do in reply?

As a teenager, when confronted with a social interaction I did not understand, I checked the database of Stephen King or Chris Claremont characters and tried to find a character moment that most matched what this real person was saying to me. I would then review the descriptive text from the appropriate passage, figure out what the real person talking to me meant, and then answer. It's a cumbersome work-around, to be sure. And eventually I learned smoother ways of talking to humans. But it worked for me.

It worked for me as long as I was prepared for some social interactions to be contemptuous, hateful, or vile.

It was actually incredibly useful.

For the first time in my life, I understood what catcalling was intended to do. (Put me in my place, remind me I was a worthless female object to be used by men.) I understood what being called a dyke meant, and why it was bad (because I didn't want or need men). I understood why being fat was bad and wrong. (I was selfish and weak and destroyed other people's lives with my selfishness, of which fatness was merely an external manifestation.)

At least I'm white. I was spared the need to understand all of those insults and microaggressions on any personal level.

I remember one occasion of catcalling, when I was about thirteen years old, which actually made me want to grin. I understood what the guy was saying! And implying! And it was awful and scary and I really wanted him to go away, but I *understood!*

Thank you, Stephen King!

I've said before, in other essays, that Chris Claremont's writing on X-Men comics are what enabled me to come out to myself as a person who was attracted to women. But it was Stephen King who told me that I was queer. Queer as in strange, other, probably disgusting, and very much to be feared and hated. Not merely for whom I wanted to have sex with but for all those other reasons. Lesbian, fat, female—there was no way I was ever going to be a person that other people viewed neutrally. The internal monologue of the people I met would always judge me and find me wanting, exactly the way that all his characters were disgusted by fat lesbians.

To this day, when I am angry, I model my invective on the patterns I learned from Stephen King. Always insult people for things they can't help. Tear at the ways they need others, the relationships they depend on. Make sure to describe attributes they can't change with the most disgusting analogies. Highlight weakness and make sure to call it a failure of character and will.

I try very hard to not let these angry rants escape into the open.

But when the self-critical asshole who lives in my head gets restive and bored and wants to find something to criticize in me, that voice also uses the language of Stephen King. I've read a lot of King over the years. I'm pretty good at his insults at this point.

And yet. And yet.

And yet I would not give up knowing what I know. Especially now that I have gotten older and learned more. More about the world, more about other people. My theory of mind has grown vastly more complex. At forty-two years old I understand people better than I did when I was thirteen, or twenty, or thirty. As mixed and complicated as the lessons of Stephen King are, I would not part with them.

King taught me how to hate, including how and why I ought to hate myself. But he also taught me that those voices of hate—the ones he created and I then allowed in my mind—were *wrong*.

Stephen King stories feature the most unlikely of heroes. More importantly, they feature the most unlikely of survivors. A teenager can outwit and escape from vampires. A child can take down the secret societies of the federal government. Children can defeat alien evil. Women, people of color, the elderly, and the disabled can save humanity after the apocalypse. This continues even in King's more recent stories. The protagonists of Mr. Mercedes are an elderly white guy with health problems, an African-American teenage boy, and a forty-something woman with emotional and mental complications.

You might be hated, feared, and an object of contempt, King whispers to me. *But you are a badass motherfucker and you will outlive all the evil bastards in the world.*

He's right. I am a badass motherfucker. I am a fat, middle-aged queer lady of dubious health and slightly complex mental landscape. The number of insults a King antagonist could throw at me are legion. The language of hate is bound up for me in my identity. But those words of hate are the badges by which I know I will ultimately thrive. I am a badass motherfucker, and so are you.

The outsiders, the strange, the disliked and marginalized—we are the survivors of Stephen King novels. Queers. Queers in all senses of the word, we are the ones who outlast evil, who save the world, who see the sun rise after the terror is destroyed.

Queers destroy horror.

Why, yes. Yes, we do.

***

Sigrid Ellis is co-editor of the Hugo-nominated *Queers Dig Time Lords* and *Chicks Dig Comics* anthologies. She edits the best-selling *Pretty Deadly* from Image Comics. She is the flash-fiction editor of Queers Destroy Science Fiction! from *Lightspeed Magazine*. She edited the Hugo-nominated *Apex Magazine* for 2014. She lives with her partner, their two homeschooled children, her partner's boyfriend, and a host of vertebrate and invertebrate pets in Saint Paul, MN.

CREATURES OF THE NIGHT:
A SHORT HISTORY OF QUEER HORROR

CATHERINE LUNDOFF

QUEER-FLAVORED HORROR TALES first appeared in the Gothic novels, vampire tales, and ghost stories of the eighteenth century. I am using the term "queer" here as shorthand for lesbian, gay, bisexual and/or transgender (LGBT), but it was once a popular term to describe stories about the strange and horrific. "Queer" has amongst its early definitions the following: weird, bizarre, strange, unnatural. In eighteenth-century horrific literature, homosexuality, whether implied or explicit, was the corruption eating away at the heart of civilization: hidden, monstrous, and menacing.

Due to the legal and social consequences of being out, early LGBT writers often only became visible as the result of suffering a disaster of some sort. Gay nobleman William Beckford, author of *The History of the Caliph Vathek* (1786), a dark fantasy awash with demons and evil magic, died in financial and social exile in France when he had to flee England amid rumors of his illegal sexuality. Dr. John Polidori, Lord Byron's physician and rumored lover, author of the first vampire story published in English, *The Vampyre* (1819), committed suicide amidst whispers that Byron had rejected him. Acclaimed gay playwright and novelist Oscar Wilde, author of the classic horror tale *The Picture of Dorian Gray* (1890) and other stories, was famously imprisoned and ruined as the result of his overt expression of what his lover termed the "love that dare not speak its name."

Women are harder to find in the lists of queer writers, but queer monsters of the feminine persuasion are far from absent from the early tales of terror. Female monsters and other creatures of the night wore their queerness as subtext, a barely contained corruption that would drive them to conquer even Death itself. They returned to haunt those they could not love in life as ghostly companions or vampiric friends, threatening the sanity and well-being of their loved ones.

Christina Rossetti's darkly fantastical poem *Goblin Market* (1862) is filled with so much lesbian sexual imagery ("Hug me, kiss me, suck my juices") that both the poet and her poem are now claimed by historians of lesbian and bisexual women's writing. Yet it is not insignificant that Rossetti described her protagonists as "sisters" and claimed it was a children's poem while she was still alive. The alternatives were too dangerous to consider.

The most famous female vampire of the nineteenth century was, without question, Sheridan Le Fanu's *Carmilla* (Carmilla, 1872). His tale of a mysterious young woman who drains her bosom companion, Laura, of life and energy until Laura's father intervenes to rescue her, enshrined the lesbian vampire in the Victorian imagination. Le Fanu himself was heterosexual, as far as historians know, and the story itself is deeply homophobic, associating lesbianism with vampirism, death, and corruption. And yet, the tale retains a hypnotic power, one that keeps the story in print while inspiring multiple movies and even a contemporary web series, which you can find at *bit.ly/1LovtAx*.

Vampires were certainly not the only queer creatures to be discovered by readers looking for a good chilling read. Most Victorian-era women writers tried their hands at ghost stories at one time or another. Ghost stories were hugely popular in the later nineteenth and early twentieth century, and that popularity drew writers like Edith Wharton, Sarah Orne Jewett, and Louisa May Alcott. These writers followed in the tradition of Gothic novelists like Walpole and Radcliffe, who had captivated large audiences with their tales of ghostly phantasms in the late 1700s. It was a fad that never quite faded away, though as with many other things, the stories changed when the Victorians got a hold of them.

Ghost stories became domestic tales, metaphors for the smothering domesticity that middle and upper class Victorian-era women often experienced. But they were also an outlet for longings that were otherwise too improper and scandalous to commit to the page: it was far safer to express your love for your heart's companion on the printed page when either you or she was deceased than when both of you were alive. Ghosts, spiritualists, and women who loved other women were closely integrated with the movements for women's suffrage in both the United States and England

This was also a time period when "Boston Marriages," households formed by two unmarried (from a heterosexual standpoint) women who were sometimes lovers and sometimes very close friends, increased in both number and visibility. The combination of domesticity and desire, whether thwarted or consummated, influenced a number of writers to use ghost stories as a vehicle to express that same love whose overt expression had ruined Oscar Wilde.

Elizabeth Stuart Phelps' "Since I Died" (1873) features the ghostly reminiscences of one half of a couple who lingers after her death to watch her beloved companion mourn her. Alice Brown's "There and Here" (1897) features another survivor of a Boston Marriage haunted by the spirit of her lost beloved. Lesbian writer Vernon Lee (the pseudonym of Violet Paget) wrote a number of ghost and horror stories, including "The Doll" (1872), the tale of a woman obsessed with a doll that she believes to be haunted. Her subsequent decision to destroy it with fire may suggest an attempt to exorcise the author's same-sex longings as much as an effort to free a trapped spirit.

Oscar Wilde wrote the occasional ghost story too, but one of the most famous ghost stories written by a queer author of this time period was Henry James' *The Turn of the Screw* (1898). This novella is often read as a classic Gothic ghost story with queer subtext, one which touches almost every character, from the children to the ghosts.

The advent of film brought new interpretations of both horror and queer representation. With the introduction of the Hollywood Production Code (adopted 1930, implemented in 1934), overt depictions of queer characters on screen became a thing of the past for as long as it was in effect. Homosexuality was implied in terms and descriptions recognized by a knowledgeable audience, though not a general one, until the 1960s in the U.S. (films made in other countries occasionally got a pass). There were, of course, some exceptions made for openly queer characters as long as they died horribly in films both horrific and mainstream, thereby serving as an example to us all.

Films like the vampire classic *Dracula's Daughter* (1936) and monster films by gay director James Whale, such as *Bride of Frankenstein* (1935), are often interpreted by contemporary audiences as classic examples of queer subtext in Code-era films. Overtly queer horror cinema didn't really come into its own until the 1960s, with films like *The Haunting* (1963), which features an out lesbian psychic, followed by *The Vampire Lovers* (1970), which was Hammer Studios' rather more explicit than the original version of *Carmilla*. *Daughters of Darkness* (1970) featured the notorious Countess Elizabeth of Bathory as a lesbian vampire.

In the meantime, portrayals of queer characters in queer horror fiction were primarily limited to villains and victims throughout the pulp fiction era, until Shirley Jackson began publishing in the 1950s. Her novels *Hangsaman* (1951) and *The Haunting of Hill House* (1959) included several sympathetic characters who can be read fairly easily as queer. Jackson is often described in contemporary analyses as a queer/bisexual author due to both her relationships off the page and these novels and other works with significant queer content.

In the 1970s, representation and visibility for LGBTQ people rose to new heights. The decade included the aftermath of the 1969 Stonewall Riots as well as the 1977 election and subsequent assassination in 1978 of the first openly gay elected official in the U.S., Harvey Milk. Within the science fiction and fantasy genre, new out queer authors writing queer-themed work found success and a readership open to their ideas; these included Samuel Delany, Joanna Russ, Thomas Disch, and Elizabeth Lynn. While none of these authors wrote what is generally considered horror, some of their works did spill over into dark fantasy and related areas.

Despite the increased influence of LGBT authors in the field, the writer who arguably most fueled mainstream awareness of horror featuring LGBT characters was Anne Rice. Her novel *Interview with the Vampire* (1976) and the books that followed changed how vampires have been depicted ever since, for better or for worse. Rice's vampires are emotionally omnisexual beings, unconfined by human morals and capable of same-sex love without judgment, and their popularity fueled a drastic shift in the portrayal of both vampires and homosexuality in horror.

In contrast, writers like Jeffrey McMahan and Jody Scott saw their particular takes on queer vampirism in books like *Somewhere in the Night* (1981), which includes both humorous and compassionate vampires and *I, Vampire* (1984), which is both surreal and satirical, published by small gay or feminist presses willing to take a chance on unique voices. Also writing in the vampire subgenre was lesbian author Jewelle Gomez, who wrote a series of linked stories about an immortal African-American vampire named Gilda who is more teacher than predator.

I would be remiss if I failed to mention that one of the most famous queer vampire movies of all time was released in the early 1980s. *The Hunger* (1983), starring queer icons Catherine Deneuve, David Bowie, and Susan Sarandon, has retained its popularity and held up well. And at the other end of the campy scale and released a few years earlier, *The Rocky Horror Picture Show* (1975) still inspires many fans to crossdress and sing along to a film that celebrates cross dressing, bisexuality and horror/science fiction cinema.

The 1990s saw a substantial spike in the amount of attention and visibility given to queer horror due to both positive events, like increased acceptance, and negative ones, such as the impact of HIV/AIDS, which became visible in the 1980s. The latter worked its way into many queer narratives, including queer horror. Vampirism began to be read as a metaphor for the disease and its impacts as much because of the association with blood-born transmission as the homoerotic elements of vampire lore. As the decade wore on, fiction echoed reality as vampires and werewolves and other creatures became increasingly concerned with achieving civil rights, as depicted in popular series like Laurell K. Hamilton's Anita Blake books and Charlaine Harris' Southern Vampire series.

Unsurprisingly, this uptick in the popularity of supernatural critters was reflected in the queer presses as well as the mainstream ones. Editor Pam Keesey published three anthologies of lesbian horror: *Daughters of Darkness: Lesbian Vampire Tales* (1993), *Dark Angels: Lesbian Vampire Erotica* (1995) and *Women Who Run with Werewolves* (1996), all from Cleis Press. These were joined by editor Victoria Brownworth's anthology *Night Bites: Vampire Stories by Women* (Seal Press, 1996) while Michael Rowe and Thomas Roche co-edited *Brothers of the Night: Gay Vampire Stories* (Cleis Press, 1997).

Several queer-identified authors who would go on to win acclaim in the horror genre made their debuts in the 1990s. These included author Poppy Z. Brite (Billy Martin), who saw the publication of several novels and collections featuring gay and bisexual male protagonists, including *Lost Souls* (1992) and *Exquisite Corpse* (1996), while Caitlín R. Kiernan, writer for *The Dreaming*, a *Sandman* series spinoff, made her novel debut with *Silk* (1998). Author Clive Barker was already well known as the author of the *Books of Blood Vol. 1-6* (1984-85) and *The Hellbound Heart* (1986) when he came out in 1996. His work went on to include movies, comics, and more books, thereby guaranteeing his place as one of the most famous LGBT horror writers in the world. Many of his stories include queer protagonists, including *Imajica* (1991).

Early 2000 saw another major coming out, this time of a fictional character. The

TV show *Buffy: The Vampire Slayer* began airing in 1997, with an ensemble cast playing Buffy and her high school friends and support system. The show followed them through various perils, then on to college where Buffy's best friend, the neophyte witch Willow Rosenberg, meets and falls for fellow witch Tara Maclay. After several episodes that show their relationship building, Willow introduces Tara to Buffy and her other friends as her girlfriend in the season four episode "New Moon Rising," which aired in May of 2000.

Queers fans and allies invested heavily in their relationship, which was one of the first out and positive portrayals of a lesbian couple on primetime television. Consequently, many of them felt betrayed when Tara was killed in the season six episode "Seeing Red" (air date May 2002). Show runners, including Joss Whedon, were unprepared for the negative reaction because they were apparently unaware of the long and distressing tradition of redshirting queer female characters. Whedon subsequently apologized and Willow, after embracing her evil side long enough to avenge Tara, continued to identify as a lesbian and eventually acquired a new girlfriend, the slayer-in-training Kennedy, in season seven.

A number of queer horror anthologies were published during the 2000s, including editors Nicola Griffith and Stephen Pagel's *Bending the Landscape: Horror* (2001), editor Michael Rowe's *Queer Fear* (2000) and *Queer Fear II* (2002), and editors Vince Liaguno and Chad Helder's *Unspeakable Horror: From the Shadows of the Closet* (2008). Along with books like editor Greg Herren's *Shadows of the Night: Queer Tales of the Uncanny and Unusual*, these focused attention on a new generation of queer horror writers, including Michael Thomas Ford and Thomas Roche.

Other queer horror writers who achieved recognition during this decade included Lee Thomas, a Bram Stoker Award winner for his novel *Stained* (2004) and a Lambda Award Winner for his novel *Dust of Wonderland* (2007). Caitlín R. Kiernan and Clive Barker continued writing and publishing horror throughout the decade, with Kiernan winning one of the first Shirley Jackson Awards for her novel *The Red Tree* (2009). The decade also saw a resurgence in queer ghost stories, including Christopher Barzak's novel *One for Sorrow* (2007), Sarah Waters's novel *Affinity* (1999), and my anthology *Haunted Hearths and Sapphic Shades: Lesbian Ghost Stories* (2008); and vampire stories, with Rick Reed's *In the Blood* (2007), among other titles.

Queer horror has only grown as a subgenre expanding beyond fiction to influence popular contemporary TV shows like *Penny Dreadful, American Horror Story*, and *True Blood*, as well as films like *Let the Right One In* (2008) and *Paranorman* (2012). Since I really can't do justice to the breadth of queer horror-themed books, erotica, cable TV, movie, and comic book titles that came out during the last couple of decades here, please see the following for further reading and watching.

Resources

- Gaylactic Spectrum Awards: spectrumawards.org

- Golden Crown Literary Awards for Lesbian Literature (Speculative Fiction Category): goldencrown.org/page-1158930

- Lambda Literary Awards (Science Fiction, Fantasy and Horror): bit.ly/lambda_sf

- Queer Horror Awards: queerhorror.com/awards

- The Shirley Jackson Awards: shirleyjacksonawards.org

- "The Fear of Gay Men: A Roundtable Discussion on the New Queer Horror": bit.ly/scribe_gay_men

- "There's Something Inside of Me: Coming Out as a Gay Horror Fan": bit.ly/buzzfeed_coming_out

- Lesbian Film Review: lesbian-films.com/category/horror

- "Vampires Are Us": glreview.org/article/vampires-are-us

Catherine Lundoff is an award-winning author and editor from Minneapolis, where she lives with her fabulous wife and cats. She toils in IT by day and writes all the things by night, including a series for *SF Signal* on LGBT science fiction and fantasy and lots of tales about things going bump in the night. She has stories forthcoming in *Tales of the Unanticipated, The Mammoth Book of Jack the Ripper Tales* and *The Mammoth Book of Professor Moriarty Adventures.* Her novel *Medusa's Touch* (written as Emily L. Byrne) is forthcoming from Queen of Swords Press. You can find more on her website at catherinelundoff.com.

EFFECTING CHANGE AND SUBVERSION THROUGH SLUSH PILE POLITICS

MICHAEL MATHESON

FOR THE LAST three and a half years I've been working with slush piles in a variety of capacities. Sometimes for *Apex Magazine*, sometimes for publishing houses like ChiZine Publications, Exile Editions, or Explicit Books. Sometimes working directly on anthologies such as *Fearful Symmetries, Glitter & Mayhem, The Humanity of Monsters, Start a Revolution*, and *This Patchwork Flesh*. Those three and a half years of slush reading have reinforced an opinion I've held most of the fourteen years I've been freelance editing:

All stories, all narratives really, are conversation. What those conversations are saying depends on several things: who's doing the telling, what they're talking about, and why the conversation is happening. All true whether or not the stories contain queer content. But when you look at slush piles in the abstract, they're very seldom reflective of the conversations, queer-related or not, being had in *published* fiction.

The conversations occurring in both published and unpublished short fiction are the result of similar factors: the socio-economic and socio-political realities that shape what gets written, what gets published, and the social media interaction around what is published. But the material that's *published* is overwhelmingly an active conversation, focused on larger questions of identity, representation, and a quest for both internal and external understanding—any body of published work is a communal investigation into questions we want answered, whether that community's local, international, or global.

By contrast, the material in slush piles that remains permanently unpublished is having a defunct conversation. The stories that are unpublishable are asking questions that are already answered, or trying to have a conversation in terms that are outmoded and obsolete.

Consequently, there are two similar but divergent conversations occurring. Both conversations react to a wealth of published material, but only one set actively communicates with the body of published work it's addressing. There are a number of factors that produce the difference between these conversations:

The first and foremost is that *you* inform the work you create; your experiences, as well as your economic, political, and cultural realities, form the basis of the work you create.

It's extremely difficult to write entirely outside of your own experience. Whatever your aims or intent, what ends up on the page reflects your lived experience in some way.

The *best* parts of what make it into the slush pile are some form of lived experience, even when the worldbuilding and other elements are fantastical or otherwise non-realist. Work that doesn't feel invested in some way—that doesn't feel lived in—doesn't make it through the slush pile. That uninvested work doesn't help further or shape the conversation. Instead, you end up with people writing fiction, as evidenced by the slush piles I've been party to, writing uninvested work that emulates what they *expect* the cultural conversation to be.

Most slush isn't bad or unutterably terrible, despite the common misconception. Most slush pile fiction is either boring or mediocre; it's unengaging in terms of themes, ideologies, or understandings of identity. It doesn't *say* anything or touch off discussions that take us into new and interesting territory. It rehashes older material, or draws upon material from earlier eras (often pulp-era fiction, or the Golden Age of SF) without understanding that the conversation has since widened.

That last issue is a function of new writers coming to classic or much-lauded work and attempting to reignite the conversations they find there. Conversations whose time has passed.

Slush piles are full of stories in which women are there merely as victims. Or stories with women in them who couldn't pass Kelly Sue DeConnick's Sexy Lamp Test: Does a woman in this story do anything or say anything relevant to the story, excluding acting as a motivating factor or quest trophy? Stories with racist, bigoted, or queerphobic content in period storytelling—because everybody was doing it then, right, and that's totally historically accurate? (The counterargument to this is a story like Kai Ashante Wilson's "The Devil in America.") And stories that exist merely to degrade a character or group.

See, unexceptional fiction is content to skim the surface of an idea. Whereas exceptional fiction is dizzying and heady in its aims. It embraces the sense of awe that informs great fiction. You feel the crush of it beating against your ribcage. Sometimes so quietly it's all but a whisper, but you *know* it when you find it.

Exceptional fiction does two things:

First, it fires on all cylinders. Fiction is an act of juggling component pieces, and even the best stories can only pull off so many tricks at once, and inevitably something suffers. Sometimes the prose is too loose or too dry, the plot poorly paced, or the subtext misfires and you end up saying things you didn't intend to say. So a piece that's pitch perfect is an extraordinary accomplishment. A merely competent piece will be one an editor enjoys and knows needs to be shared; an exceptional piece is one that sets the editor digging into it, trying to figure out how the hell it was machined so perfectly.

Second, exceptional fiction changes the course of the conversation by either advancing the conversation, or rewriting it entirely. If we're very lucky, it does so permanently. I would argue that exceptional *queer* fiction reshapes the conversation by naturalizing queer identity and representation.

You produce more diverse content in fiction by naturalizing diversity. Doing so is how you get people to sit up and pay attention. When you present the reader with diverse characters and identities in fiction—which is, after all, a more accurate representation of the state of affairs outside of fiction—and do it repeatedly, diversity becomes the normalized state.

This is because the majority of conversation about queer content suggests that being queer is in and of itself something exceptional, and the thing the story should focus on. Except, when the exceptionalism of queerness is the focus of a story, the story Others queerness instead of naturalizing it.

You make diversity a normal thing in fiction by not making the work about a character's queerness, their race, their neuroatypicality, or any other form of diversity as the foregrounding feature. Instead, you make that story about how the character moves through the narrative trajectory of the piece. Woman warrior defeats ancient evil, is lauded as heroine, marries princess. Deep-space astronaut survives destruction of orbital space station, now must figure out how to survive to get home to see his husband again. And so on. If a character in a story is queer in some respect, but that queerness never plays a central role, or is even just mentioned in passing? That's still a queer narrative. It's representational politics at work. You want to see diverse content in published work? Build it into the background and the foreground of the story and it saturates the work you're creating.

The only reason straight white male characterizations in North American and European fictions are so dominant is because they've been viewed so long as the default states for storytelling. If you work from the basis that white, male, and straight is your tabula rasa, then the act of writing about race, femaleness, and queerness becomes falsely perceived as a needless complication. But the assumption of default state is false bias: there is no default state for characterization in storytelling, let alone in queer storytelling.

Here's the thing:

I've done a lot of editing one way or another in the last decade and a half. And that idea that queer stories are principally about being queer comes up all the time. But it never came up quite so dramatically as when I was trying to put together two anthologies, *Start a Revolution* and *This Patchwork Flesh*. These books had the stated intention of featuring protagonists who fell somewhere along the larger QUILTBAG (and beyond) spectrum, but whose queerness was not the central narrative and focus.

Start a Revolution, an anthology themed around revolutions literal and more personal, was especially bad for submissions of stories that were about how being queer was itself revolutionary. There are a number of reasons for this narrative showing up so frequently, but I'm going to lay at least some of the blame for it on how the majority of LGBTQ+ presses shape the conversation around queer identity. By pushing the idea that a story must be centrally about *being* queer in order to be representational of queer storytelling, the conversation has moved to being queer as an act of exceptionalism and away from normalization of queer identity.

Which brings us back to what I was talking about earlier in terms of *exceptional* fiction. See, the best things I've seen in the slush pile, and ultimately the things I recommended to senior editors or took for anthologies, were stories that decentralized being somewhere on the QUILTBAG spectrum. The stories I gravitated to were stories in which the queerness of the characters was a function of the story, not the main feature.

Work that features diversity without being exoticizing or appropriative does so by having diverse characters move through stories that don't have the nature of their diversity as the focal point. Failing to do so leaves you with storytelling like the curebie narrative. Ultimately destructive narratives supposing that autistic or otherwise neuroatypical characters just need "fixing," curebie narratives are stories in which neurotypical characters, through science or magic, "fix" neuroatypical characters by rendering them neurotypical as well; they suggest that, clearly, not being "normal" is a terrible thing, and these poor, malformed characters must wish they weren't so monstrous. The "curebie" narrative is a deeply fucking terrifying narrative structure, because it's a short hop, skip, and a jump from suggesting that fixing people so you're less terrified of them is a normal course of action, to sterilization and eugenics narratives. And there's a precedent for that leap: neuroatypicality and autism have historically been "treated" through the application of invasive medical treatments, heavy pharmacology, and eugenics primarily through sterilization—the same set of methods historically used to "fix" queer people. On the whole that's something I suspect most people who write curebie narratives don't actually consider hard enough, or editors would see far fewer of those style of stories showing up in slush piles.

Now, the majority of the stories with queer content that I've seen in slush piles fail at being good representations because they exoticize queer identity. And that happens because most people produce what they *think* the conversation about queer identity is.

Sometimes that's a function of very white, usually straight, writers trying to produce what they think, or have internalized, is the experience of the Other. The conversation about diversity, in all its forms, invites writers to create wider representation, so you're going to get people writing experiences of lives other than their own. And you always hope that people writing about other cultures and trying to envision what it's like to be the Other creates space for diverse writers to be able to submit their work and shift the conversation to a wider range of voices—or at least that attempts by writers of one culture to capture the voices of another come off in respectful and careful storytelling. It certainly can, and frequently does. But sometimes you also get something less desirable.

Given how prevalent the calls for diversity and representation are, an unscrupulous writer can use diversity as a gimmick to the point where it becomes a shortcut to publication.

Nowhere has the argument that diversity is just a set of brownie points we're all trying to score been more prevalent than in the interminable screeds coming out of the Sad/Rabid Puppies and Gamergate camps. Which is total bullshit. People of colour, queer writers, and neuroatypical writers aren't writing from their experience just to get published. The primary reason to write stories with diverse characters is that diversity is a lived, internal experience. Writing diversity from an internal perspective is including yourself in the conversation. Appropriating diversity, however, is a function of entitlement.

That appropriation, that entitlement, shows up in the way we talk about diversity itself. "Diversity," as descriptor, can function as a colonialist and dismissive act exactly because it positions anything non-white, non-male, and non-heteronormative as non-primary or Other. It's not self-descriptive language, it's ascriptive language—and thereby exoticizing. And that exoticism, relating to all kinds of diversity, queer content included, shows up all too frequently in slush piles. Especially in horror venues, where the history of the genre has really not been good on diverse representation.

In my time as a submissions editor with *Apex*, I saw some of the worst exoticism, entitlement, and appropriation of diversity I've come across anywhere doing editorial work. You combine a publication that focuses on horror fiction and dark fantasy with a lot of white North American writers idolizing horror fiction's historical body of work, with its hugely problematic issues around representation, and you tend to get stories that either pay lip service to diversity, or that fly in the face of it entirely. This often occurred in combination with the three principal story types that made up the bulk of *Apex*'s slush pile: the serial killer story (a disturbing number of these written by Texans—your guess as to why is as good as mine; I have no working theory there), the cannibalism story, and the rape/revenge-fantasy story.

The lack of diversity in multiple respects in the *Apex* slush pile was discouraging, not least of all in terms of the general lack of queer content coming across the transom. And it wasn't just *Apex* having those issues. Many venues are welcoming to queer/LGBTQ+/ QUILTBAG fiction, but don't receive it in the slush pile. Yes, many *are* intentionally or unintentionally unwelcoming, and the submissions calls and guidelines put out often lead to white, straight writers appropriating diversity instead of people of colour, queer writers, and neuroatypical writers getting their own work published. But there are venues that manage to actually run diverse and diverse-authored content, and do it consistently. Flawed as those diversity statements and calls sometimes are, they're part of the necessary work of soliciting work from diverse writers in order to have the material to run.

It takes that consistent publication of more than token amounts of diverse and diverse-authored content to prove that a venue is actually interested in diversity. Otherwise, rightly or wrongly, a venue is going to be seen as just trying to make hay out of diversity itself. Especially since the magazines that curate diverse content on a regular basis do it *noticeably* well: *Crossed Genres, Strange Horizons, Shimmer, Clarkesworld, Ideomancer, Tor.com, Lightspeed, Nightmare, GigaNotoSaurus, Unlikely Story,* and *Lackington's,* among others.

Anthologies, too, have to get diversity right, and a publisher has to do it repeatedly across multiple projects in order for the publisher to be considered welcoming to diverse and diverse-authored content. The editors of those anthologies also have to prove that they can consistently curate diverse-authored content across multiple projects. Seeing publications getting it right or trying to do so was one of the things that made reading slush for the *Glitter & Mayhem* anthology way back when such a pleasure. Not everything that came in for that anthology was perfect. But the bulk of what I saw in my portion of that slush pile were pieces that were going hammer and tongs at diversity, representation, and general oddity in the best possible sense.

It's funny, too, because you find that effective diverse content crops up in places you wouldn't expect. All kinds of diverse content showed up in the slush pile for the *Fearful Symmetries* anthology, often in completely normalized, rather than exoticized, contexts. I say that with such shock because the bulk of horror fiction is just *appallingly* bad at doing diversity and representation well. This is primarily because horror fiction less frequently focuses on the uncanny side of horror, the numinous or otherwise transformative, and is instead transgressive and victim-oriented. Transgression itself is not my problem here, but rather who that transgression is perpetrated against and how. Because the different ways in which violence is directed in horror fiction perpetuates, by example, the idea of a stratification of victimhood: Who should you care more about as a victim? What skin colour, race, and other orientations do you most readily identify with?

Those stratifications of victimhood, and many of the functions of horror as transgressive wish-fulfillment fantasy, play into a fascinating, if disturbing, affirmation of heteronormative gender roles: Men prey on women. Men rescue women. These two functions are established as natural, and reinforced by their repetition. When women prey on men there's subversion at work (with the qualification that this, too, can be a misogynistic trope). And when women rescue men there's an upheaval of social roles that is totally intolerable to a wide subset of people. But you have to enact, and keep enacting, upheaval if you want to create space for diverse content. The sheer weight of fiction that elides diverse content is staggering, and requires a tectonic shift to redress. In earlier eras of fiction, the elision of diversity was both an act of suppression and an appalling obliviousness to the racist, queerphobic, and otherwise dismissive agenda underlying the worldview of so many published writers. In modern fiction, that same elision is simply unforgivable.

We all need to be creating upheaval in fiction. The representation of underrepresented groups and cultures in Western literature pushes against the bulwark of colonialist, hegemonic, heteronormative, white-centric narratives. They are reshaping the field. They are actively changing the conversation.

That's the kind of thing you always want to see in a slush pile, whether the stories are queer-centric or otherwise. Because as an editor, you always want to see the things that push the conversation further. And as a writer, you always hope you're writing the piece that makes that happen.

❦

Michael Matheson is a pansexual, genderfluid writer, poet, editor, book reviewer, occasional anthologist, and Clarion West (2014) graduate. Their fiction and poetry has appeared or is forthcoming in a number of venues, including *Ideomancer*, *Stone Telling*, and a handful of anthologies. Their first anthology as editor, *The Humanity of Monsters*, came out from ChiZine Publications in September. They can be found on Twitter @sekisetsu or otherwise online at michaelmatheson.wordpress.com.

PUTTING IT ALL
THE WAY IN:
NAKED LUNCH AND THE
BODY HORROR OF
WILLIAM S. BURROUGHS

EVAN J. PETERSON

AT TEN YEARS old, I first encountered William S. Burroughs' work—on film. My father would take me to the video store, and I would run my fingers along the slick VHS boxes and admire the lurid cover art of screaming mouths, rotting zombies, and unnamable things emerging from basements, satellite dishes, and body cavities. Like most budding horror fans born after the '70s, my love of the genre was built on videos rather than late night horror hosts or EC comics.

The box for *Naked Lunch* was different. It wasn't the imagery (a sharply dressed Peter Weller looking up at a reptilian mugwump) but rather the title; the words didn't make sense to me. "Naked" aroused my interest. Even prepubescent, I was aware of and fascinated by sexuality. But what did that have to do with "lunch"? Just as incongruous, the back of the box featured an image of a hovering typewriter that was perhaps eating a man's face.

My dad, a postflowerchild, let me rent and watch it. My mother was furious.

The film, a surreal amalgamation of several Burroughs texts as well as his wild biography, fascinated me with its insect fetishism and its thoroughly unglamorous presentation of narcotic addiction. Even more fascinating than that was the exploration of homosexuality.

Although the film stuck with me throughout my life, I didn't read *Naked Lunch* or any of Burroughs' writing itself until grad school at age twenty-four. Nonetheless, the intersection of horror and queerness was there for me long before. Throughout high school I read Clive Barker and Anne Rice, devouring but also studying the way they normalized and even romanticized male homosexuality in their work. When I finally read *Naked Lunch* (and *The Wild Boys* and *Junky* and *Queer*) for a Burroughs reading group, I was revolted, more than a little triggered, enraptured, and hooked.

Naked Lunch is absolutely a work of horror, though it's many other things as well. It's difficult (and unnecessary) to categorize, slipping between detective noir, caustic and hilarious satire, gleeful science fiction, occult fantasy, throat-spasming body horror, and addiction memoir. Burroughs demonstrates just how arbitrary genre can be—and what could be queerer than that?

It's precisely the body horror, not despite but in addition to his humor and absurdist satire, that shows us how truly queer his body of work remains.

The simple and pure homosexuality was enough to horrify the readers of the '50s. To many overly sensitive and fundamentally conservative readers, a dick in an ass is body horror. So are rimjobs, which Burroughs never shied away from. Had he lived long enough, it would be priceless to hear his thoughts on newly emerging fetishes such as pup play.

But of course the sexuality in *Naked Lunch* almost always leads into the fantastic, usually a dark fantastic. One of the most memorable scenes of the book starts with a heterosexual encounter (albeit quite focused on Johnny's ass) between Johnny and Mary, which leads into a homosexual one between Johnny and Mark, which then leads into several elaborate and sexualized executions by hanging as characters kill one another, transform into one another, die, come back, transform again. Deadly sexual hangings are common scenes in the book, all the more freakish and frightening as some of them appear to be consensual or at least enjoyed by those whose necks are breaking.

When Burroughs chose to defend his work, he explained that scenes such as these were a satire of the American bloodlust for capital punishment. This claim fits the tone and content, though I think he also got off on writing it. Those characters hanged while getting fucked are often very young red-haired guys. At the time I first read the book, the fact that I myself was very much Burroughs' type was not lost on me, causing me to set the book down and take a breather several times during the reading of it.

I soon discovered that erotic body horror can be found across the scope of Burroughs' work. *The Wild Boys* contains a passage about the ectoplasmic zimbu, reincarnated entities created through occult sex rituals, their colorful ectoplasm clinging to the cocks of those who brought them back into form. Before the zimbu, the wild boys cloned themselves through cell samples biopsied from the inside of their rectums. All of this is told in painstaking detail as Burroughs deftly mingles science fiction with fantasy into his raunchy comic-bookish universe.

But queer sex is only one way into body horror in the Burroughs canon. Burroughs is as well known for his excruciatingly confessional descriptions of heroin addiction as he is for his carnivalesque sex. He describes shooting up in pus-weeping veins, or if he can't find a needle, using a pin to open up his vein and squeezing a medicine dropper full of heroin or morphine or god knows what narcotic into the ragged hole.

Plenty of existential horror permeates the work as well—Burroughs wrote frequently about Control, a shadowy force that constantly seeks to keep people from exploring, expressing, and being what would now popularly be called "authentic." Telepathic, drug-induced, and/or occult means are used to keep characters in line or frame them, torture them, and do all manner of nasty things. Burroughs weaves in Lovecraftian cosmic horror at times and just as easily employs Sartrean and Nietzchean nihilism. The most palpable horror in his work, however, is grounded in the body.

His monsters are also a mindfuck delight. In Spare Ass Annie, a spoken routine set to music in collaboration with the Disposable Heroes of Hiphoprisy, Burroughs describes the title character as having "an auxiliary asshole in the middle of her forehead like a baleful bronze eye." She lives in a town full of monsters that also includes Centipeter, a man-centipede chimera that constantly sexually harasses the townsfolk. These monsters are born to women who've been caged in fresh human bones, somehow touched by malevolent gods that enjoy watching human debasement and humiliation.

The talking asshole with its hook-like teeth, the mugwumps with their black boney beaks and addictive semen, the Reptiles with their flexible bones and green fans of cartilage: the monsters are everywhere in Burroughs, whether magical or science fictional or human or just plain inscrutable.

He was such a bizarre genius that the only director to ever successfully adapt his work into a feature film has been David Cronenberg. Cronenberg reigned through the '80s as the undisputed king of body horror on film, especially science fictional body horror with Scanners, Videodrome, and his brilliant remake of The Fly. Cronenberg's film treatment of Naked Lunch features a buffet of squishy Burroughsian perversities: beetles with talking rectums, centipede sex murder in a giant birdcage, and people sucking psychotropic jism out of the phalluses growing from aliens' heads. Fittingly, Cronenberg described Burroughs' sexuality as an "alien sexuality." Burroughs' art, like Cronenberg's, fetishizes the capital-O-Other.

Cronenberg, it should be noted, has frequently employed homoeroticism in his work, knowing how psychologically disquieting and arousing it can be to many audience members. However, unlike Burroughs or Samuel R. Delany, Cronenberg whips his crypto-gay cock out but, as Delany would say, never puts it all the way in. In Naked Lunch, for instance, main character William Lee (Burroughs' early pen name) wakes up in bed with another man and constantly explores the idea of homosexuality, but we only ever see him make out with a woman—while getting dry humped by a typewriter-turned-fleshy-sex-mutant, but still.

The takeaway? Even the director of Rabid, in which porn star Marilyn Chambers undergoes experimental plastic surgery that gives her a phallic, blood-draining tentacle that turns people into contagious zombies, has shied away from getting too gay on screen, even when homosexual identity crisis is a core theme of the work.

But gay isn't the same as queer.

Burroughs disliked the term "gay" and rejected the label in favor of "queer," one of the earliest people to do so. "Gay" is a euphemism. "Queer" is a reappropriated slur; it's outré, unapologetic, and frequently considered offensive. While "gay" conjures a specific subculture with specific tastes, "queer" is a word that implies homosexuality but goes far beyond it. "Queer," like Burroughs and his work, is transgressive, intentionally positioned against category and easy definition, and grounded in the body. Queerness is about unstably gendered (and non-gendered) bodies and the sexual anatomy and activity of those bodies. Queerness does not conform, even and especially to a homosexual mainstream. Queerness destabilizes gender and sex just as Burroughs' work destabilizes grammar and genre. Queerness disrupts the status quo—like horror and science fiction.

Burroughs remains one of the most dangerous and important intellectual perverts of the twentieth century. His perversions were philosophical, a popular literature of obscenity eroding the conservative norms of the late '50s and early '60s from the ground up. He was certainly a proto-cyberpunk and -splatterpunk, but more importantly, he was a proto-punk, influencing such rockstars as Iggy Pop, Throbbing Gristle, The Dead Kennedys, Kurt Cobain, and even David Bowie.

William S. Burroughs blazed for decades like a junky-fag Godzilla, an iconoclast for whom nothing was sacred but human life and freedom. He isn't remembered as a "horror" writer because he never allowed himself to be ghettoed into a specific genre. We should all be that good at what we do.

Evan J. Peterson is the author of *Skin Job* and *The Midnight Channel* and editor of the Lambda Literary Award finalist *Ghosts in Gaslight, Monsters in Steam: Gay City 5*. His journalism, fiction, nonfiction, and poetry can be found in *Weird Tales*, *The Stranger*, *The Rumpus*, *Unspeakable Horror 2*, *The Queer South* anthology, *Arcana: The Tarot Poetry Anthology* and *Drawn to Marvel: Poems from the Comic Books*. He is the Editor-in-Chief of Minor Arcana Press and a 2015 Clarion West graduate. Evanjpeterson.com can tell you more.

QUEERS DESTROY HORROR!
HORROR!
ROUNDTABLE INTERVIEW

MEGAN ARKENBERG

WHAT IS IT like to be a queer horror writer in 2015? We caught up with four up-and-coming writers of the dark, surreal, and horrific to ask about their experiences in the genre. Meghan McCarron's genre-bending stories have been finalists for the Nebula and World Fantasy Awards, and she is one of the fiction editors at *Interfictions*. Brit Mandelo is the senior fiction editor at *Strange Horizons* and the editor of the critically acclaimed anthology *Beyond Binary: Genderqueer and Sexually Fluid Speculative Fiction*; her fiction has been nominated for the Nebula Award and the Lambda Literary Award. Rahul Kanakia's short fiction has appeared in *Clarkesworld*, *Apex*, *Nature*, and many other places, and his first novel, *Enter Title Here*, was published by Disney-Hyperion earlier this fall. Carrie Cuinn is the editor of Dagan Books and the quarterly magazine *Lakeside Circus*; her short fiction has appeared in a variety of places, including her latest collection, *Women and Other Constructs*. Here, they offer their insights into genre, identity, and the strange attractions of fear.

Thank you for taking part in our roundtable! I'd like to start by asking about your relationship to the label "queer horror writer." Is this a description you would use for yourself? How do you classify your work?

Meghan McCarron: Like every other writer and queer person, I thrash around when it comes to labels. Like, queer best gets at the shape of my sexuality and gender expression, but you know, I'm not sure how well my life embodies the revolutionary side of the word. I write stories with vampires and monsters and ghosts (so many ghosts), but also I am terrified of most horror movies.

I am delighted to be called a horror writer, even as I ask questions like, "Can I be a horror writer if I was too scared to see *It Follows*? If I stopped reading *House of Leaves* when the book told me to stop reading it because I was too scared to go on?" This is a 100% true story.

I was a huge horror reader as a kid. Not sure why I fell off that wagon, but some of it was due to the fact the "adult" horror I encountered in the late 1990's didn't speak to me the way *Point Horror*, the grindhouse for girls, did. That and my inability, at that age, to take pleasure in stories that end with characters consigned to certain doom. I had trouble with the weekly situational reset on sitcoms. Seinfeld was enough of a horror story.

Brit Mandelo: Thanks for having me! This issue is a neat project—loving the whole "Queers Destroy . . ." ethos.

I'm definitely queer and definitely a writer, but I actually wouldn't say I write horror fiction. I suspect the stuff I tend to lean toward falls far more under the header "dark fantasy," because the affective punch I'm often looking for—both when I write, and when I'm reading other people's work—isn't the sensation of horror or fear; it's that soft, gut-twisting *upsetting* feeling instead. Not scary, but thought-provoking or unsettling, maybe? Though I have written one more traditional horror piece, "The Writ of Years," which was my take on a sort of classic faux-Lovecraftian thing, except without pronouns. (And on that note, I've found it very interesting to see how reviewers gender the protagonist. A rare few of them get that there's a *reason* for the lack of gendered terms.)

I certainly gravitate toward queer issues and characters, though, because that's what reflects the world I live in. There's also an affinity, I think, between dealing with the discomforts and dislocations of contemporary life as a queer person that can be dealt with in some interesting ways in dark fiction; there's a connection—I think a lot of people would agree—between horror and queer literature. I grew up on it, at least: I was a huge fan of Poppy Z. Brite when I was a youngling. But I wouldn't say I write it. I could get behind the "dark fiction" thing a bit more, but it's also a little reductive as a label (in the way of labels, I suppose).

Rahul Kanakia: I readily call myself queer, but "horror writer" is not a description I've ever applied to myself. Almost all of my stories are dark, and some have been published in horror magazines, but in general I've always found it hard to demarcate the boundary between horror and the other speculative genres.

Carrie Cuinn: I don't usually think of myself as a horror writer, because I usually think of myself as just *a writer*. I write everything: lit, SF, magic realism, nonfiction; even poetry and screenplays. But I do write horror too; it's the first kind of writing I was drawn to, and no matter what else I write, I always come back to it. Even when I'm doing other kinds of writing, there are still elements of horror in it, because fear, loss, and uncertainty are universal themes.

"Queer" is a fine label that I use depending on the circumstances—when it's appropriate to tack on an appellation for one's sexuality, because of the particular project I'm involved in. If the project is about sex, if it's about being queer, then absolutely, I've got nothing to hide. I think, though, that too often markets or editors want you to include that in your bio as a selling point, a way to make money off of the exoticness of your inclusion, and so I usually leave it out. We rarely see straight writers describing themselves as "heterosexual horror authors," so why should *my* sexuality be something to trade on?

Rahul: That's an interesting thought, Carrie. I feel like straight writers don't describe themselves as "heterosexual horror writers" because they don't need to. It's assumed. But, in situations where their sexuality is in doubt, artists aren't shy about correcting the impression that they might be queer (e.g. Michael Chabon and James Franco, despite their subject matter, are quick enough to avow their straightness). As queer writers, we belong to a community of both writers and readers who are hungry to see other queer writers. Personally, although I was never shy about my queerness on my blog, I never made an issue of it in my author bio, and it wasn't much of a theme in my work. But somehow, through some strange mechanism—maybe nothing more than gossip?—people began to speak of me online as a queer writer. I have found it neither harmful nor helpful, career-wise, but there is something comfortable about it, and I think it has led me, over time, to be less wary about writing on queer themes.

Meghan: It is the strangest thing, to out yourself as a writer. But I do agree that visibility is invaluable, if not for me, then for every other LGBT person writing out there. And, let's face it: all we have as writers is ourselves, our perspectives, and our stories. No one has to hew to writing about any one aspect of themselves, but if thinking of myself as a queer writer helps me dig into those issues in my work, I think that's a positive thing. The question reminds me a bit of all of the pronoun stickers made available at Wiscon this year. I chose the sticker reading "no preferred pronoun," because it was true. But I've never said that out loud before. The labeling was liberating. It deepened my sense of self.

What initially drew you to horror or dark fiction, and what draws you now?

Meghan: In 2009, the bookstore where I worked got in a new anthology of historic ghost stories. I read the whole thing, and contracted this mania for ghosts. The specific inspiration for that mania is tucked away in my subconscious, but I think it's a combination of the rich history of ghosts in American short fiction, and the incredible power they have to address big questions of loss and grief. Ghosts are often tricksters, too, which is a great plot mechanism.

As for the larger question of horror, I'm really not quite sure. I generally do not know why I write about the things I write about, or in general why I like the things I like. Sometimes I suspect that's a legacy of being heavily closeted. More generously, it keeps my creative process mysterious in a useful way.

One thought: I grew up Catholic, and Catholicism involves some gruesome shit. I definitely used to stare at gory crucifixes and think about how Jesus suffered—that was supposed to bring me closer to God, plus it killed time during math class. That wound in his side, man! I still remember a vivid description of the water and blood flowing out from that wound. I don't even want to know if that was in the Bible or just something a nun told me. Like I said: useful mystery.

Perhaps my Catholicism is also why I'm less drawn to true, hopeless horror. I've been trained to expect a resurrection.

Brit: I appreciate stories that leave me feeling struck, even blindsided, emotionally and psychologically. Some folks can do that with joyful and pleasant stuff; in the end, though, I'd say it often comes from darker fiction, stories dealing with difficult and unpleasant things in honest and provocative ways. For example, I think that books like Kiernan's *The Red Tree* and *The Drowning Girl* make a good illustration of what I think uncanny or dark fiction can do, in both directions: to upset you and to offer you some kind of hope.

I think maybe it's more that I like stories that have a hell of a lot of affect, whether that's pleasant or unpleasant for me? And horror is certainly a genre of affect and intensity, more generally dark fiction, too.

Rahul: I remember that when I was young (and I'm talking fourth or fifth grade) I loved to read about the Holocaust, and I went through what felt like dozens of Holocaust-themed kids' novels. As late as my teen years, I could not get enough of the Holocaust. Today, that's incomprehensible to me. Nowadays, as I'm approaching age thirty, I do my best to avoid all Holocaust-related fictions. I'm not sure what accounts for this change (and it's possible that I am an outlier here, since Holocaust novels do well in the adult genres, too).

Standing at the remove of years, I struggle to articulate what it was about the Holocaust that appealed to me so much. There's something terrifying about even putting the words "Holocaust" and "appealed" in the same sentence. Because horror stories contain a disquieting truth about human nature. If you see a movie that happens to contain some horrific element, it's easy to allow your feelings to pass uninterrogated. But when you're seeking something out, over and over, you have to face up to the notion that you're deriving some pleasure from this topic. I think there is something in the human psyche that delights in hatred and destruction. For instance, whenever there's a natural disaster on the news, I'm horrified and feel terrible for the people who are suffering, but there's also a part of me that's awed by the scope of the destruction. It's a very ugly emotion, and it's something I try not to think about. Bad novels and television shows are those that allow me to experience that delight without questioning it, while good ones are those which hold it up to the light and expose it. Although, honestly, whether a given work of dark fiction is good or bad, it's still profiting from the same impulses. Even a show that's as complex and uncomfortable as *The Sopranos*, for instance, draws its fundamental appeal from my delight at seeing mobsters exercise their will to power.

Carrie: Humanity survived until now by forming collectives and working together against outside dangers. Because you needed a tribe to support you, casting someone out almost always meant their death. When we grow up knowing we're different from those around us, we live aware of the risk we take every time we expose our true selves to another person. We can do our best to fit in, or stand out in a way that changes the people around us, but that fear is always in us, no matter how far down we bury it or how safe we think our lives are at that moment. Even though humans no longer need to be homogenous in order to be safe, there are still many who resist change out of fear, misunderstanding, or a need to control. We grow up in a world that's often waiting for us to be unlike the rest, defying categorization—and then that's it, we're out.

That fear affects us no matter what makes us different—our sexuality, gender presentation, race, family dynamic, physical or mental ability, it doesn't matter. In a way, I think that's what makes horror and dark fiction so appealing to anyone on that spectrum of difference: you recognize something true to your life, even if the person in the story doesn't look or act like you. The story is what you recognize, and there's some comfort in a familiar feeling, even when it's fear.

Over the decades, writers and literary critics have made all kinds of connections between horror tropes and queer identities: the vampire's bite represents forbidden sexual desires, the werewolf's uneasy merger of two selves parallels the experience of being closeted, and so on. Do you see a particular relationship between queerness and the horror elements of your work? Or do suggestions like these make you roll your eyes?

Meghan: Personally, the fun of writing in genre is the tropes and all their baggage. All that cultural power is extremely enticing.

Over the past ten years, I've been exploring, obsessively, the process of finding a queer identity. That exploration has involved a lot of monsters. A vampire and a ghost are alive and dead, a werewolf is a person and a wolf, etc. I don't think queers are monstrous, but I do think queer sexuality often involves boundary-crossing—and monsters straddle boundaries. They're liminal.

I do think, like Brit and the others mentioned, that there's a danger of queer horror trending into a sad and doomed kind of place. But we should be able to have our miserable, nightmarish hopelessness without it suggesting some equal hopelessness in our romantic lives.

Brit: As I noted before, I think that historically it's hard to deny that queer writers have written a lot of horror fiction—and that something about dealing with feelings of abjection, fear, and othering in fiction kind of tends to create dark stories. There's also, of course, a strong field of writing by queer folks that *isn't* horror. Because, you know, there are a lot of things to write about besides how sad and doomed we all are, et cetera. So I resist a sort of totalizing equation of queerness with horror, but that doesn't mean that horror doesn't *also* contain elements of queerness and otherness that speak to people—if that makes sense.

On the work I've done, though, I think that it's often less about queerness and horror being linked and more about the fact that I sometimes write darker fiction and I mostly write about queer people, so. It maybe evens out into an interesting relation, but I've also written science fiction starring queer folks and regular old fantasy starring queer folks and contemporary speculative stuff with queer folks and—you get my drift. But I do think that dark fiction lets us explore issues of loss and pain, fear and despair, all of those raw human feelings; I think it also offers a unique opportunity to represent the fraught relationship between otherness and those feelings. So there's a sideways kind of linkage, then.

Rahul: It took me years to realize that a significant portion of my writing was driven by my horror over my own queerness. For instance, for years I would write story after story about doublings: clones, evil twins, alter egos, mirror universes, etc. And I'd think, hmm, that's an odd theme, isn't it? Why am I so obsessed with men who're forced to face their own denatured bodies?

Carrie: I think for some authors, sure, their queerness is expressed in the horror elements of their work, but all queer writers everywhere? Ridiculous. That's like saying one's inability to be attracted to a person who isn't an opposite of the binary sexual dynamic they impose on their perspective of humanity is expressed in science fiction as a preference for big, shiny, metal, phallic-shaped rockets. Sure, for some people, it is. For others, they just like space transportation, and write about the most culturally recognizable forms of it.

My queerness informs my writing in the best ways, I think. It's made me more open minded, more cognizant of people's differences and similarities. I can see what's beautiful, or terrifying, in others, in ways that people who aren't queer may not. I understand horror, and fear, and having to run, to hide . . . And because I recognize darkness when I see it, it's easier to write about.

Queers Destroy Horror!, the title of this special issue, parodies the negative responses that are sometimes sparked by queer content in the horror genre. Has your work garnered certain responses based on either queer content or your own identity?

Meghan: I've had random online reviewers wonder aloud about my mental stability, and I've gotten a number of ignorantly handled "positive" reviews. I'm not sure if that's so much because of the queer content of my stories than the frank and sometimes fucked up sex I've written.

What jumps to mind is how I've tried to "destroy" horror in workshop. Contrary to my previous point about hopelessness and queerness needing to be separated in horror, I never, ever, ever, ever want to read a story that ends with one half of a same-sex couple dying, leaving the other tragically alone. Someone has to die at the end of a horror story, is the problem. I submit that gay couples should get a ten year reprieve. In 2025, they can start dying tragically again.

Brit: The immediate thought I had to this was, "well, everyone gets yelled at on the internet, right?"—though some folks get yelled at more than others, sure. I've had more negative interactions as a critic writing about and trying to draw attention to queer content in the speculative field, though, than I have as a fiction writer—which is interesting to me in its own right.

But probably the thing that irks me more than specifically rude negative responses to queer content are the responses that elide the issues of gender and desire. I sort of expect that some people are just, well, hateful assholes. Like I noted before, though, I'm more frustrated by readings that seem to erase the protagonists' identities. This is particularly true of stories with genderqueer characters, or asexual characters, or bisexual characters—situations where it's easy for someone to overwrite the complexities or nuances of gender and sexuality into something more binary. Being a queer and genderqueer person myself, it gets under my skin a little more than I'd like sometimes.

Overall, though: I think the field of speculative fiction—including the darker end—has been growing more and more inclusive, though the shift causes plenty of conflicts still.

Rahul: Honestly, no. I've published a number of queer stories at this point and haven't yet gotten an overtly bigoted response.

Carrie: My identity is not just as a queer person, but also as a woman, which is a category of horror writer that still struggles with negativity and abuse, because a lot of horror fans are straight, white, male, and looking for hate porn—that kind of story which is satisfying to read because it's violent, sometimes sexually so, and whose victims are usually women. Even people who don't think they'd ever like *that sort of story* buy in droves the exact same tale, as long as one man saves one woman in the end. Being a woman who writes scary stories means you are sometimes putting yourself out there to be commented on and criticized by people who'd much rather see you as a victim than an author.

Being queer means you're doing the same thing, but instead of a victim, many would rather see you as the monster.

I think I'm best known as an editor of queer horror for my work on *Cthulhurotica*, an anthology that subverted H.P. Lovecraft's racist, homophobic, and misogynistic view by using his settings but populating them with a wide spectrum of characters. Including, yes, sexually active characters. It's definitely exposed me to a certain segment of his fanbase who were rabidly opposed to seeing the Mythos in a new way. At the same time, there were huge numbers of people who loved what we did and couldn't wait to see more.

Rahul: I think Brit makes a really interesting point regarding erasure of queer readings. I remember growing up and imbibing the idea, from somewhere in the speculative fiction world, that queer readings of literature were "overreaching." They were critics imposing a reading onto a text "that just isn't there." By and large, I think that populist art forms in general tend to have a suspicion of the critic and of any reading of the text that's not right at surface level. The argument is, well, we're inside these characters' heads, so if they're gay, why don't they just say it.

But the result, for me, of that thinking was that I didn't understand any conception of gender or of desire that didn't fit exactly into preconceived notions. Some of my favorite creators were right out there, faithfully transcribing or transmitting the messiness that exists in peoples' heads, but I didn't see that. To me it was all overreaching. It's the job of the writer to show us the things that are in plain sight but rarely seen. However, it's also the job of the reader to try to go there and to strip ourselves of preconceptions and see things in a different way.

(This leaves aside, of course, the whole question of reading meanings into a text that an author didn't intend. That too is a completely valid activity. For instance, I recently saw a production of *Twelfth Night* that played up the possibility that Sir Andrew's real attraction was for Sir Toby. Now, did Shakespeare intend that? Who knows and who cares? The real fun was in seeing the words in a new light.)

Much as we can point to Mary Shelley as the woman who invented science fiction, we can also argue that queer people created horror. The eighteenth-century Gothic novelists Horace Walpole and William Beckford had well-known relationships with young men, while the influential ghost story writers M. R. James and Henry James might be claimed as asexual. Does this history of the genre seem useful or important to you?

Brit: Well, this might be the scholar in me, but I think it's always important to know you've got a history—to know that things aren't written on sand, and that other folks have come before and can offer a sort of genealogical tracer to the types of work that different types of people have done. It's interesting to look at the ways in which genre fiction has been used to theorize and represent marginalized identities for decades upon decades—ever since the novel form was the weird new thing for ladies, et cetera. Connections to the past remind us of the fact that we aren't alone, to some extent.

And, in more recent terms, things like the history of the plague years of the AIDS epidemic are in some sense only accessible in affective terms to people as young as I am *through narrative*. Some of that fiction is going to be weird and dark and upsetting, because the time was weird and dark and upsetting, though that wasn't all it was to the people who survived it. It's important to mark our experiences, to share them, to communicate narratively to other narrative-seeking creatures. It's sort of a thing humans do, I'd say, and I think it's important.

Rahul: It was pretty late in the history of the Western novel before an explicitly queer individual could be portrayed as anything other than haunted and doomed. Even queer authors like Baldwin wrote books like *Giovanni's Room*, where a same-sex relationship— almost as a matter of course—becomes obsessive and murderous. Before that, you have all the doomed, decrepit relationships in Proust's novel or Thomas Mann's Aschenbach, wasting away in *Death in Venice*. There's a sense of self-loathing and despair buried so deeply inside all of these novels that it seems to spring from the essential nature of the protagonists' desires. Any queer person reading these books would have a difficult time coming away from them without feeling as though same-sex desire was a flawed, horrific impulse.

When viewed within that environment of disgust, horror novels almost offer a more hopeful view of same-sex desire, in that the darkness is segregated and is explicitly contrasted with the light. For instance, Beckford's Vathek is, like the characters in Baldwin and Proust and Mann, obsessed with the pursuit of pleasure. And, like them, he comes to a bad end. But at least he manages to achieve a sort of majesty. He's an anti-hero: someone in control of his destiny; a person who proceeds forward in full knowledge of the possible consequences.

And when he is cast down, it's not—as in these other novels—because of some internal rot in his soul. Instead, it's an external punishment visited upon him by the forces of Hell. It's not a hopeful vision of the passions, but it is, in some ways, a more nuanced one.

Meghan: Totally! Yes! Any and all queer lineages please! Honestly, that's the sum of my reaction. I like what Brit and Rahul had to say about how fiction has evolved to process the dark side of the queer experience, whatever that dark side might be.

Carrie: I think it's useful to see this as part of the history of genre, but it's just the most recent tip of the iceberg. The horror label may be new, but writing about and telling stories about horror are as old as humanity. We have always huddled around a fire, warning of the dangers in the dark, or the secret monsters lurking within our midst. How many stories of shape changers or possession or witches were really about regular people who just happened to be a little different? Hiding yourself from ignorant townspeople isn't a new phenomenon. Neither is being queer.

Finally, what are the current trends in horror that interest or excite you? What's coming up next for your own work?

Meghan: I'm excited about the ongoing conversation about, and critique of, Lovecraft's racism. I'm excited to see great horror writers like Nathan Ballingrud become popular far outside the normal bounds of the genre. I'm excited to see a larger number of writers examining Poe, I'm excited about the unstoppable groundswell of Shirley Jackson worship, I'm excited about the Shirley Jackson Award. This is not nearly queer enough a list of things. Here is a queer thing—I am very excited for *Blood: Stories*, Matthew Cheney's collection from Black Lawrence Press. I don't think he would call himself a horror writer, but the title story, "Blood," is dark as fuck.

I've recently completed a fantasy novel, which is not horror but some terrible things do happen and also there is a ghost; I can't put down the ghosts. I'm also working on a cycle of stories about a deadly flu outbreak in New York City, another horrible thing that is not horror. As a writer, I'm always trying to terrify myself. It's great how many different genres you can do that in.

Brit: I like seeing more nonbinary characters in fiction, and I like seeing more stories that deal with issues of gender and sexuality, obviously—things that I do think are happening more and more in dark fiction. I also like darker stories with meta elements that explore the things the genre is doing and can do, more explicitly. I'm excited about things like this special issue, drawing attention to all the awesome and varied ways queer writers and stories can adapt and employ the tools of genre writing.

As for me, I have a few short stories that I've been working on, and I just finished a second Master's degree program. So, that sort of ate up a lot of writing time I'll have back now. I look forward to settling down to do more work again; I also look forward to writing more criticism. I've been working on an article about the two Kiernan novels I mentioned previously that I hope will be picked up somewhere, too.

Rahul: Is it awful for me to say that I don't read very much contemporary fiction nowadays? Certainly not enough to be able to opine on the trends within any particular genre.

As for my own work, I can tell you that I'm writing young adult and middle grade novels, and the YA field, in particular, tends to be very trend-driven. For some reason, certain motifs or sub-genres will catch on and tons of books will be purchased and published, while others will go completely fallow. Recently, there was a trend for YA thrillers, including many with traditional horror elements. I have no idea about the source of that trend, since it doesn't seem tied to any particular kidlit bestseller (I suppose, if anything, it was an outgrowth of the success of *Gone Girl*).

Given my own early fascination with Holocaust novels, I've always felt that teens have an appetite for dark fiction, and I know that when I'm writing for kids I never worry that my work is too dark, because I think kids have a real fascination with death and with the darker side of life. If anything, the stumbling block here isn't the kids, it's the editors. I recently wrote a middle-grade thriller—a novel about a boy who becomes convinced that all the other kids at his twelfth birthday party have entered into a conspiracy to humiliate him—and, due to my agent's intuition that its bleakness would make it a hard sell, I'm currently in the process of giving it a happier ending.

Carrie: My favorite current trend is the one toward greater inclusivity. The same old stories over and over again have gotten stale, haven't they? Allowing a more inclusive take on what "horror" is enriches the genre—think of Nathan Ballingrud's award-winning work, which can just as easily be described as "magic realism" as horror, and yet is generally considered to be fresh, and brilliant. Allowing more diverse creators and characters means there are new stories and new variations on old favorites. That's better for everyone.

I've actually got a couple of short stories, and a novel, that I'm working on now which fall into the "horror" category. The upcoming trend which interests me most in my own work is that I'm planning to start working a little less toward the end of the year, so I can devote more to my writing. (I currently work two full-time jobs, which leaves almost no time for anything else.) I miss having the luxury of time, of being able to take a story idea and put it on the page, instead of having to wait for days or weeks before I catch enough of a break to scribble some words down. Once that changes, you can expect to see a lot more fiction from me!

ARTISTS' SPOTLIGHT:
FIVE QUEER ARTISTS DESTROYING HORROR ART

CORY SKERRY &
MEGAN ARKENBERG

QUEER HORROR ART is the tl;dr of our most disturbing moments. We who let our subconscious bleed onto canvas, paper, and clay are compelled to remark upon the world with our hands and voices. At least for us, the darkness in our history is an orchard of inspiration.

It's a history I like to see flayed and stitched back together in different iterations, examining the unique ways in which we understand the sickness in the human condition. The variety in the GSM spectrum gives our community strength, and I think that variety is also the key to Destroying horror, where we are usually seen as anything but the protagonist.

When I selected artists for this special issue, I looked for work in which the creator's gaze was strong and easily distinguished from the heteronormative, cissexual gaze that dominates most horror art. It was more difficult to find queer artists than I expected, because not everyone announces their queer status, but the art and GSRM communities were helpful in sharing their favorites. In honor of the symbolism behind the spectrum, I narrowed my choices with the intent of representing disparate styles, media, and processes: KG Schmidt's crisp lines and comfortable elegance; Elizabeth Leggett's subtle, textured surrealism; Eliza Gauger's unapologetically weird chameleonism; my own splashy, gritty ink work; and of course, AJ Jones's eerie, illuminated struggles.

I'd like to introduce you to our Queers Destroy Horror artists. I hope their art enhances—and possibly reflects—your own experience.

AJ JONES

What attracts you to horror and dark subject matter?

I suppose I've always been drawn to darker, slightly bloody subjects and drippy, rusty environments; I'm not sure why, but horror movies, books, games, I'm really into all of it!

To what extent do you feel being queer influences your art?

Being queer influences pretty much every aspect of my life; I view the world through queer lenses. I discovered this when a professor of mine would question the strangest things about subjects in my illustrations, and I just realized that he and I experienced completely different worlds on a day to day basis. I'm pretty deeply immersed in queer culture, from my circle of friends to the media I consume, it all influences the content I create.

How do your own fears interact with your art?

Recently I've had a fascination with painting things I used to be uncomfortable with, and making them appealing to me—not necessarily making horrific things beautiful, but making them a bit more surreal.

You're involved in a collaborative art blog, Lot No. 3, which showcases original "dark and surreal" content. Can you tell us a bit about how this project started, and what it does for you as an artist to be producing work on a new theme each week?

Lot No. 3 began when my roommates and I decided that we really needed to start producing finished work on the regular, and one of the things we had in common was that we all gravitated towards darker themes and subject matters. So we started the blog as a really casual way to hold ourselves accountable to just finish something, whether we've spent thirty hours or one hour on it.

One of the aspects of your work that has changed the least over the years is your propensity for dramatic lighting. What would you say has changed the most, and how does it complement the way you play with light?

Even as a beginning artist I embraced values and contrast and darker, heavier marks, but recently I've been trying to play with lost edges and letting things disappear and fade into the shadows. Something that has drastically changed is the color palette I work with. It's gone from super dark, less saturated colors to brighter, heavier saturation. I also often bring in extra, internal light sources, which I've certainly gotten more bold with.

Eliza Gauger

What attracts you to horror and dark subject matter?

People ask me this a lot and it never fails to catch me by surprise because I don't think of my art as being "dark." I've learned to say disclaimers when I'm showing my art to someone because I've learned that what I feel is "normal" or "true" or "beautiful" or even "realistic" will usually strike people as ugly or unnerving.

To what extent do you feel being queer influences your art?

Queerness has driven me to focus very much on "monstrousness" as subject matter, or rather, depicting what feels "right" to me and which usually ends up appearing monstrous. And most of my work has a sexual or fetishistic tone even when it is not explicit. Feeling alienated and, often, as if I'm hiding myself or my desire in an effort to keep people around me from being confused or upset, leads to a sort of "ghost at the window" perspective. I'm the ghost.

How do your own fears interact with your art?

My own particular traumas inform a lot of what I choose to draw in terms of the process of drawing being a literal "objectification" of an idea or a person—you can turn someone into a piece of paper with marks on it through the process of drawing, which reduces threat. It's like taking an entire dimension of existence away from them. I've drawn several people before I met them. A lot of my art is a combination of hostile or confrontational, and tender or comforting, because I feel ambivalent and dichotomous about just about everything.

The occult plays a large part in both your comforting "Problem Glyphs" project as well as a more unsettling role in the forthcoming comic book *Black Hole Wizard*. How does it feel to approach one subject from two disparate paradigms?

I've never been a "true" occultist in that I have never really stuck to studying the tomes and then practicing the rituals or recipes, despite being thrown up against the idea a lot in my life. I was a tween Wiccan like everyone else but didn't agree with the touchy-feely stuff about no curses, no bad vibes, etc. And the gender binarism in most alchemical/neopagan stuff is just ridiculous. All the phallic green god vs. yoni earth goddess stuff, I mean where did that leave me? It's such a patriarchal lens with which to view paganism, and it's ahistorical at best—in a huge number of magical traditions, gender weirdness and queerness was a part of the liminalism inherent to magic workers. You find it everywhere.

I just talked a lot about all the things occultism isn't to me, as opposed to what it is, sorry. The approach to occultism I think is most interesting and productive is semi-Jungian, although there are serious gender problems there, too. "Problem Glyphs" pulls on Jungian archetypes but also makes up a lot of its own, or revives lesser-used meanings. It's an intuitive process of constant self-reference and cross-reference with reference material. *Black Hole Wizard* probably cleaves more to some external or collaborative concepts of "occultism", demons, magic(k), and so on, as well as pop cultural Metal subculture stuff. This is necessary for the process of making a comic book with someone (in this case, *BHW* writer Simon Berman). So everything I do for *BHW* is something he's signed off on, or was his idea in the first place. It's much more structured than "Problem Glyphs," which is extremely organic.

With media that ranges from digital to oil paint to a Sharpie on a mailing label, which do you find yourself returning to the most, and why?

Probably just pencil. Ever since I attended a classical atelier and went through the absolutely soul-destroying, daily, grass roots classical cast drawing process, turning out photorealistic pencil drawings of plaster casts of classical art, I've had a much more thorough understanding of contour, shadow, and the physical memory of rendering. You can do anything with a pencil and a gum eraser. Drawing is the cornerstone of everything else, everything. If you can draw you can do anything else with a massive head start. "Well drawn is well enough painted."

Elizabeth Leggett

What attracts you to horror and dark subject matter?

It is hard not to love perfectly delivered shock and awe! That moment in a story where you cannot really believe the writer is taking you down *that* Rabbit Hole, but you are so caught up in the whole experience that you just throw sanity over your shoulder and go with them, is fantastic. It is that cresting over the first serious hill on the roller coaster you kept having second thoughts about riding the whole time you were in line. It is a delicious gut punch. What is there not to love?

To what extent do you feel being queer influences your art?

Illustrating beautiful women was my first hint to myself that I was not straight. I remember my first fascination was with a long-haired brunette in first grade. She was always very serious and I remember trying to memorize what she looked like in different lighting. I tried to draw her, but did not ever capture her. At first, I did not understand, I just felt compelled to illustrate females. I guess both loves are tangled together.

How do your own fears interact with your art?

Tough question. The most honest response I can offer is that if the subject makes me exceptionally uncomfortable to create, I need to do it. I use my aversion as a compass to lead me to more powerful pieces. Sometimes, I am not even aware of the triggers beforehand. Art illuminates soul?

There's a distinctive textural quality to your paintings that creates an otherworldly effect. How did you acquire this aspect of your style, and what drove you to keep exploring and strengthening it?

I was a traditional artist until my late twenties, but around 1995-1996, I shifted to digital. The market was beginning to require graphic program awareness, I had returned to school so money was tight and paint is expensive, and Adobe offered teaching students remarkable deals. I was also missing deadlines working traditionally, which is never, ever good. My first tablet was a monster! I guess I was too stubborn to learn the "right" way to use digital tools. I just fiddled around until I manhandled it to recreate what I had done before.

What kind of relationship do you see between the mood of your subject and the mood of the landscape in which you place them?

Most of my professional work is creating illustrations for short stories and novel covers. The idea is to create curiosity and interest without spoilers. That being said, I enjoy it a great deal when there can be discordance between subject and landscape. I think it makes a better overall composition. (This can be especially true for horror!)

KG SCHMIDT

What attracts you to horror and dark subject matter?

When I was growing up, I looked for safe spaces to acquaint myself with taboo subjects I ran into on a daily basis and desperately wanted to understand: mental illness; inappropriate thoughts, feelings and appetites; death; grief; futility; helplessness; the unknown, invisible webs of social and environmental danger and pitfalls. Nonfiction was helpful, but I learned that the horror and dark fantasy section of the library was where they kept all the good stuff. Stories filed under horror and dark fantasy didn't try to feed me a happy ending—I was given electrifying scenarios and left with open-ended "IT'S NOT OVER YET" conclusions. Since that was my life at the time, I found that message more uplifting than stories with more conventionally happy endings.

To what extent do you feel being queer influences your art?

This is an odd question. It feels a lot like when I was asked how "being a woman" influenced my artwork—or when people tried to figure out if I was a man or a woman based on the style I chose to draw in. Are you asking me how queer my art is, or how my experience as a queer person shows up in my work? I certainly draw for a lot of queer clients, and a substantial part of my body of work depicts people who happen to be queer, in situations which reveal or explore that facet of their being. And then there's, you know, a couple decades of formal training, experimentation, research, and daily practice, and that has definitely influenced my art. My goal has always been to express the empathy and interest I felt in what I was drawing, but I don't feel that discipline or empathy are directly tied to me being queer.

How do your own fears interact with your art?

Extensively! I'll start a project and I won't finish it for years because I'm afraid of what kind of attention it will attract to me. And other times, I hurl my id at the screen, hit upload, and run like hell. And my id will be, like, fluffy baby animals curled up in a basket or something. And then everyone will know I like fluffy baby animals, and that is terrifying, because maybe someone has the opinion that the baby animals are problematic, or indicative of some deep wrongness in me, or that I'm wasting my time and talent on all these fluffy baby animals instead of making real art, whatever that is. Why fluffy baby animals? What are these fluffy baby animals really saying? How are fluffy baby animals addressing a larger social, political, or economic issue? Can I qualify my enjoyment of fluffy baby animals with a 140 page doctorate thesis and a thirty-minute PowerPoint presentation? What kind of artist am I if I'm not using my love for fluffy baby animals to get into fights on the internet? Questions like these are the armature my fears grow themselves around. I'm facing them head-on whenever I make something, and again when I publish it online.

How organic is the development of the (often complex) composition in your work?

Depends on how complete the piece is in my mind before I start working—it's a lot like cooking. Sometimes I have a selection of powerful visual elements which go together, but I have to put some forethought and planning into composing the piece before I sit down and actually do it—equivalent to flipping through my favorite recipes and working from one or two of those. Sometimes the pieces fall into place while I'm engaged in the process of the piece, and it evolves under my hands into something different from what I initially pictured—maybe I have to substitute some basic ingredients, experiment—use the butt of the spatula handle for something different than its intended purpose because I don't have a mortar and pestle on hand. And then, sometimes, a bunch of simple successful dishes accumulate over time, and I get to make something using all of those experiments, which tastes amazing. And of course, more often than I'd like to admit, I prepare the ingredients disastrously out of order or overcook something, or burn something I forgot to stir constantly, and I am obliged to eat my own mistakes while resolving not to do *that* again.

Physical intimacy and solitude both play strong roles in your work. What draws you to these two different moods?

That's a very personal question. Well, I am drawn to these two moods because I was the sad fat dragon with no friends and I yearned for friendships based on mutual delight, respect, and understanding—where we could just *hug* each other and it wouldn't feel dangerous or weird. But I hadn't met any of those friends in person yet. So I drew lots of pictures where people who liked each other and felt safe in each other's presence got to snuggle a lot, and when I hit the internet, I posted them up online, where people understood what they were looking at. And that was enough to take the sharper edges off of a rather lonely chapter of my life. Physical intimacy connects me with other people, and solitude connects me with myself. Striking a healthy balance between the two has proven integral to keeping me happy and centered, both as an artist and as a human being. Refusing to conflate interaction with intimacy or connectivity with a connection to self generates a perpetual tension within me, a part of my daily experience that I draw constant inspiration from.

PLUNDERPUSS

What attracts you to horror and dark subject matter?

I don't know, but it's been this way as long as I can remember. My parents are fond of texting me snapshots of the humiliatingly awful dark poetry I wrote when I was young enough that learning to pee in the toilet was still on my résumé. Maybe it was a way for my wee mind to process the gore in those National Geographic documentaries I loved so much, or maybe it was the older brother I idolized letting me watch R-rated horror films when he was babysitting me (highlight: watched a miniature dinosaur eat a dude's genitals, not even kidding). But it's always been *Ghostbusters* and naming the monster under the bed and forcing myself to walk down dark stairs without the light on just to see if I could do it.

To what extent do you feel being queer influences your art?

Monsters are a solid metaphor for the unknown, for the Other. When I first became cognizant of my bisexuality and gender nonconformity, we lived in an inbred mill town in backwoods Idaho, an hour from the nearest chain fast food restaurant. I was definitely the Other, just one pissed off redneck away from becoming a sad news story. That internalized fear of torches and pitchforks has guided me to depict the hidden, the liminal, and the feared in ways that focus on their beauty, complexity, necessity, and even sometimes their cuddliness.

How do your own fears interact with your art?

The few times in my life that I've actually been terrified were almost exclusively because someone wanted to kick my ass. It's strange because I know I can take a punch, but I also never know how far someone is going to go. The type of fears I depict in my art are really just delighted escapism: the disturbing, the weird, but most of all, the highly unlikely. The subject matter that really scares me also, somewhat paradoxically, bores me. Given the choice, I would paint a monster with shark teeth and tentacles over a scene of two men passing an entire group of strangers on the street, with one guy in the big group turning toward the two with his fists up. Even though when it happened I almost had to take "peeing in the toilet" off my résumé, I don't find that scene visually inspiring.

Many of your images feature a striking contrast between the subject in the foreground and a vividly colored and textured background. What do you see as the relationship between these various elements of a piece?

Perhaps because I'm a long-time fan of comics and street art, I developed an appreciation for a gritty "canvas" with natural textures (like brick or metal) supporting a brightly colored graphic foreground (like spray paint or stark ink). I see the contrast as a tool for adjusting how seriously the viewer takes the image. If I'm trying to unsettle the viewer, I shrink the contrast so it seems more "possible," but if I'm just trying to explore a "what if," I let my aesthetic preferences win.

In addition to your illustration work, you write speculative fiction. How does the process of creating a story compare to the process of creating visual art (or vice versa)?

It used to have very little in common, but after attending Clarion West, I realized I could apply concepts like contour, chiaroscuro, and composition to stories. Some of them already had parallels (I think of composition as analogous to plot structure, for example). When I'm imagining either a story or an illustration, I start with a brief piece of inspiration—an image, a few words of dialog, a "what if"—and either write the first scene or do a sketch to see if my idea is strong enough to support a finished work.

ARTISTS' GALLERY

Art by Eliza Gauger

Art by Eliza Gauger

Art by KG Schmidt

Art by KG Schmidt

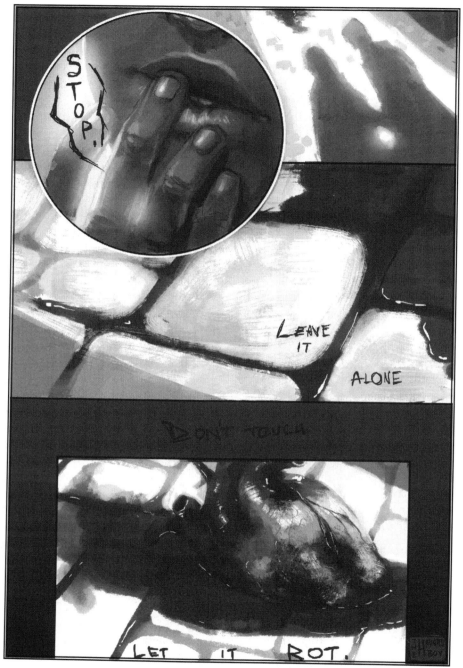

ART BY AJ JONES

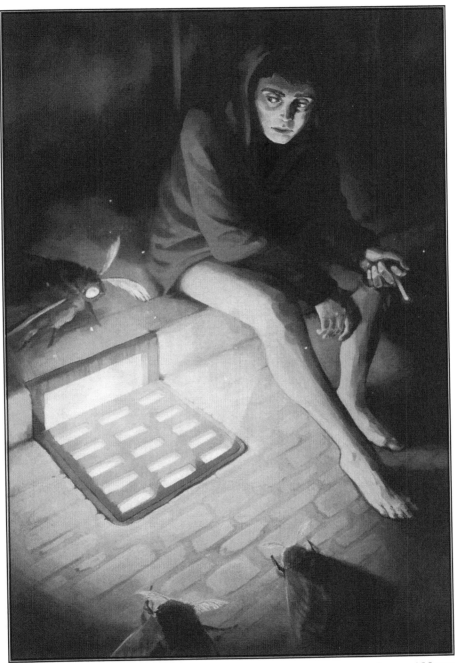

ART BY AJ JONES

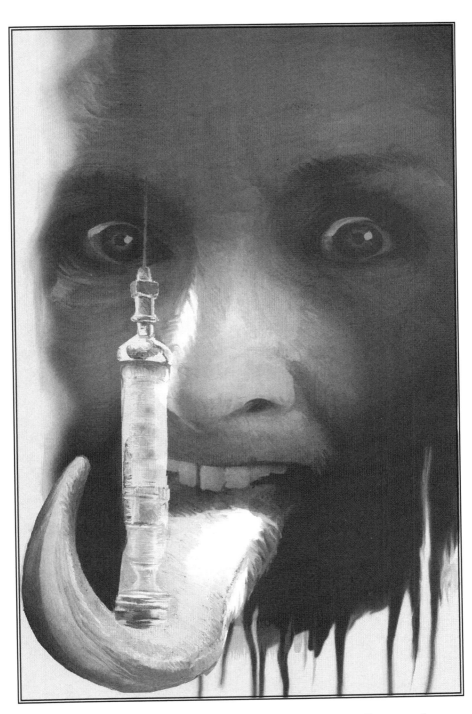

ART BY ELIZABETH LEGGETT

ART BY PLUNDERPUSS

ART BY PLUNDERPUSS

AUTHOR SPOTLIGHT:
MATTHEW BRIGHT

TRACI CASTLEBERRY

So. Why Dorian Gray?

Because I have a disturbing weakness for the Victorian gothic, and if you're playing in that wheelhouse Dorian Gray is as queer as they come. Oscar Wilde was a genius, Dorian is his finest creation, and if you're going to steal, steal from the best.

Putting Dorian's love of beauty up against a disease that ravages that same beauty seems like the perfect vehicle to showcase his narcissism. How did you come up with that idea?

As per any writer brain, I jump from one interest to the next, and writing this happened to coincide with a fascination with AIDs-era San Francisco and the Castro. Put the immortal, ageless Dorian into that, and the contrast jumps right out. Gay culture has always had a thing about youth and beauty, and Dorian Gray sums it up rather succinctly; place that in a time when all those things were being cruelly taken away, and it's even more tragic.

The repetitive lines about the appearance of the dying men serve to heighten Dorian's obsession with looks as well as the desperation of that era. Can you tell us more about your thoughts on those?

Before I wrote the story, I'd watched the documentary *We Were Here*, and there was one part that stuck with me. One of the survivors talked about how, after burying one partner, he immediately launched into other relationships, which ultimately ended in death too. He said that, even though each new relationship might be cut short, the fleetingness of everything was what made them launch so much faster into the next relationship, and it became a cycle. That's what the repetition was about: Dorian jumping to the next man, then the next and the next, and not looking back.

Dorian is actually somewhat dislikable from a moral standpoint, yet here he's managing to be sympathetic as well. How did you manage to keep Dorian's recognizable features while also making him your own?

Dorian sold his soul for immortality and left behind everyone he knew to die: I'm not sure likeable is the first thing on his mind. But I suppose in this story he's just another survivor, portrait or not, through a terrible era, which makes him easier to understand. His guilt at the end is the same as described by many of the real-life survivors of the epidemic.

You've mentioned that this story is part of a series featuring Victorian gothic characters transposed into twenty-first century LGBT history. Can you tell us more about that?

"Part of a series" might be a strong description, as they're still in the early stages of planning, but I'm in the process of shaping a collection to go alongside "Golden Hair." Dracula knocking around Stonewall, Carmilla munching on suffragettes, a gender-swapped Spring-Heeled Jack, the Lost Boys in the trenches, Sherlock Holmes at the Hundred Guineas Club . . .

I know you do a lot of art and design as well. How does story affect your art and vice versa? Do you approach them the same or differently?

I've never thought of them being connected, but Golden Hair, Red Lips started with one image—the sign that read "there's something out there"—and worked out from there, which is the same approach I take to design and art.

Got any forthcoming projects you'd like to tell us about?

After many, many years of procrastination I've finally completed the first draft of a novel—a sort of steampunk Victorian detective pastiche featuring Oscar Wilde, Arthur Conan Doyle, and Queen Victoria as the detective's sidekicks. With any luck, that'll be the next thing I shepherd into the world . . .

AUTHOR SPOTLIGHT:
KELLEY ESKRIDGE

TRACI CASTLEBERRY

"Alien Jane" is about twenty years old now. Where did the story come from, and how have your thoughts on it changed, if at all, in that time?

The story came from a segment on the TV show *60 Minutes* about congenital insensitivity to pain. People with CIP don't feel pain at all, although they feel other physical sensations. But pain messages simply don't get through. It's very dangerous: kids with CIP can maim or kill themselves just by doing kid stuff.

At that time, there was little awareness about the condition, and families were on their own to deal with it. I've always been drawn to stories of how we isolate ourselves or are isolated by others. I decided to explore the emotional pain of othering through the absence of physical pain. I still think the story does that. As long as there is othering, some of us will be aliens.

Although that makes it sound as if I had a Grand Theme in mind. I did not. I write from character, and the coolest plot devices in the world don't work for me unless I can connect them to characters I care about. I'll never be a "big idea" writer. I'm a writer who explores personal choices that have big consequences.

Setting a story in a mental ward seems like one of the most overdone kinds of horror stories, yet "Alien Jane" avoids the usual clichés. Why set the story there, and did you consciously try to stay away from or subvert the stereotypes?

Three of my relatives have experienced time on psychiatric wards, locked and open. It's not a cliché to me.

Side trip into the notion of *Write what you know*: the experience of spending time on a ward with someone I love while they were tranked to the back teeth or just coming out of the fugue of ECT does not automatically make the setting of "Alien Jane" authentic. Doing something is not the same as writing it. But the more we're willing to stop and sit with our memories and our own experiences, to notice the specific details, to sift through the particulars of reality, the more authenticity we can bring to . . . well, everything, but certainly to writing.

I set the story on the ward because I wanted a confined space for Rita and Jane to collide in. I wanted the constant promise of cure, the sense of forced intimacy, the "for your own good" excuse for control. I wanted a setting where pain mattered, where pain in all its forms was the purpose of the community.

A setting that matters to the characters becomes its own kind of character, its own kind of relationship, in a story.

In your essay, "War Machine, Time Machine," you mention that the stories you loved best involved a woman finding her strength and discovering her power. That certainly happens in "Alien Jane." Why does this remain an important theme in your stories?

You know, I want to respond with something profound, but the only true answer is: because.

In the same essay, you mention that you don't consider "Alien Jane" queer although many categorize it as "lesbian." How do you categorize it, if at all? And if you don't, why not?

I categorize it as a story. About people, some of whom love each other and some of whom do themselves or each other great harm. That's what people do.

I struggle with the notion of categorization, as you'll know from reading the essay. But on a deep level I'm beginning to understand the power of tagging (thank you, internet). I see categories and tags as essentially different. Tagging is inclusive: the point is to have all the tags that people might find significant. Categories, however, are like buckets or boxes or bathrooms: I think our cultural assumption is that things can't truly belong in more than one at the same time.

I think this is changing, and I am delighted. Now that I've found a way to describe things that feels naturally inclusive and expansive and particular, I'm happy to tag my work and myself as queer. Because I don't have to prioritize the story, or myself, as one thing above all others.

Rita is lesbian and angry and smart and fucked up and frightened and loving and female and young and Latina and she likes broccoli. She is all the things she is. She is a particular person, and this is her particular story. But no one ever categorizes it as a Latina story, or as a vegetarian story, or a feminist story. Why not? What's that about? Categories are reductive, and I think we too often use them to separate people rather than bring people together.

You also say that to you, the word "queer" is a meta-descriptor, "implying relativity, fluidity, defiance of categories," which allows you to define it any way you want. How does your work reflect this idea?

I am always exploring what it is to be human. All the things we are; the infinite permutations of us. Fuck categories. I'm in a constant process of discovering myself and becoming more of who I am.

I see my body of work as queer because, to the best of my ability, it includes rather than excludes women, people of color, people who have all different kinds of sex, and genderqueer people who are sexy as hell and don't apologize and don't explain. My people are as human as I can make them, and I think that "human" is a wide open space where anything is possible.

In the "War Machine, Time Machine" essay, I wrote that I don't define myself as queer. That has changed. I tag myself as queer routinely now. I'm publicly and proudly queer because I'm bisexual. I'm publicly and proudly queer because I am married to a woman. Personally and privately, I also feel queer in the culture because I'm a woman over fifty who still shows skin. I recently got my first tattoo. At every opportunity I dance like a crazy kid until I am soaked with sweat. I am trying to carve out a screenwriting career in an industry in which I am considered both unfuckable and invisible, so when I say, *Your categories are bullshit and here I am with my visible fuckable strong powerful characters*, to them I am queer as hell. Queer means that I am here to tell all the human stories, and I belong here, and I am to be reckoned with.

I know you've been working hard on your Solitaire screenplay. Anything you'd like to tell us about that?

By the time this goes to print, the film (now titled *OtherLife*) will have completed shooting in Australia. I'm enormously proud of the script, and the brilliant, creative team who have embraced it. They are making the story their own in ways that surprise and delight me.

I should also say that *OtherLife* is only loosely based on *Solitaire*. Anyone who expects to see the characters or events of the book on the screen will be disappointed. The heart of the film, as in the book, is Ren's journey into herself through the mechanism of virtual confinement, but the film story is utterly different.

I'm good with that: it relieves all of us involved from choosing what moments of the book to keep and what to jettison. We kept the core of the character, the deep needs and feelings that drive her, and built our film story around that.

People ask if it was hard for me as the author to step into the lead screenwriter role after the initial draft of the adaptation was completed—after the story was already changed so much from the book. The answer is no, it wasn't hard at all. It was liberating. Any author who believes her story is too sacred to subject it to the demands of a different medium ought not to option it to the movies. Don't send your kid to rock camp with a cello and be surprised when she comes home with an electric violin; don't be surprised that she plays a different song.

What can we look forward to seeing from you in the future?
I don't know. Something that compels me. And there will be humans.

AUTHOR SPOTLIGHT:
LEE THOMAS

ARLEY SORG

"The Lord of Corrosion" is really focused on family, and a lot of time is invested in building and exploring different facets and kinds of familial relationships. How does this story represent your experiences, feelings, and beliefs around family?

I suppose the primary family relationship in the story is a bit of wishful thinking on my part. I was never close to my family. It's not an issue of animosity or resentment. We were just brought up with an "every person for him/herself" kind of vibe, and we all had extremely different interests. The kind of family connection that many people inherently understand is lost on me, so occasionally I try to explore family dynamics in my work. At times, the characters are disconnected from one other in a way I can relate to, and other times they operate in a more "traditional," cohesive manner, as they do in this story.

One of the most startling and relatable moments for me was the scene where Sofia asks, "What's wrong with me?" It's a deft demonstration of the internalization of hate. What were the challenges of writing a piece so carefully focused on hate, and how did you deal with them?

Well, that's exactly it. One insidious aspect of prejudice is the effect it has on a person's self-worth. That's the metaphor behind "The Lord of Corrosion." Not only does the title represent a monster, but it also represents the cultural messaging that can eat away at a person's self-esteem. For a child like Sofia, she has no concept of being different, because her fathers didn't raise her to think in prejudicial terms. Then an outside influence arrives that acts as her first introduction to this kind of hate. In her mind, the influence (Gundy Morgan) is an adult, a power figure, and she is too young to know that power figures aren't always right. She's never learned to question such attacks, just as most children haven't. The emotional abuse she endures in a very direct manner represents both the blatant and the subtle destructive messaging that comes from our culture.

Growing up gay and having spent no real time in the closet, I was constantly struggling to keep negative messaging out, or at the very least, trying to view it objectively. I had to believe that if I was "an abomination," "a perversion," "a second class citizen," it had nothing to do with me, but rather was the result of a cultural construct and a set of definitions that benefited certain groups. I figured it was a given people were going to victimize me, but that didn't mean I had to accept the role of victim, because the minute I claimed that role, they would win. I would have defined myself as weak, as "lesser." Fortunately, we've made some progress away from the mindset I encountered as a young adult, but the negative messaging, whether in regard to the LGBTQ community or in regard to race, is far from gone.

Daddy Gundy strikes me as a really great larger-than-life antagonist, with a name and personality that I can easily visualize growing in power and reappearing in sequels or longer works. The ending is wonderful but also potentially ambiguous—especially in the horror field! Is this a character you plan to revisit? Was he inspired by real people or events?

I might not be done with Gundy Morgan yet. I couldn't fit all of him into this story. It was already at novelette length, and I didn't think additional details about the character were necessary to effectively tell the tale. My initial approach to the material was significantly different. It started out as a story that blossomed into a novella-length work, which I had to put aside because it was running far beyond the word count Wendy [Wagner] had requested. "The Lord of Corrosion" was my second run at the material, in which I refocused the action and pushed Gundy further into the background. There's a lot to explore with this premise and these characters, and I intend to return to all of this in a longer form so I can dig deeper into some of the ideas. I just need to let it simmer a little longer before diving in. As for my inspiration, Gundy is simply a composite—a personification of racist hypocrisy and social power structures that support intolerance. Real world personalities that informed Gundy's character are easy enough to find. Many of them are running for office.

I really enjoyed this story and I'm looking forward to reading more of your work. What are you working on now, and what can we anticipate seeing from you in the future?

Thank you! My most recent release is a mini-collection from Cemetery Dance, called *Cemetery Dance Selects: Lee Thomas*. It's a kind of "Greatest Hits" of my previously published short fiction. Plus, I have several short stories appearing in the near future, including "The Grief Frequency" in *Unspeakable Horror II*, and "Pincushion" in *Vicious Circle*. I've just completed a novella about a gay mobster, facing supernatural forces, called *Minotaur*, and I'm deep into the first draft of a Young Adult novel set during the Great Depression, which also deals with gangsters and a magic system based in ancient metal objects.

AUTHOR SPOTLIGHT:
CAITLÍN R. KIERNAN

ROBYN LUPO

What was it that drew you to tell "Rats Live on No Evil Star"? When you set out to write this one, how did your own understanding and or experience of mental illness inform your writing?

You have to understand, I wrote this story way back in 1998. Or maybe 1997. I'm honestly not even sure which year. So, any recollections about how it occurred to me or what my motivations were, are murky at best. I'm working from memories that may be eighteen years old, and I've written almost two hundred short stories and nine novels since then. But I was living in a loft by the railroad tracks in Birmingham, Alabama, situated pretty much where the story is set. And the west-facing windows, tall windows, had an unobstructed view of the sky. The sky has always been difficult for me. I'd go so far as to say I have a phobia of the sky. And I think that's what's at the heart of this story. And, too, I was reading an awful lot of Charles Fort at the time.

This story tends to evoke feelings of dread; what do you think draws us to read on the darker side of speculative? Is the answer the same for writers—do you think what motivates you to capture a dark current in your work is along the same lines as someone reading it?

I can't speak for other people. I honestly have no idea what attracts other people to the morbid, the dark, the macabre. Likewise, I have never understood why some people like what I write. It's fortunate that they do, obviously. As for myself, my attraction to the weird—which is the word I'm mostly comfortable with—goes very far back into my childhood. I was reading Alfred Hitchcock anthologies by second grade. My mother read me Dracula when I was in fourth grade. In the past I've answered this question by recourse to Poe's "Alone": "And the cloud that took the form/(When the rest of Heaven was blue)/ Of a demon in my view." It's the lens through which I see the world, for whatever reason. But I cannot, with any confidence, say why that is.

Both Olan and Jessie have stories that seem to bolster them and support them, and Olan reports certain works make him nervous. What written works have supported or inspired you lately? Are there any works that make you nervous?

Truthfully, I rarely read fiction. I largely stopped reading fiction back in the late nineties. I think the last novel that really floored me and had a tremendous effect on my own work was Mark Z. Danielewski's *House of Leaves*, and it was published fifteen years ago. When I do read fiction now, it's usually old favorites like Angela Carter, Shirley Jackson, Cormac McCarthy, Harlan Ellison, Ray Bradbury. Works that make me nervous? That actually inspire in me a sense of dread? Well, the authors I've named. And Charles Fort. The man was a crank, but he knew how to use words to achieve an unsettling effect.

What's next for you?

Right now I'm about to begin the screenplay for my novel *The Red Tree*, which was optioned this summer. After that, I'll be writing my next novel, *Interstate Love Song*. I'm also proofreading my next three collections right now, *Houses Under the Sea: Mythos Tales*, *Beneath an Oil-Dark Sea: The Best of Caitlín R. Kiernan* (Volume Two), and *Cambrian Tales*. The first of those three will be released by Centipede Press, and the latter two by Subterranean Press. The third is a volume of juvenilia including writing from college, high school, and junior high. And I'm still getting *Sirenia Digest* out monthly.

AUTHOR SPOTLIGHT:
SUNNY MORAINE

SANDRA ODELL

From the first paragraph "Dispatches From A Hole In The World" resonates with a loneliness that settles in the bones. How did you come to write this particular story?

It's an incredibly personal story. It's difficult for me to always be sure exactly where these things come from, but I do know that an enormous amount of it arose from the past couple of years in my graduate program, which have been very difficult and have left me feeling like I'm in a bit of a wilderness period where a lot of personal connections are fraying and the future is increasingly unclear. That's been extremely anxiety-making, and I decided to try to get something of a handle on it by pumping it into fiction. I also have a tendency to vanish into large projects, especially emotionally powerful ones, and that can be disturbing. It felt right to deal with it here too.

The narrative voice reflects a character familiar with the ins and outs of academia, the daily grind of research and reporting. What experience do you have in the hallowed halls of higher education?

I'm a doctoral candidate going into my seventh year and I'm stalled at the dissertation phase—which, like I said above, has generated an enormous amount of anxiety. But there was a lot of anxiety prior to that, in terms of completing intensive coursework and training in research methods. Aside from that, graduate school can just be *brutal* in general. It can be and often is punishing both mentally and emotionally—sometimes also physically, if it makes it hard to take care of yourself—and I think there's the seed of some very effective psychological horror hiding in that kind of ordeal. You can form deep relationships with the people who go through it with you, but it can also be frighteningly isolating at times.

The story hinges on the sense of immediacy that comes from social media. That sense of connection leads to a form of voyeurism where some would say that every aspect of our lives is laid bare for the world to see. What is it about the realities of social media that lend themselves so well to horror fiction?

I think a lot of it is what you're saying—the question of what's seen and not seen, who controls movement across the spectrum of private and public, who really is *watching* and what they want. But I think there are also questions of how we understand our own experience of reality and our place in it. What documentation and sharing actually do to our memories. There's this dominant narrative—less dominant now, I think, and fortunately so—that lots and lots of sharing and documentation damage one's ability to be fully present in the moment, or render that experience less legitimate in some way, but I think it's worth considering what it actually does do. Whether there's a kind of observer effect, where documentation of something literally changes that thing.

One of the things that's most terrifying to me—and which I deal with somewhat for mental illness/cognitive disability reasons—is the idea that one's own perceptions and memories are highly unreliable. I don't mean in the sense that people often misremember details or miss things as they happen; I'm talking about wholesale manufacture of vivid experiences and an inability to tell the difference between the memory of an actual event and the memory of a dream. I wanted to write about that, and combining documentation of horrific things with it felt very natural.

To me, the real horror of this story is the very real comparison to the early years of the AIDS epidemic when everyone wanted to do something yet no one knew what. Men and women died by the thousands and the queer community rallied around its own even when the rest of the world would have preferred turning a blind eye. Such horrors influence our daily lives, often shaping the world around us. As a queer writer, what are your thoughts on how stories help us work through the fear of matters beyond our control?

I think writing about frightening things is a very primal way in which we cope with them; we've probably been telling horror stories since we first began telling stories at all. But for people who face oppression and marginalization and daily peril because of who they are, I think fiction is even more powerful, because telling stories is a form of resistance. Taking these things that seem overwhelming, that often seem too dominant to fight, and incorporating them into fictional worlds—even ones where endings aren't necessarily happy and goodness doesn't necessarily triumph—is a way of stepping beyond and even above these things. You can shrink them down to an approachable scale and understand them better, and that's a claim to power. It might not change your day-to-day in a dramatic sense, but anything that helps you claw your way upward means so much.

And I love how it works for things both internal and external. Those of us who fall within oppressed categories of identity obviously deal with external threats, but those external threats cause enormous inner pain and turmoil, and fiction can help us grapple with those things, drag them outside ourselves, and face them down as the enemies they are. I think that's incredibly valuable and important.

Queer writers such as Poppy Z. Brite, Vincent Varga, and Felice Picano are familiar names in the horror community, but the underrepresentation of queer writers in any form of genre fiction continues to be a concern. Many are afraid their works will be labeled for "gay audiences," others worry that their work won't be welcome in a time when markets loudly proclaim support of "diversity" yet don't have the numbers to support their claims. If you could speak to young queer writers first setting a bloody pen nib to paper, what would you tell them about making their voices heard?

Just tell your stories. Tell them honestly and truly and don't worry—in the moment—about who the audience is or how they'll be marketed and sold, or what people will think. Writing with the door closed is such an old piece of writing advice that I think it's almost cliché at this point, but it's also true. If you let all the other stuff in, it'll get between you and the things you need to be digging into in order to do good work.

And dig into the pain. I don't think it's useful to tell someone to be fearless, because fear is part of it; you have to go into the dark and ugly and painful things in your life *with* the fear, not in spite of it. When I decided I needed to write about the worst parts of my experience, I embraced all the negative feelings associated with them and did my best to harness them. I tried—as well as I could—to use the terror and the rage rather than attempting to get some kind of distance from it. That's enormously hard, and I'm still learning how to do it, but especially when you've been through bad times because of who you are, dragging that terror and rage into the light and making art from it is, like I said above, resistance. And it's powerful.

Being afraid of everything external to the work . . . That'll hurt the work. I think what you're describing is too often a reality and I think it needs to be fought, but the writing absolutely has to come first. And if you're going to fight those things, great writing in your arsenal is probably one of the best weapons you can have.

AUTHOR SPOTLIGHT:
ALYSSA WONG

SANDRA ODELL

Some writers feel a slow build up is necessary when writing horror, but you waste no time diving into the darkness in "Hungry Daughters of Starving Mothers," creating a vivid immediacy that continues to the end. When writing short fiction, how conscious are you of story pacing and voice?

Very. One of the things I love about short fiction is how condensed it is; it requires diligence and constant attention to make it work on both the sentence level and overall story arc. The challenge of getting creative within strict confines of form is one that I enjoy. Plus, I like stories that start and end with a bang, and I feel that short fiction is particularly well suited for that.

Shapechangers are a favorite horror trope, and you add to that concept with a deliberate exploration of the outsider, of queer identity, that enriches the tale. What inspired this story?

I'd been writing a lot of dark, heavy stories, and I wanted to write something light and funny about girls trying to find love in the big city. What I ended up with instead was a story about a predatory city and a girl who doesn't believe she can or should encounter true love. So, super light and funny!

I love shapechangers. I wanted to couple that physical fluidity with a protagonist who has a very strong sense of identity. No matter what she looks like, she always knows who she is and what she's doing. It's that intentionality that I really like about her. She knows herself very well, and she believes that her existence makes her inherently monstrous—which is something that I remember internalizing when I was very young and bogged down with queer Christian guilt.

The integration of both the queer and cultural elements of the story is seamlessly engaging. How much of you rests behind the lines?

Oof. Actually, for this story, I spliced a bunch of my friends' dating mishaps together and integrated them into the plot. I also lived in NYC for a while, which helped me write about the city on a more personal level.

For this story, I wanted to write about a variety of queer Asian American ladies. Luckily, I know many queer Asian American ladies, and our myriad experiences—both the commonalities and the differences—helped me put together a number of characters whose lives I felt were plausible in this setting. They're not meant to be representative of Every Queer Asian American Woman, because I believe that the idea of an extant One True Narrative is total bullshit. But they're people I felt that I could have met, and I'm okay with that.

Too often the representation of Asians in fiction was relegated to the "exotic oriental" or the "cultural victim to show relevance." Likewise, queers are pigeon-holed as "psycho-killers" or "misunderstood best friends." Growing up, how did such representations influence the girl who would become the woman you are today? How do you hope your own writing will influence others?

I grew up in a conservative, Evangelical Christian bubble with pretty strictly controlled media, and I didn't see much queer representation at all. The first positive queer female representation I encountered was probably in Tamora Pierce's *The Will of the Empress*, where one of the protagonists discovers her attraction to another woman. It's treated beautifully. I remember reading that book over and over, always coming back to that same scene, too afraid to admit the reason why to myself.

I also didn't see much representation in terms of Asian characters. Whenever an Asian (and rarely Asian American, if ever) girl showed up in media, she was small and demure, an exotic oddity, a prize to be won or a tragic lover abandoned after a war (thank you, *Madame Butterfly* and *Miss Saigon*). Add to that the pressure to conform to the submissive model of femininity espoused by my Evangelical background and you have a veritable Venn diagram of unhealthy modeling.

When I write, I want to remind people that we aren't there for "flavor;" we exist in stories as we do in real life, not to fulfill some agenda, but because we can't not exist. I write stories for the kid I used to be, so afraid of being abnormal, so eager for any kind of positive validation in media that girls like me could be fierce, ugly, deadly, soft, good, bad, anything and everything. That we were more than our stereotypes, that we contained so many permutations and variants that we couldn't be held back. And I write to let all of the other sad, queer, Asian American kids know that there's someone out there who might share some of their experiences, and that we aren't alone.

If you could speak to readers afraid to explore the works of queer writers for fear of catching "the gays," what would you tell them?

I think it's important to know yourself. If you're a reader who doesn't want to read queer fiction, whether for personal ideological reasons or because it makes you uncomfortable,

I see that. And I understand, because I've been there.

At the same time, the human experience is so vast and rich, and I believe that queerness is a large part of that. Maybe you're not queer, but you know someone who is; maybe reading stories featuring queer characters or by queer writers will help you understand that person better, or better pinpoint what about queerness makes you uncomfortable.

Ultimately, it's up to you. The stories should always be about the characters, and if those characters don't speak to you, then the reason why is something important to understand about yourself.

What scares Alyssa Wong? What sends a shiver up your spine?

Now that seems like imprudent information to reveal! (It's okay, I'll tell you anyway.)

I hate bugs. Like, gut instinct revulsion. Which, of course, means that I can't stop writing about them. I write about things that deeply interest me, and for me, fear is a type of mandatory interest.

AUTHOR SPOTLIGHT:
CHUCK PALAHNIUK

ARLEY SORG

"Let's See What Happens" develops incredible momentum. It almost reads like a screenplay, with lots of action and dialogue. Parts of it capture a stream of consciousness feeling. The barreling pace matches the unhinging of the mother and father, flinging the reader along into their crazy. Yet there are plot elements that are very deliberately explored / unveiled. Ultimately, the sense of relationship between parents and child is completely transformed, perhaps even reversed in specific ways. How did you develop this story and its style? What was the process for writing the piece?

The piece began as a wreck. In the first draft Heather brought home a new chum who lectured the family about God. The chum's name was "Party Doll" which was also the original title of the piece. This was too, too much up front when I was really trying to arrive at the run-on church scenes. Lately when writing, I've been trying to use unlikely words as conjunctions. Here I wanted to use Now, Next, and Always as the touchstones to hold together a long string of actions. The sequences in church—the now, next, always bits—are the sizzle of the story. Finally I jettisoned Party Doll, stripped down the traditional narrative scenes that connect the church scenes, extended the church scenes, and the story began to work. My belief is that since word processing software prompts writers to perfect grammar and spelling—thus making storytelling as easy as snapping a photo—writers should experiment as painters were forced to move beyond classic figurative work. Stories should become more expressionistic and take greater risks with language.

Throughout the tale Heather's parents are referred to as "Heather's mom" and "Heather's dad," even in moments that are far more focused on the parents, which I think gives the sense of everything being in relation to Heather. There's also a lot of interesting language play, where saying one thing means another thing, which is thematically aligned to the plot. What is the intended effect of using titles instead of names for the parents?

To me, an actual name is the most trivial, abstract aspect of a character. Heather and Brian, having names, become the least interesting parts of the story; having a name seems to resolve them and preclude their development. But characters known by their roles—Heather's mother and father, the snake man of the temple—they have a greater reality and status in my mind, because they've been given an identity that relates to something in the world. Their role-based names also echo the language of folk tales wherein we'd see Coyote, then Coyote's wife and Coyote's baby. This ranking of character role vs. proper name is my way to suggest something mythic is happening.

The story immediately delves into a topic (religion) that is, for many people, heated and emotional. While the main characters make fairly caustic, derisive statements in the beginning of the tale, by the end their own imperfections and mistakes are revealed. If anything, the religious experience could be seen as validated by the turnabouts at the end. As the author, is creating a message central to the piece; is there a message you hope to convey to readers; or is this just a wild story with an interesting setting and messed up characters?

My writing peers and editors have been prompting me to write more happy endings. The last thing I want to do is deliver a message. We're already so immersed in social engineering that nobody needs me foisting more life lessons on them. Instead, my goal is to experiment with new ways to make storytelling fresh and dynamic. The mechanics of a story excite me far more than the propaganda.

I can't stop thinking about that flyer. It's so unique, so particular in its details. The preacher with the snake is a fairly well-known type, but that flyer lends the entire piece a sense of grounding in the real for me. What parts of your own history are represented in this story? Which characters do you relate to the most and in what ways?

The flyer is the only through-line object, and each time we revisit it the flyer accrues importance. It also reflects Heather's degrading idea of salvation. While it's not there, physically, at the end, it has manifested in the actual Heaven it promised. The brochure dies and is resurrected along with Heather. As for my experience, in high school I loved to attend Holy Roller tent revivals with friends. They were the only thing close to a mosh pit in the small farming town where I grew up. It was a revelation to see adults act out in such loud, violent, cathartic ways.

Reading this was like getting in a car with no seat belt, watching wide-eyed as the driver accelerates, and blazing through turns along a curvy mountain road. I found it engaging, provoking, enjoyable and very memorable. What are you working on now that you're excited about?

For the time being I'm writing the script for the next *Fight Club* comic sequel, another ten installments. On the first ten, I held back a bit, trying to let readers adjust to a new medium. But for the next ten I can go wild, with greater skills and confidence. I've also co-written a screenplay from my novel *Lullaby*, and it might need some on-going tweaks. Between everything else I'm writing short stories, trying to find one with a strong enough premise to expand into a new novel. If all else fails, my next book will be another collection of stories. Thank you for your generous enthusiasm about "Let's See What Happens."

COMING ATTRACTIONS

Coming up in November, in *Nightmare* . . .

We have original fiction from Matthew Kressel ("Demon in Aisle 6") and Silvia Moreno-Garcia ("Lacrimosa"), along with reprints by Gemma Files ("The Emperor's Old Bones") and F. Paul Wilson ("Soft").

We also have the latest installment of our column on horror, "The H Word," plus author spotlights with our authors, a showcase on our cover artist, and a feature interview with Kim Leggett.

It's another great issue, so be sure to check it out. And while you're at it, tell a friend about *Nightmare*.

Looking ahead beyond next month, we've got new fiction on the way from Dennis Etchison, Nisi Shawl, Caspian Gray and many more.

Thanks for reading!

SUBSCRIPTIONS & EBOOKS

If you enjoy reading *Nightmare*, please consider subscribing. It's a great way to support the magazine, and you'll get your issues in the convenient ebook format of your choice. You can subscribe directly from our website, via Weightless Books, or via Amazon.com. For more information, visit **nightmare-magazine.com/subscribe**.

We also have individual ebook issues available at a variety of ebook vendors, and we now have Ebook Bundles available in the Nightmare ebookstore, where you can buy in bulk and save! Buying a Bundle gets you a copy of every issue published during the named period. Buying either of the half-year Bundles saves you $3 (so you're basically getting one issue for free), or if you spring for the Year One Bundle, you'll save $11 off the cover price. So if you need to catch up on *Nightmare*, that's a great way to do so. Visit **nightmare-magazine.com/store** for more information.

STAY
CONNECTED

Magazine Website
www.nightmare-magazine.com

Destroy Projects Website
www.destroysf.com

Newsletter
www.nightmare-magazine.com/newsletter

RSS Feed
www.nightmare-magazine.com/rss-2

Podcast Feed
www.nightmare-magazine.com/itunes-rss

Twitter
www.twitter.com/nightmaremag

Facebook
www.facebook.com/NightmareMagazine

Subscribe
www.nightmare-magazine.com/subscribe

ABOUT THE
QUEERS DESTROY
HORROR! TEAM

Wendy N. Wagner, Guest Editor-in-Chief, Fiction Editor, & Managing Editor

Wendy N. Wagner is the author of *Skinwalkers*, a Pathfinder Tales novel inspired by Viking lore. She's published more than thirty short stories in anthologies like *Cthulhu Fhtagn!*, *Armored*, and *The Way of the Wizard*, and magazines like *Beneath Ceaseless Skies* and *Farrago's Wainscot*. She serves as the managing/associate editor of *Lightspeed* and *Nightmare* magazines. She is also the non-fiction editor of Women Destroy Science Fiction!, which was named one of *NPR*'s Best Books of 2014. She lives in Oregon with her very understanding family.

Megan Arkenberg, Nonfiction Editor

Megan Arkenberg is a Milwaukee native transplanted to Northern California. Her work has appeared in *Clarkesworld*, *Asimov's*, *Strange Horizons*, Ellen Datlow's *Best Horror of the Year*, and dozens of other places. She procrastinates by editing the fantasy e-zine *Mirror Dance*.

Robyn Lupo, Poetry Editor

Robyn Lupo has been known to lurk around Southwestern Ontario, complaining about the weather. She helped destroy flash-sized science fiction in 2014 and hopes to wreck poetry for decent people everywhere soon.

Paul Boehmer, Podcast Narrator

Paul Boehmer attended his first Shakespearean play while in high school; he knew then that he was destined to become the classically trained actor he is today. Graduating with a Masters Degree, Paul was cast as Hamlet by the very stage actor who inspired his career path. A nod from the Universe he'd chosen aright! Paul has worked on Broadway and extensively in Regional Theatre; coinciding with another of his passions, science fiction, Paul has been cast in various roles in many episodes of *Star Trek*. Paul's love of literature

181

and learning led him by nature to his work as a narrator for *Books on Tape*, his latest endeavour. Paul is married to the love of his life, Offir, and they live in Los Angeles with their two midnight-rambling tomcats, Dread and David.

Cecil Baldwin, Podcast Host

Cecil Baldwin is the narrator of the hit podcast *Welcome To Night Vale*. He is an active ensemble member of the New York Neo-Futurists, creating original work for the long-running show *Too Much Light Makes The Baby Go Blind*. Cecil has also performed at The Shakespeare Theatre DC, Studio Theatre (including the world premier production of Neil Labute's Autobahn), The Kennedy Center, The National Players, LaMaMa E.T.C., Emerging Artists Theatre, The Assembly, Rorschach Theatre and at the Upright Citizens Brigade. Film credits include *The Fool in Lear* with Paul Sorvino, *Open Cam*, and sundry national commercials.

Craig Laurance Gidney, Assistant Editor

Craig Laurance Gidney writes both contemporary, young adult and genre fiction. Gidney's first collection, *Sea, Swallow Me and Other Stories* was a finalist for the 2009 Lambda Literary Award in the Science Fiction/Fantasy and Horror category. *Bereft* (Tiny Satchel Press), a YA novel, appeared in 2013. *Skin Deep Magic* (Rebel Satori Press) is his third book. Gidney lives and writes in his native Washington, DC.

Lisa Nohealani Morton, Assistant Editor

Born and raised in Honolulu, Lisa Nohealani Morton lives in Washington, DC. By day she is a mild-mannered database wrangler, computer programmer, and all-around data geek, and by night she writes science fiction, fantasy, and combinations of the two. Her short fiction has appeared in publications such as *Lightspeed*, *Daily Science Fiction*, and the anthology *Hellebore and Rue*. She can be found on Twitter as @lnmorton.

Traci Castleberry, Spotlights Editor and Editorial Assistant

Traci Castleberry lives in the Arizona desert. By night, she works the graveyard shift at a hotel and enjoys catching creepy-crawlies like snakes, scorpions, tarantulas, and Gila monsters. By day, she's the willing servant of two cats and a Lipizzan mare who has a habit of arranging the universe. She's attended Clarion, Taos Toolbox, and the Lambda Literary Retreat for Emerging LGBT Writers and has been a judge for the Lambda Literary Awards. Her publications include stories in *Daughters of Frankenstein*, *Suffered from the Night*, and *Lace and Blade 2* as herself while her alter ego, Evey Brett, has written books including *Capriole*, *Levade*, and *Passage* and has numerous short stories with Cleis Press, Lethe Press, Pathfinder Web Fiction and elsewhere. She can be found online at eveybrett. wordpress.com.

Sandra Odell, Author Spotlight Interviewer

Sandra Odell is a forty-seven-year old, happily married mother of two, an avid reader, compulsive writer, and rabid chocoholic. Her work has appeared in such venues as *Jim Baen's UNIVERSE, Daily Science Fiction, Crossed Genres, Pseudopod*, and *The Drabblecast*. She is hard at work plotting her second novel or world domination. Whichever comes first.

Arley Sorg, Author Spotlight Interviewer

Arley Sorg grew up in England, Hawaii and Colorado. He went to Pitzer College and studied Asian Religions. He lives in Oakland, and most often writes in local coffee shops. He has a number of short stories out at various markets and is hammering out a novel. A 2014 Odyssey Writing Workshop graduate, he works at *Locus Magazine*. He's soldering together a novel, has thrown a few short stories into orbit, and hopes to launch more.

Cory Skerry, Art Director & Illustrator

Cory Skerry lives in the Northwest U.S. with his partner and a menagerie that includes a bonafide dragon. He spends his time peddling (or meddling with) art supplies and writing about impossible things. When he dies, he would like science to put his brain into a giant octopus body, with which he promises to be very responsible and not even slightly shipwrecky. More of his nonsense can be found at plunderpuss.net.

AJ Jones, Cover Artist

AJ is an illustrator and part-time comic artist who loves painting with dramatic lighting and colors that make little sense. She is currently working on *The Kinsey House* webcomic with her partner in crime, Errow (wife goals), and is excited to grow even more as an artist and storyteller because of it (life goals).

Elizabeth Leggett, Illustrator

Elizabeth Leggett has illustrated for Lethe Press, *Spectrum22*, ArtOrder's INSPIRED, *Infected By Art Vol 3*,Quillrunner Publishing, Quiet Thunder Publishing, Little Springs Design, S.J. Tucker, and private collectors. She was cover artist and art director for *Lightspeed's* special issues Women Destroy Fantasy! and Queers Destroy Science Fiction!. In 2013, she published a full 78 card tarot and successfully Kickstarted the project. In 2015, she won the Hugo Award in the Fan Artist category.

KG Schmidt, Illustrator

KG Schmidt is a freelance illustrator and independent comic artist living and working in the Pacific Northwest. He has been networking with clients and peers, and putting his work up on various online galleries catering to queer and adult audiences for 12 years. He studied animation at Portland Art Institute, and graduated from PNCA with a Bachelor's in Fine Art in 2011. He interned at Periscope Studios in the winter of 2013, where he completed *The Creativitree*, his first independent publication. His style is heavily influenced by his rural upbringing, and the aesthetic sensibilities of his grandfather, a World War I-and-II era poster stamp enthusiast. He still tucks himself into bed armed with Erte, Mucha, and Heinrich Kley artbooks for when things go bump in the night.

Eliza Gauger, Illustrator

Eliza Gauger is a writer, artist, and the creator of occult psychotherapy project *Problem Glyphs*, SF collaboration with Warren Ellis *Deep Map Pilots*, doom space metal comic *Black Hole Wizard* with writer Simon Berman, and the reimagining of the cult underground webcomic, *Jerkcity HD*. Gauger is represented and collected in Seattle, San Francisco, Berlin, Munich, and New York. Upcoming illustrations and stories by Gauger will appear in Queers Destroy Science Fiction! and Queers Destroy Horror!, as well as guest pages in *BARTKIRA*. Gauger is indifferent about their pronouns, and passionate about drawing the perfect aquiline nose.

Additional Special Issue Staff

We made every effort to involve queer production staff whenever possible, but, as with the Women Destroy projects, we involved some allies on the production side of things. (Note: Copy Editing, though it has "Editing" right in the name, is actually a production job. Similarly, Audio Editing is a production task as well.)

- **Publisher** John Joseph Adams (ally)
- **Associate Publisher/Director of Special Projects** Christie Yant (ally)
- **Podcast Producer** Stefan Rudnicki (ally)
- **Audio Editors** Jim Freund (ally) & Jack Kincaid (ally)
- **Copy Editor** C. Liddle
- **Proofreaders** Anthony R. Cardno, Jill Seidenstein, Melissa V. Hofelich & Lisa Nohealani Morton
- **Submissions Readers** Robyn Lupo & Sandra Odell
- **Book Production and Layout** Matthew Bright of Inkspiral Design
- **Crowdfunding Logo Design** Julia Sevin

the *Finest* SCIENCE FICTION FANTASY & HORROR

IT'S DANGEROUS TO GO ALONE! TAKE THIS.

Press Start to Play

Foreword by **Ernest Cline**, author of *Ready Player One*

Including stories by **Andy Weir, Marc Laidlaw, Seanan McGuire, Austin Grossman, Holly Black, Rhianna Pratchett, and Hugh Howey**

Edited by **Daniel H. Wilson** and **John Joseph Adams**

You are standing in a room filled with books, faced with a difficult decision. Suddenly, one with a distinctive cover catches your eye. It is a ground-breaking anthology of short stories from award-winning writers and game-industry titans who have embarked on a quest to explore what happens when video games and science fiction collide.

From text-based adventures to first-person shooters, dungeon crawlers to horror games, these twenty-six stories play with our notion of what video games can be—and what they can become—in smart and singular ways. With a foreword from Ernest Cline, bestselling author of *Ready Player One*.

Your inventory includes keys, a cell phone, and a wallet. What would you like to do?

>__

STORIES BY:

Charlie Jane Anders
Chris Avellone
Jessica Barber
Marguerite K. Bennett
Holly Black
T. C. Boyle
Cory Doctorow
Nicole Feldringer
Austin Grossman
Hugh Howey
David Barr Kirtley
Chris Kluwe
Marc Laidlaw

Yoon Ha Lee
Ken Liu
S. R. Mastrantone
Seanan McGuire
Micky Neilson
Rhianna Pratchett
Hiroshi Sakurazaka
Catherynne M. Valente
Robin Wasserman
Andy Weir
Django Wexler
Daniel H. Wilson
Charles Yu

PRESS START TO PLAY

Available wherever books are sold Vintage Books

New From Titan Books

Titan Books

Weird Western / May 13, 2014 / 464 pages

trade paperback / 978-1-781-16450-1 / $16.95

ebook / 978-1-781-16451-8/ $7.49

www.johnjosephadams.com/dead-mans-hand

DEAD MAN'S HAND

edited by John Joseph Adams

From a kill-or-be-killed gunfight with a vampire to an encounter in a steampunk bordello, the weird western is a dark, gritty tale where the protagonist might be playing poker with a sorcerous deck of cards, or facing an alien on the streets of a dusty frontier town. Here are twenty-three original tales—stories of the Old West infused with elements of the fantastic—produced specifically for this volume by many of today's finest writers, including new work by Hugh Howey, Seanan McGuire, Kelley Armstrong, Jonathan Maberry, Alistair Reynolds, Elizabeth Bear, Joe R. Lansdale, Tad Williams, and many others.

WASTELANDS 2

edited by John Joseph Adams

For decades, the apocalypse and its aftermath have yielded some of the most exciting short stories of all time. From David Brin's seminal "The Postman" to Hugh Howey's "Deep Blood Kettle" and Tananarive Due's prescient "Patient Zero," the end of the world continues to thrill. This companion volume to the critically-acclaimed Wastelands offers thirty of the finest examples of post-apocalyptic short fiction, including works by George R.R. Martin, Junot Díaz, Seanan McGuire, Paolo Bacigalupi, and more. Award-winning editor John Joseph Adams has once again assembled a who's who of short fiction, and the result is nothing short of mind-blowing.

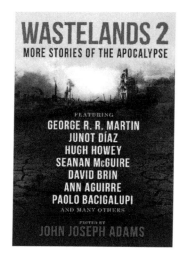

Titan Books

Apocalypse Fiction / Feb 24, 2015 / 523 pages

trade paperback / 978-1-783-29150-2 / $14.95

ebook / 978-1-783-29152-6 / $7.49

www.johnjosephadams.com/wastelands-2

Also New in 2015

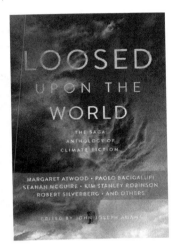

Saga Press

Climate Fiction / September 15, 2015 / 592 pages

hardcover / 978-1-481-45307-3 / $27.99

trade paperback / 978-1481450300 / $16.99

ebook / 978-1-481-45031-7 / $11.99

www.johnjosephadams.com/loosed

LOOSED UPON THE WORLD
edited by John Joseph Adams

This is the definitive collection of climate fiction from John Joseph Adams, the acclaimed editor of *The Best American Science Fiction & Fantasy* and *Wastelands*. These provocative stories explore our present and speculate about all of our tomorrows through terrifying struggle, and hope.

Join the bestselling authors Margaret Atwood, Paolo Bacigalupi, Nancy Kress, Kim Stanley Robinson, Jim Shepard, and over twenty others as they presciently explore the greatest threat to our future. This is a collection that will challenge readers to look at the world they live in as if for the first time.

OPERATION ARCANA
edited by John Joseph Adams

In the realms of fantasy, the battlefield is where heroism comes alive, magic is unleashed, and legends are made and unmade. Now acclaimed editor John Joseph Adams is sounding the battle cry and sixteen of today's top authors are reporting for duty, spinning never-before-published, spellbinding tales of military fantasy, including Glen Cook, Elizabeth Moon, Myke Cole, Seanan McGuire, Simon R. Green, Tanya Huff, Carrie Vaughn, and many others. *Operation Arcana* is a must for any military buff or fantasy fan. You'll never look at war the same way again.

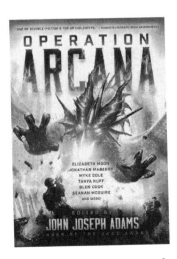

Baen Books

Military Fantasy / March 3, 2015 / 320 pages

trade paperback / 978-1476780368 / $15.00

ebook $8.99 / audiobook $24.50

www.johnjosephadams.com/operation-arcana

THE APOCALYPSE TRIPTYCH

EDITED BY JOHN JOSEPH ADAMS AND HUGH HOWEY

BEFORE THE APOCALYPSE
MARCH 2014

Trade Paperback ($17.95)
Ebook ($4.99)
Audiobook ($24.95)
ISBN: 978-1495471179

DURING THE APOCALYPSE
SEPTEMBER 2014

Trade Paperback ($17.95)
Ebook ($6.99)
Audiobook ($24.95)
ISBN: 978-1497484375

AFTER THE APOCALYPSE
MAY 2015

Trade Paperback ($17.95)
Ebook ($6.99)
Audiobook ($24.95)
ISBN: 978-1497484405

FEATURING ALL-NEW, NEVER-BEFORE-PUBLISHED STORIES BY

Charlie Jane Anders	Tobias S. Buckell	Sarah Langan	Leife Shallcross
Megan Arkenberg	Tananarive Due	Ken Liu	Scott Sigler
Chris Avellone	Jamie Ford	Jonathan Maberry	Carrie Vaughn
Paolo Bacigalupi	Mira Grant	Matthew Mather	Robin Wasserman
Elizabeth Bear	Hugh Howey	Jack McDevitt	David Wellington
Annie Bellet	Jake Kerr	Seanan McGuire	Daniel H. Wilson
Desirina Boskovich	Nancy Kress	Will McIntosh	Ben H. Winters

WWW.JOHNJOSEPHADAMS.COM/APOCALYPSE-TRIPTYCH

58302908R00109

Made in the USA
Charleston, SC
08 July 2016